MARIA NOLAN

THE

SHADOW OF THE

HILL

A NOVEL

2

Maria Nolan, is a founding member of Focal, The Wexford Literary Festival (2013) and its current Secretary. Maria is a Wordsmith, Feature Writer and Photographer with a monthly publication, the *Slaneynews*, and has worked in the past with the People Newspapers having her own page Town and County Life in the Enniscorthy Guardian for over 3 years.

Maria is a Civil Servant with the Department of Agriculture and lives in her beloved Enniscorthy with her husband Jim and their dog Oscar and records all things literary and cultural in the town.

Her short stories, poetry and Travel Articles have been published in several anthologies and chronicles including *Irelands Own, From Wexford With Love, Love & Loss* and *The Scaldy Detail*.

For my mother Maeve Doyle, my Godmother Peg Walsh, and my fairy Godmother Marie Harrison, all of the McDonald line.

Introduction

I have wanted to write a book from the very first moment I read one, and that was a very long time ago.

So, what took me so long you might ask and, all I can say in my defence, is that I have been too busy living, to take the time and apply the discipline that is required to produce a novel.

It took a world pandemic, Covid 19, when life as we knew it ceased, for me to take the time to sit down and begin to write.

Not that I hadn't always written, being Secretary of Rapparees/Starlights GAA Club for over twenty years, Secretary of the Co. Wexford Strawberry Fair, Secretary of the Enniscorthy Chamber of Commerce and Secretary of Wexford Literary Festival I have written enough Minutes in my time to fill a library.

This book began as a story I wanted to build around my great grandfather's family, The McDonalds, the thirteen children of Thomas and Mary McDonald, and in particular, the seven daughters who went to England and became nurses and teachers there.

But when I began to write, it not only became a story of a family, but also of a town, my town Enniscorthy, and a people, the Enniscorthy people and their history, in challenging times, from around 1885 to 1916.

This is a novel and a work of fiction populated by both real and invented people. All historical references and facts are researched, and to the very best of my knowledge accurate, but my characters both real and invented are my versions of these people, and how they may have reacted and interacted, and I hope I have done them all justice.

My story is very much interlaced with historic moments and as my characters, real and fictitious, zigzag in and out through the pages of history I try to give them a variety of voices, ideologies, beliefs and principles, in an effort to explore and understand our various degrees of Irishness and the problems and dilemmas that brings.

The Shadow of the Hill, is of course historical fiction and I hope a very good story, but I also would like to think that it does in some way demonstrate how we are all shades of our past and even though at times, we may wish to blot it out, that ancient shadow has a habit of creeping up on us and seeking us out no matter where we are.

I am indebted to the following writers and authors for their excellent research and writing:

Colm Tóibín – Enniscorthy – A History

Dan Walsh – Hunting with the Bree

Helen Ashdown – The Last Surrender

And I would like to thank special friends and authors, Carmel Harrington, for always encouraging me to write, Sheila Forsey, for being kind enough to take the time to read and appraise the first part of this book, reassuring me that it was worth finishing, Caroline Busher, Felicity Hayes McCoy, Eamonn and Drucilla Wall, Paul O`Reilly, Joe Neal for supporting all my literary endeavours, and friend and colleague Anne Gilpin, who has always been there with support and assistance and who very generously gave of her time to proof read this novel.

A most sincere word of thanks to friend and author Derek Meyler, whose expert advice and knowledge proved invaluable when it came to the practicalities of self-publishing, and to all my friends and colleagues on the Wexford Literary Festival Committee, especially inspiring Chairman Richie Cotter, Anne Gilpin, Roisin Williams, Edel Kelly, Jarlath Glynn, Carol Long, Elizabeth Whyte, Jonathan King for their continued support and encouragement, not just for me, but for all new and existing writers.

To my dear friend and Wexford Ambassador Anne Doyle for her continued promotion and endorsement of me and all things literary in Wexford.

Frank Corcoran editor and owner of the *Slaneynews*, for his continued interest and patronage of everything I have written for the publication over the past ten years, thank you most sincerely Frank for providing me with a constant focus and purpose for my writing and for continually challenging my literary talents.

To my husband Jim for his culinary expertise, seeing to it that I always had a proper dinner, something that I might otherwise have overlooked.

Last and by no means least, my grateful thanks to friend and artist Larry Dunne who designed the front cover. Larry is a local artist with oodles of talent and I just love his work, so as soon as I came up with the title, I knew immediately that he was the one to create the artwork to go with it, and I wasn't disappointed. Thank you so much Larry for turning my book into a work of art.

I hope I have created something that you, the reader, will find both enjoyable and entertaining and thank you so much for choosing this book.

If you wish to make a comment please feel free to do so on my Facebook page, all comments are welcome, but please do remember `it`s nice to be kind`……… only joking!

Maria Nolan

As a footnote I just want to mention that the word `quare` is a Wexford colloquialism meaning very, i.e. quare good, meaning very good, or it can also mean odd or strange i.e that`s a quare thing, meaning that`s a strange thing.

The Shadow of the Hill

Part I

Chapter 1

Leaning over the bridge as the sun was slowly sinking in the Enniscorthy sky Thomas McDonald exhaled with satisfaction as he gazed towards the Island where his horses grazed. It was a beautiful June evening with the setting sun glistened on the river Slaney like tiny mercurial fairies dancing a jig on its still waters.

Thomas McDonald loved his town of steep hills, elegant Cathedral and stately Castle and the meandering river that divided it, and liked nothing better than to spend treasured time, of an evening, staring at its beauty and absorbing its splendour, but on this evening, he wasn't just admiring the beauty of it, he was counting the magnificent brown trout gliding just beneath the surface before taking great leaps into the air as if celebrating the glories of the day past and giving thanks to the Universe in grateful synchronisation.

`Myself and William must come down later with the rods`, he thought, `a few of those lovely brown boys would feed the whole lot of us for a day or two, come to think of it, if we sold them it could feed us for a good while more.'

Feeding his large family of thirteen was never very far from Thomas's mind and sure how could it be, all those hungry little mouths were his responsibility, and had to be fed. They were his children, and he had to do his best by them and now that they were getting older he worried even more about them and worried how he would be able to provide a good life for all of them.

It was approaching the turn of the century and although Enniscorthy had begun to prosper a little, it had taken considerable time for it to emerge from the grey shroud of Famine, even if the town had not been as cruelly decimated as other parts of the country.

To give them their due, and Thomas was nothing if not a fair-minded man, the towns ruling classes had done their best to do the decent thing, providing work and even a certain amount of aid for the impoverished and afflicted.

The local landlords, Portsmouth and Carew, weren't the worst of them, it had to be acknowledged, and as far back as 1840, had made sizeable donations to the General Relief Committee of the Enniscorthy Union, allowing them to acquire lands and build a Workhouse in the town capable of accommodating some 600 people. By 1848, deep in the throes of the Great Hunger, there were one thousand and thirty-eight miserable souls housed there: men, women and children.

Lord Carew himself had been elected Chairman of the Union and in 1846 both landlords along with many of the guardians of the Union, prominent businessmen of the town, made generous contributions to alleviate the suffering of Famine victims.

Yes, Thomas affirmed, Enniscorthy had surfaced from her darkest period, scarred and limping, but a lot less so than most, and had even begun to thrive a little with the arrival of the Davis brothers, Samuel and Abraham who had started milling flour in the town when Thomas was only a chap and were now providing high quality employment at their Mill at Fairfield, and the brothers from Wales, Samuel and John Buttle who established a pork and bacon factory a few years before and were another great source of work in the locality even if each week the "killing day" evoked a horrific gene memory in local people of the tragic Battle of Vinegar as the waters of the Slaney ran blood red and the almost human squealing of the pigs could be heard all over town, reminiscent of ghosts from the past reliving the terror of that fateful day."

`Still`, Thomas thought, `the factory is providing plenty of jobs and along with the Mill and the Rock Factory might just help stem the haemorrhage of our children to England and America.'

That persistent bleed was the stuff of nightmares and disturbed the sleep of Irish parents since Black `47, Thomas being no exception.

The Rock Factory at Springvalley was of particular interest to Thomas. As a horse dealer he had been delighted to see Michael Breen come up from Killurin to set up business in the town and begin manufacturing horse drawn carriages that were now being sought by the gentry for miles around, even as far away as Dublin, with Thomas only too happy to provide the horses for them.

Thomas was a proud and honest man and he took both satisfaction and pleasure in his animals. He had a keen eye and was known to be a good judge of horse flesh, his horses were well bred, well fed, meticulously cared for and in demand. He was building up a reputation in the locality especially among the landed gentry where he was gaining trust and even admiration.

With a degree of contentment the big man gazed, once again, towards the Island where his horses were now silhouetted against the setting sun and whilst not exactly praising or exalting himself in any way, cos that would surely be a sin, he admitted, only to himself mind you, that he was doing alright.

God had blessed himself and his wife Mary with all of thirteen children, a baker's dozen, all of them surviving the rigours of childbirth and infancy which was both an achievement and an exception in the times. It did of course help that Mary was a midwife and had not only birthed all her own children, from Maryanne who was approaching her twentieth year right down to the youngest JohnJoe who had just come into the world, but had birthed almost every child in the surrounding Parish as well.

Mary McDonald was recognised for miles around as a gifted Midwife "better than any doctor" according to the local women and so well thought of that even Lady Gray, herself, of the Brownswood Estate, had called on her to attend at the birth of her fifth child and was so delighted with her beautiful, healthy daughter, Eileen, proclaiming that it had been her easiest and most relaxed labour due to the care, attention and knowledge of the skilled, young midwife Mary Power, that she presented Mary and Thomas with a beautiful wedding gift of a silver tea service and had been kind to them ever since.

When a horse needed clipping or shoeing on the Brownswood Estate, Thomas McDonald was called upon and when a work horse needed to be bought he was given the task of sourcing and purchasing, which was almost a fulltime job with the Estate now boasting a stable block for over twenty horses.

Thomas couldn't believe his good fortune and knew exactly how lucky he was to be trusted by and in the employ of Lady Eveleen Gray.

There had been little interaction between the Pounden family of Brownswood and the Enniscorthy community since John Pounden had died violently at the hands of the rebels during the 1798 Rebellion.

Captain Pounden had been in command of his infantry at the Battle of the Duffry Gate on 28th May 1798, when the rebels led by Fr. John Murphy stampeded cattle into his lines of Yoemen, injuring and maiming in a frenzy of horns and hooves, followed immediately by a wave of weapon wielding Pikemen. The injured Pounden was piked to death.

Mistrust and insecurity had festered on both sides in the intervening years compounded even further by the marriage of Jeremiah Pounden to Jane Stuart, a member of the Scottish nobility and ninth in line to the British throne, doing little to endear them to the Enniscorthy townspeople who had suffered severely at the hands of the Crown in the wake of the Rising.

Jeremiah`s daughter Eveleen inherited the Scottish title of Baroness Gray when her Uncle, Lord Moray, died in Scotland in 1895, and insisted on being addressed as Lady Gray, further alienating her from the ordinary people of Enniscorthy born from the ashes and suckled on the aftermath of Rebellion leaving them with scant regard and even less respect for either titles or royalty.

But Eveleen Pounden was a bit of a rebel herself, eloping with Scottish artist James Maclaren Smith, ten years her senior, shortly after her 21st birthday, and although always giving the appearance of aloofness and detachment she formed a bond with Mary Power during her confinement and labour and continued to keep an eye on Mary`s life as she married and bore her own children.

When Lady Gray became aware of Thomas McDonalds growing reputation with horses she instructed her farm Manager Jack Harris to seek him out and give him work at the Brownswood stables.

Having a great love of horses herself and often visiting the stables when Thomas was at work there to hear the news of Mary and the birth of their latest child, she began to encourage Thomas to bring some of the older children to work with him.

`There`s lots of work and lots of room here for them` she told him.

Thomas was always very grateful for the work on the Estate and grateful for Lady Gray`s offer and would be grateful, he thought, going forward, for anything that the good lady might be able to do for his children. He was a proud Enniscorthy man and very proud of all his children, they were well mannered, knowing their place but intelligent and confident when addressed as he had taught them to be. `You will never meet anyone any better or worse than yourselves in the eyes of God` he told them `so be respectful of all but don`t be afraid to speak up for yourself when spoken to.'

Lady Gray had recognised their attributes from early childhood and encouraged Jack Harris to find odd jobs around the estate for William and his brothers Thomas and Michael as they got older, with William, to her delight showing the same flair for horses as his father and in Maryanne, the eldest girl, she immediately recognised the same kindness and care complimented by practicality and the ability to cope that she had witnessed in the child`s mother, which became all the more apparent with the outbreak of smallpox in the town of Enniscorthy in 1895.

That same year Lady Gray`s daughter Ethel and son in law Henry Tufnell Campbell persuaded her to completely reconstruct Brownswood House, much to the annoyance of her youngest child Eileen who dearly loved her Georgian home just as it was with the five bays, the pillared porch and the eave roof, epitomising relaxed and understated elegance.

But much to Eileen`s irritation her opinions and preferences were dismissed, and popular architect of the day Sir Thomas Drew was called on to turn her beautiful family home into "a magnificent specimen of Elizabethan architecture".

Men were brought on to the Estate from the town and environs to begin work on the mansion without realising that they carried with them the dreaded smallpox.

When members of her household staff fell ill with the disease Lady Gray sent for Maryanne and Mary McDonald to nurse them. Mary declined having too many young children at home herself to take the risk, and besides, she was pregnant again and hadn`t long to go, but the fifteen year old Maryanne volunteered and moved on to the Brownswood Estate, nursing the sick with sympathy, efficiency and kindness and little regard for her own safety.

`Maryanne has a true vocation you know` Lady Gray told Thomas when the epidemic had past `and it shouldn`t be lost to humanity due to circumstances, when the time comes I hope you will allow me to use my influence to see that she follows her path.'

Thomas McDonald assured her ladyship that he would never stand in the way of the betterment of any of his children.

....

`What's the house like now Thomas?` Mary McDonald asked of her husband in late 1896 when construction work had been completed at Brownswood.

`God Mary it's a quare fine looking job, fit for a King to live in with all its towers and ornamentation` Thomas said as he sat in close to the fire `though not everybody's cup of tea now mind you`, he continued, `sure the young missus goes mad about it, "an abomination" she called it the other day and I heard her say it out straight to Ethel and Henry when they were saddling up to go out riding the next morning. Not afraid to say what she thinks that one, she hates it, but you know something, I'm not at all sure that she's all that wrong, but then who am I to cast an opinion on such a grand building, indeed who am I to complain at all` Thomas went on becoming a little more animated, `sure the new stable block is the best I've seen on any Estate in these parts and beyond, and I have an inkling that herself might be going to ask me to manage it. Now wouldn't that be something Mary McDonald? We could start thinking about moving out of the Shannon altogether and finding somewhere with a bit more room for all of us.'

`More room would be a gift from God himself` Mary replied `but moving out of the Shannon I'm not so sure I'd want that, the people here have been good friends and neighbours to us over the years and I wouldn't want them thinking that we were getting above our station, sure you know what they're like around here for that.'

`Ah Musha Mary mo chroi` Thomas uttered despairingly `sure we can't always be worrying about what people will think now can we? You and me have to think about what's best for all these young ones, it's not about us anymore Moll, it's about making a good future for all of these.`

`I know that Thomas and I appreciate that you are always thinking of your family and not beyond in the Public House gulping down bottles of stout and mouthing out of ya when you come home, like many a man` Mary replied `and all you children should be very grateful to your father

15

for the good life he gives us, do you hear me now` she said looking around the room at her brood `but you need to be careful too now Thomas and don`t get too far ahead of yourself and bring all that envy and begrudgery down on top of us like a ton of bricks. You know what this town is like, they`re just waiting for you to raise your head above the gutter to step on ya and grind ya right back down into it, especially if you are raising yourself up with hard work and honesty` she concluded.

`Ah will ya listen to her now`, Thomas said jokingly, `and her the very best of friends with her ladyship, sure isn`t she always asking after ya.`

`I`m not joking now mind Thomas` Mary continued with a worried countenance, `there`s many that have long memories in this town and they won`t take too kindly to you getting uppity and parading around with the Poundens of Brownswood.`

`What are you talking about parading around with them?` Thomas asked irritated.

`Oh sure didn't I tell ye, you were seen up at the Dublin Horse Show going around with Lady Gray herself, sure wasn`t it the talk of the town for weeks afterwards.`

`And what if I was, I was only giving her ladyship an opinion on the horses and very much appreciated it was too I can tell ya` Thomas retorted `and as for long memories there`s nothing they can say there Mary Power all the McDonalds bore their pikes proudly on Vinegar Hill and beyond.`

`I know they did and so did the Powers I`ll have ya know` she snapped immediately.

`Not a word can be said against either the Powers or the McDonalds Mary, you know that, and I know that, and besides it was a long time ago now, we`ve all moved on, Enniscorthy has moved on, and these children here in front of us will surely want to move on and make better lives for themselves. This town made its stand on Vinegar Hill and proud we are of it, but sure where did it get us Moll, it brought nothing only years of terrible sorrow and hardship mostly on the women and children and old people who were left behind in fear and poverty. And sure we were only picking ourselves up out of the squalor and casting off the terror when the nightmare of the Famine descended upon us shrouding us in its vile mist. We`ve had enough heartbreak, suffering and destitution in this country Mary, it`s time for us all to forget the past and think about making a better future together not more trouble for ourselves and each other` Thomas concluded.

`Oh I know husband, but not everyone thinks like you do, I`m only saying be careful is all, there will always be people who will want to take you down Thomas McDonald that`s just life and you children would do well to listen to that too, thread softly is my advice to you` Mary said to her family.

`They`ll do no such thing Mary McDonald`, Thomas said looking around the room, `never let small minded people stop you from bettering yourselves or being what you want to be`, he told his children.

`But what if it was some of the bigger people, some of your betters like, stopping you from being what you wanted to be or making yourself better, what would you do then Da` asked William who had been following his parents conversation closely.

`Small mindedness is not confined to the poor and underprivileged William`, Thomas explained to his fourteen year old son, `there has to be someone in authority, someone has to run things but that doesn`t mean that they always run them right.`

`So what do you do when they don`t then Da` William inquired `do you do what they did on Vinegar Hill and fight against them and try to get them go home and leave us alone here in Ireland to run ourselves.`

`Well now that`s a hard one William`, his father said pensively, `if many of ourselves that I know are anything to go by, they wouldn`t run an errand never mind a town or a county or a country. It`s all about respect you see, Will, if we have respect for one another then it really doesn't matter who's in charge as long as things are fair for everyone.`

`But if they're not fair Da` the boy continued `like it's not fair that the English are over here in our country telling us what to do, is it, sure what's wrong with their own country, it must be a terrible place altogether if they don't want to stay there.`

`Do ya know William I've asked myself the same question many's a time and never came up with a decent answer and you're right, there's nothing fair about it, you're not going to get an argument on that but if we can't get rid of them, and God knows we have tried often enough with little or no success, then we have to learn to live with them and even use them to make life better for ourselves.' Thomas went on, `Would you consider Lady Gray now to be English, William, or you Maryanne, do you think of her as English and our enemy?`

`I don't really Da` Maryanne answered `and sure I don't think she thinks she's English either and Eileen certainly doesn't, she's always saying that she's Irish and sure she is, isn't she.`

`Well she was born here in Ireland, Maryanne, to an Irish mother, and the Pounden family have lived here in Enniscorthy for generations but what really makes her Irish is that she thinks of Ireland as her home the same as you and me`. `What do you think William, is she English?` Thomas posed the question to his son.

`Well she's very wealthy and lives in that grand big house and has servants and horses and stables and talks different that we do`

`And does that make her English William and our enemy?` his father asked.

`Well no Da it doesn't, sure she's very good and all to us, isn't she, but the lads in school say that all them wealthy people are English and they stole our land from us and only for them we could be living in big houses and have servants and horses and all and sometimes they call me a lackey because we work for her, especially you Da` he added in a small voice.

`Do they now William, well maybe the very next time they say something like that to you, you could ask them what`s the difference in their fathers working in the pork and bacon factory owned by two brothers who came over here, not too long ago from Wales, sure are they not more English than Lady Gray.`

This seemed to placate the confused William who was trying very hard to understand his heritage and all that went with it, but he was delighted to have an answer for the lads in school the next time they referred to his father as "her Ladyship`s lackey".

`They`re all very fine words and sentiments Thomas McDonald` Mary interjected `and I know you`re a good man trying to be fair to all and trying to make a good life for us all, but you mark my words, the mistrust, and yes, even hatred, is always just a scratch beneath the skin and the itch will begin to needle soon again take it from me.`

`Is something going to happen to us Da?` a sleepy curly headed Michael asked in a small voice.

`Nothing is going to happen to any of us Micilin, I`ll make sure of that` Thomas told his second son but he had to concede, if only to himself, that there was a ring of truth in his wife`s warnings.

`We are a nation of begrudgers, God help us` Thomas mused `a quare people we are alright, always blaming the English for keeping us down and here we are, all the while doing our livin` best to beat each other down.`

But just in that instant, Thomas McDonald felt his flesh crawl, like someone had walked on his grave, as a tremor of foreboding, like he had never experienced before passed through his being, affirming to his subconscious mind, that his perceived prosperity and hob knobbing with the titled and wealthy could come at a very costly price for himself and his family.

Chapter 2

The beginnings of an itch that would eventually have to be scratched came two years later with the centenary Commemorations of the 1798 Rebellion.

Things had gone well for the McDonald family in those two years with Lady Gray bestowing the position of Manager of the Brownswood stables on Thomas, along with his eldest son William as a most willing, able and talented apprentice.

The McDonald family, despite Mary`s reservations, had moved to a larger residence at Court Street, Enniscorthy, and true to her word Lady Gray, who spent a lot of her time at her London residence in Kensington had used her influence with her acquaintance a Miss Marion Brew, Lady Superintendent of the Royal London Hospital at Great Ormonde Street, to get Maryanne accepted to do her nurses training.

This may not have been seen as such a good thing by all the McDonalds as Maryanne was a second mother to all of them and a tremendous help to her mother Mary, but it was a marvellous opportunity and no one wanted to stand in her way.

`I will miss her terribly` Mary cried to Thomas one night when they were alone in bed `what are we all going to do without Maryanne? She is the best child anyone could have, never a cross word out of her and not a jealous bone in her body, she has looked after all her siblings almost from the time she could mind herself.  She`ll make a great nurse though, wont she Thomas?`

`She will Moll` Thomas said warmly `and she`ll make us all proud I have no doubt.`

Maryanne left Enniscorthy that April in an avalanche of mixed emotions, it broke her kind and loving heart to leave the bosom of her family and her hometown, and the fear of the unknown in a strange land was overwhelming, but she was being gifted the opportunity of doing what she wanted to do with her life and despite her anxiety, trepidation and sadness she knew she couldn't let the chance escape her.

After many lengthy and tearful "goodbyes" she departed with Lady Eveleen and Eileen, who were planning to spend some time at their Kensington residence while Maryanne settled into her new life, leaving in her wake a gaping void in the lives of those she loved and left behind in Enniscorthy.

....

'98 Clubs and Committees had sprung up all over the county that year as Wexford made plans, to remember and honour those who fought and died one hundred years before.

The Enniscorthy Committee were busy with preparations for the commemoration of the Battle of Vinegar Hill to be held on Whit Sunday, 29th May.

Thomas and Mary both felt a surge of pride and admiration when the sixteen year old William announced that he had volunteered himself to march to Vinegar Hill in the Parade as a pikeman, like those who went before him.

Thomas, himself, being of fine stature and a recognised, able horseman had been approached by the Committee to re-enact the role of rebel leader Myles Byrne.

There was nothing else talked about in the town for weeks beforehand, the excitement and anticipation was palpable as special trains were laid on to bring in crowds from both north and south of the county, as well as spectators making the trip from Dublin, Wicklow, Carlow, Kilkenny and even from as far afield as Cork.

Thousands were expected to participate, as organised contingents from the baronies of every part of the county drilled and prepared for the greatly anticipated event.

Thomas had never seen his children as happy. They skipped and danced around the place in expectation of the great day. He couldn't help but feel a little bit sorry for his employer and the Pounden family who couldn't look forward to or participate in the commemorations like others.

'Isn't it quare, all the same' he said to Mary one evening 'it's almost like in some strange way the rebels won the day, even though they were heavily defeated, it's their descendants who can look back with pride, one hundred years later, on the stand they made and the fight they took to the might of an Empire. Isn't that a quare one now Mary but that's the way it seems.'

'Well it is surely Thomas' Mary said looking up from bathing the youngest in front of the fire 'but you know what's even quarer to my mind is that the fight on the day is always looked back at with great talk and palaver and bravado but no one ever seems to look back at, or commemorate, the misery and hunger of the women and children and the old ones left to fend for themselves. I remember hearing my grandmother talking about the indignity, the terror and the terrible humiliation of it all, not about the glory and grandeur of it, I'll have ya know.'

'Ah Ma sometimes you just have to stand up and fight when you're being beaten down, regardless of the outcome' William said defiantly 'You're the one always going on about God and religion I surely thought that you would think it right for the Catholics and their priests to stand up to them English Protestants who took our land and our language and tried to take our religion as well.'

Before Mary could reply to her son Thomas said 'It wasn't as simple as that William, there were plenty of big Protestant landowners who fought with the rebels in 1798, sure what about Bagenal Harvey, W█████████ton, Matthew Keugh, Cornelius Grogan and many others

22

and sure the North Cork Militia who fought against the rebels were all Irish speaking Catholics. It was more about the dignity and freedom of a people I think William and the right of a country to rule itself, but that's only my opinion and I know you will hear many great speeches on the Hill on the 29th that will probably tell it a whole lot better than me.`

....

The 29th May dawned a cold, crisp day with not a sign of summer on it, but the inclement weather couldn`t come close to dampening the spirit of those arriving in Enniscorthy and gathering in staggering numbers at the Fair Green for the Commemorative Procession to begin.

The McDonald household was a flurry of excitement as Mary and Elizabeth assisted Thomas and William to dress, while fourteen year old Agnes took on the task of looking after the little ones who were moving and wriggling and squirming like a bag of maggots with utter anticipation of the great day, their little faces lit up with expectation, they had never seen the like of it before.

Mary stood back admiring her men, William, young and fearless in the white shirt, black waistcoat, black trousers and green sash of the Pikemen and Thomas, handsome and heroic in full United Irishman attire, beige breeches, ruffled shirt, tapestry waistcoat, green tailcoat, black boots and wide brimmed hat with a peacock feather flying defiantly from it.

`A grand pair of smashers ye are surely` she said her heart brimming over and spilling out in a tear that she wiped quickly from her cheek. Mary realised full well the wave of republicanism bubbling just beneath the surface in Wexford, once again, and she feared for herself and her young family when the pot would come to the boil, but today she couldn`t help the surge of pride and passion she felt deep, down within her for her place and her people .

`Scratch us`, she thought, `and we still all bleed as true a shade of green as ever.`

As his children gathered at the front door, piling out on to Court Street, to wave goodbye to himself and William, as they headed for the assembly point on the Fair Green, Thomas couldn`t help thinking of all those families and all those men who set off with high hopes that day one hundred years before and he crossed himself in the memory of them and thanked them solemnly and silently for their sacrifice.

`I want ye to behave yourselves today and be good children for your mother` he told them ` don`t leave her side and don`t get lost, there will be thousands of people in town today like you`ve never seen before, but most of all I want you to enjoy and remember this day forever because you will never see it again.`

And with that a father and son headed off like many a father and son before them with pride in their hearts, passion in their guts and glory on their minds.

....

When the order rang out on the Fair Green, "Pici ar Aire" the hairs stood on the back of Thomas McDonald`s neck. From his vantage point on horseback it was like watching the manoeuvre of disciplined and experienced troops as the pikemen began their trek to Vinegar Hill, with the men from the Barony of Shelmalier taking the lead, each man marching with firm step and proud carriage remembering with dignity and bearing the men they had come to honour, as strains of national melodies, played by fife and drum bands, wafted on every breeze making Enniscorthy a sight to behold and one that would live in the collective memory for generations to come.

It took an hour for the parade to reach Vinegar Hill where thirty thousand people had gathered to bear witness to their past and revere their dead. Speeches by Sir Thomas Grattan Esmonde, grandnephew of Esmonde Kyan and Rev. Patrick Francis Kavanagh, grandnephew of Fr. Michael Murphy, drew spirited cheers from the massive crowd, electrifying the air and charging it with energy and intensity.

`The men and women of Wexford who perished on this hill one hundred years ago have not been forgotten, their spirits are still here today in Enniscorthy`, Fr. Patrick Kavanagh roared to the forty thousand strong, `For Faith and Fatherland!` he bellowed to rapturous applause and thunderous shouts of "God save Ireland" and "Erin go Bragh".

Suddenly, one of the horses spooked, reared, threw its rider and headed frantically in the direction of the crowd. Thomas and William broke ranks simultaneously, with William leaping from the ground up behind his father they took off after the escapee which they managed to restrain just as it was about to interrupt official proceedings. William leaped from his father's horse on to its back and rode to the bottom of the field where he calmed it down before returning it to its rider who was being treated by his sister Elizabeth, having sustained a bloody gash to his head in the fall.

The rider introduced himself to Elizabeth as Richard Saunders of Ballymount House and thanked William for his ` quick mind and excellent horsemanship` inquiring if William had ever ridden to hunt or at Point to Point. William told him that he was far more used to looking after horses than riding them.

`And you`, he inquired of Elizabeth, `can you ride as well as you can clean a wound?`

`We can all ride Mr. Saunders we`ve been on horses almost from the time we could walk, and we don`t get thrown from too many of them either` Elizabeth said playfully.

`Well that being the case perhaps you might consider giving me a few lessons in horsemanship` Richard Saunders said laughing at the spirited beauty in front of him.

`Well certainly not lessons in manners anyway` William said surprised by his sister`s remarks.

The pale shades of evening were cascading down the hill, as the evening sun spilled the last of its pot of gold gently out over the river Slaney, and a proud and happy people headed homewards, none of them would ever forget what they had witnessed that day and many of them would speak of it often and well into the future trying to explain to children and grandchildren what it meant to them to be there.

`Is it silly Da to say that I felt the presence of the ghosts of the Battle of Vinegar Hill today?` William asked his father later that evening `I could nearly feel the men and women of 1798 marching along beside me as we went through the town.`

`It`s not one bit silly William, the people of 1798 were with us every step of the way today` Thomas said `after the Battle of Vinegar Hill they were left to rot into the hillside because their families were too afraid to claim their bodies, and who could blame them for they were in danger of being hanged themselves if they did, but today William, today, their descendants claimed them with pride one hundred years later and honoured them with a dignity that they have long been without.`

`Remember this day forever` Thomas told his eldest son `it`s part of who we are, the blood and bone of our ancestors flowed into our river and seeped into our soil, it is what we eat and drink here in Enniscorthy and it will never let us forget.`

Elizabeth, sitting contentedly in the corner listening to the conversation, smiled, yes, she would also remember the day for a very long time to come, but for a totally different reason.

Chapter 3

Lady Eveleen Gray lost her husband James Maclaren Smith on 26th February 1900, the year of Queen Victoria`s visit to Dublin.

She had been estranged from him since 1889 when he left to live in Italy where her youngest daughter Eileen had visited him on numerous occasions but Eveleen Gray hadn`t seen him for many years, so she could scarcely claim to be heartbroken on hearing the news of his passing, and besides, she had never quite forgiven him for the slight of leaving her, and simply thought it very inconvenient that he should choose to go to his eternal reward just before the Queen was due to visit Dublin.

As ninth in line to the throne, Lady Gray had received an invitation from Queen Victoria to join her at a reception at the Vice-Regal Lodge, in the Phoenix Park on the 4th April, to commence her three-week Irish visit.

`The whole of Ireland will be there`, Eveleen mused, `damned inconsiderate of James to leave me in this dreadful predicament.`

James had ruined many things in Eveleen`s life while he was alive, but she was quite certain that he wasn`t about to ruin things now from beyond the grave and besides she had already accepted the invitation before news of his death had reached her.

So regardless of what anyone thought, and Eveleen was never one for worrying greatly about that, her trip to Dublin would go ahead as planned despite the fact that the Queen herself might not look favourably on it, having spent many years in mourning after the death of her own dearly beloved Albert.

But that was an entirely different relationship Eveleen reasoned, taking the decision to risk whatever criticism would come her way and making arrangements with Lord and Lady Iveagh to stay with them at their residence at Farmleigh, on the outskirts of the Park.

She was very much looking forward to seeing the seventy-two year old Queen, who was on her fourth, and possibly her last, visit to Ireland, and relishing the idea of seeing all the latest fashions and mingling with friends and acquaintances that she hadn`t seen in a very long time. But most of all Lady Eveleen was looking forward to riding out every day of her stay in the magnificent seventeen hundred acre Phoenix Park.

She would have liked Eileen to accompany her, but the girl had little or no time for pomp and ceremony or indeed ostentatious displays of either wealth or power, coupled with which, she had been very fond of her father and wouldn`t hear of heading off to enjoy herself so soon after his passing and wasn`t taking too kindly to her mother going either.

But even Eileen`s ire and disapproval weren`t enough to put Eveleen off the trip: she had been excited about it from the moment she received the Invitation.

The old Queen seemed to have a certain fondness for Ireland ever since her first visit back in 1849 in the wake of the Famine, visiting Killarney and apparently falling in love with it so much so that she returned to Kerry once again in 1861.

However, it had been thirty-nine years now since she last set foot in Ireland and excitement was mounting all over the country in anticipation of her arrival and Eveleen was going to make sure she didn`t miss a moment of it.

She would take Thomas and William McDonald with her to look after the horses, her own maid Mary and Thomas`s daughter Agnes, to assist. Like all Thomas`s children Agnes was kind, caring and hard-working and a most able seamstress, an attribute that might just come in extremely useful on a trip away from home. Who knew what might get torn or ripped or what button would need replacing.

Agnes had taken her sister Elizabeth's place in the Gray household when the latter went to join Maryanne in London.

Maryanne had been making quite a name for herself as a most able and compassionate nurse among the staff and patients of the Royal London Hospital and from her letters seemed to be extremely happy apart from missing her home and large family.

Superintendent Brew had had no hesitation taking on Elizabeth for nursing training on the recommendation of Maryanne, if she was anything like her sister the hospital who do well to have her, and besides, nurses were going to be in very high demand if war broke out in South Africa.

Lady Gray had been delighted, sometime later, to receive a letter from her friend Marion Brew telling her how well Elizabeth was doing and how easily she had settled in, considering the circumstances under which she had left home.

There was no doubt she had a vocation similar to Maryanne's, indeed the desire to care for others seemed to be something of a family trait, however Elizabeth's departure had been a far more traumatic and unnerving experience for the McDonald family.

....

Elizabeth McDonald thought that she had never seen anything finer than Richard Saunders even with a gash in his head and blood streaming down the left side of his face, in truth she had noticed him at the very start of the Parade, dressed as he was, in the flamboyant attire of the United Irishmen he would have been difficult to miss, cutting quite a dash sitting statuesquely atop his flighty mare, Orchid.

Well-fitting beige breeches, brown knee high boots, a ruffled cream shirt, a green sash tied to the side and the green and gold tailcoat of the United Irish, topped off with a wide brimmed brown hat with a gold feather cocked at an angle, sat well on the dark curls of Richard

Saunders and Elizabeth had him well in her sights, long before he took a topple.

When Elizabeth saw the mare rearing and throwing it`s rider she sprang into action with similar speed to her father and brother, getting to Richard`s side almost as soon as he hit the ground.

Having checked as best she knew how that there were no bones broken, she ripped a piece from her petticoat and began mopping at the cut on his head and wiping the blood from his eye.

Hitting the ground hard Richard was a little dazed from the fall but quickly realised that there was nothing seriously wrong and opening his eyes was delighted to see a most beautiful, if concerned face, staring down at him. She seemed to know what she was doing, this angel of mercy, scanning him with the pale green eyes of a cat set in an exquisitely shaped oval face of creamy complexion and framed by wisps of auburn hair wilfully escaping from the white mop cap of the pike women. She had a delicacy and strength about her all at once and Richard felt that he could have lain there looking into that kind, attractive face forever, but of course pride wouldn`t allow and he got to his feet reluctantly.

Elizabeth was quiet enjoying the pressure of Richard Saunders body leaning on hers as she helped him to his feet just as her brother William cantered up beside them.

Richard seemed to have a keen interest in horses and their riders and had been impressed with William`s fast reaction to the situation and his handling of the apparently skittish mare, prompting him to arrange a meeting with William at the Saunders stables on his next day off.

Elizabeth really wanted to go too but wasn`t quite sure how to orchestrate it, when Richard said `Oh, and I do hope you will come along with your brother, Elizabeth you seem to have a good knowledge of horses and sure you never know when your nursing skills might just be needed again, that is, if it suits you to come of course.`

`I will do my best to make it Mr. Saunders` Elizabeth said not wanting to appear too eager even though she knew she would go anywhere to see Richard Hatton again.

`Please call me Richard` he said smiling as the three of them walked slowly together down the hill as the last shadows of a summer evening rippled towards the Slaney like waves rippling to the shore.

William took to hunting like the proverbial duck to water. He was a natural and had an almost uncanny way with horses, he could get them to do just about anything for him and Richard Saunders had begun entering him in Point to Points where his ability and dexterity was winning races, and getting him noticed and selling Saunders horses.

Elizabeth was also proving herself to be an able rider, revelling in the thrill and excitement of the hunt and attracting many an admiring glance from several of the young male hunters in the Saunders pack, causing something akin to jealousy to stab at the consciousness of Richard, almost despite himself.

Elizabeth was loving this newfound freedom and the glimpses she was gleaning of a different and more exhilarating world. Her growing exuberance, passion and confidence enhanced her beauty and charm and was making her almost irresistible to the twenty-two year old Richard.

Elizabeth had never thought of herself as beautiful or special, in a family of thirteen there was no room for that kind of self-centred thinking, but she had to confess she was basking in the glow of all this unfamiliar attention and indeed getting quite carried away by it.

Richard`s mind was haunted by her. She was his first thought on awakening each morning and his last going to sleep at night, each time he saw her he knew he was more in love with her than the last, and every time she caught him looking in her direction her breath fluttered like a tiny butterfly in her chest and her heart trembled.

Elizabeth had been raised a good moral Catholic girl but she wanted Richard Saunders in every way possible to want a man; and with a passion, she could scarce admit to herself, she knew she would have him come hell or high water. From the moment their eyes had made contact, secretly in the hidden niches of their being, both of them instinctively knew that they would have to be together. It was as simple or as basic as that, once met they travelled a path of no return.

On a beautiful April morning in 1899 their chance came. When riding with the Bree Hunt Elizabeth's horse threw a shoe and Richard gallantly offered to take her back to the stables and saddle up a new mount for her. As soon as they were certain they were alone Richard looked deep into Elizabeth's eyes and their fate, whatever it would be, was sealed.

As he slipped an arm around her slim waist and bent to kiss her lips Elizabeth felt the ground slide beneath her, and when their bodies met, consumed in flames of raw passion and need, they barely had time to seek cover among the forest trees before they were swept away in a volcano of love, lust and an almost animalistic abandon.

Not a word had been spoken. There had been no need. They both knew how the other felt, being exactly what they were feeling themselves and in some strange, inexplicable way, they both realised that come what may this was always going to be the great love of their lives, however long they lived, and however many loves they might have.

For three blissful months they lived a lifetime, until the world discovered their secret and reality prepared to trample on their happiness.

....

Richard Saunders was an only son and both he, and Elizabeth, knew that his duty would always be to provide for his aging parents, continue his rich Anglo Irish line and protect and hold the land of his ancestors.

One of those ancestors, William Hatton, may well have fought with the rebels on Vinegar Hill but the world hadn`t changed sufficiently for Richard Saunders to marry and spend his life with a Catholic girl with no land and no dowry, however much he loved her. He would have to uphold his duty and life role and marry Dorothea Davis, the daughter of Samuel Davis owner of the very successful flour Mill at Enniscorthy.

Dorothea would come to the union with property and money if not beauty and grace.

Richard was distraught wondering, not just how he would explain to Elizabeth, but how he would live the rest of his life without her, for he knew deep in his heart that he could never be really happy with anyone else as long as she walked the earth.

William had finally made the decision to talk to his father about the relationship that he had seen develop and blossom between Richard Saunders and his sister. He didn`t want to reveal Elizabeth`s secret or make any kind of trouble for her but he knew that the liaison could only end badly and he wanted to get his sister out of the situation with the minimum of heartache and embarrassment to her.

William loved Elizabeth, and he had developed quite an affection for Richard Saunders, but he had heard the talk among the Saunders pack and knew that Richard was promised to Dorothea Davis and would most certainly marry her.

William didn't want to see his sister hurt any more than was necessary and certainly didn't want her to be the subject of unsavoury talk and amusement, so he sought his father`s wisdom and advice.

Thomas McDonald was heartbroken for his beautiful, spirited, daughter, when his son came to him with the news. He knew Elizabeth was headstrong and the situation would have to be handled delicately, but he also knew his girl had a strong character and an inherent pride that wouldn`t allow her to belittle herself. Armed with that knowledge he had approached Elizabeth and was both amazed and awed by her calmness and acceptance of her circumstances.

`I knew from the beginning Da that it could only end one way` she cried into his chest `but I love him and he loves me and I have no regrets. We had three wonderful months that will have to last us for the rest of our lives.`

`I know you don't want to hear it now Elizabeth`, Thomas said cradling his weeping child, `but time is a great healer and in time you will come to forget Richard Saunders and you will learn to love someone else, someone more suited to you and our way of life.`

`I will never forget Richard Saunders Da and he will never forget me. We are bound to each other forever, I know that now, and so does he and so it will be until the day we both die` Elizabeth sobbed `you were the one who always told us that we were the same as everyone else Da, well it seems you were wrong now doesn't it.`

`I am so very sorry Elizabeth for any false impressions I may have given you, and you are quite right to chastise me for them, I never meant for it to cause you hurt or harm` Thomas confessed ` how will you deal with it now, do you want me or your brother to talk to Richard for you?`

`No I want to see him one last time and say our goodbyes and don't worry about me Da I won't be letting myself down, I knew exactly where I stood from the beginning, I always knew he had a duty to his family that he would have to uphold and I respect him for that, I would expect nothing less of him.`

`You're a fine person Elizabeth` Thomas said with tears in his eyes `and I am very proud to call you daughter.`

Elizabeth's resolve waned and almost faltered several times before her meeting with Richard but in the end the two came together one last time.

Elizabeth asked Richard to remain silent, while she told him that she fully understood his commitment to his family and his kind, and to Dorothea Davis the woman he had been promised to, and she was not going to interfere in any way with that, but her parting words would remain with him forever. `You will never forget me Richard Saunders or the love we have for each other, all the days of your life. I will wander through your dreams at night and you will look for me every day in the woods where we lay, no-one will be able to take my place no matter how hard they try and at the end of your life you will look back and remember only me.`

Then Elizabeth turned and walked away leaving Richard Saunders distraught and on his knees with his head in his hands hiding tears of realisation that he had just lost the love of his lifetime.

It had taken a superhuman effort on the part of Elizabeth to keep walking, several times she felt that her legs would collapse underneath her, but love and pride carried her forward, and it was only when she knew that she was out of sight that she sank to the ground in anguish. A distant part of her had hoped against hope that Richard would come running after her saying that he would forfeit everything for a life with her.

That choice had to be his, she couldn't in anyway orchestrate it, and it hadn't happened.

Now she must do what had to be done and leave Enniscorthy forever.

She wouldn`t subject her family to the torture of watching her in abject misery as Richard Saunders got on with his life and married Dorothea Davis, she simply had to get away.

Elizabeth had already written to Maryanne who had recommended her to Superintendent Brew, who was happy to have her begin her nurses training as soon as she got to London, with all the talk about an imminent war in South Africa they were recruiting and training nurses at great speed, and Maryanne had written, saying that she had no doubt that

Elizabeth would be rushed through the process with the minimum of formality.

`Just what I need`, Elizabeth mused cynically, `a war! I will go as soon as I am trained and put as much distance as I can between myself and Richard Saunders. I may as well be miserable among the miserable, where my pain and anguish will be trivial and go unnoticed instead of remaining here, to be watched and shamed and pitied, however well-meaning the sentiments.`

In August 1899 the McDonald family of Court Street, Enniscorthy, said, yet, another tearful goodbye to a sibling about to make a new life for herself in England.

Chapter 4

Thomas and William both struggled with mixed feelings when Lady Gray informed them that they would be accompanying her horses to Dublin, staying for at least a week, perhaps longer, at Farmleigh House in the Phoenix Park for the upcoming visit of Queen Victoria.

And Thomas really wasn't looking forward to breaking the news to his wife.

'It's a wonderful honour now Moll, don' t you agree with that at least, both for myself and William, think of the people who will see our horses and how well we care for them, sure William is becoming so well known to the rich and titled that he could land a job managing a stables anywhere in the country and this is going to be yet another feather in his cap, you wouldn`t deny him that now would ya?'

'Oh indeed and you know I wouldn`t ' Mary McDonald retorted `I'm not disputing the importance of the occasion and the honour it is at all, you are well aware of my concerns Thomas McDonald and don't go pretending that you're not. Whatever excitement there is about the Queen in Dublin you know how they feel about her here in Enniscorthy. You and William were on Vinegar Hill just two short years ago for the 1798 Commemorations and you saw and felt the intense republicanism just beneath the surface here in Wexford, they won't take kindly to you and William being part of Her Majesty`s celebrations in Dublin, I can tell ya that for sure.`

'And you know my feelings Mary for my own place and my own heritage and you certainly know Williams but we are a country of many different heritages and we should try to live with and respect them all, haven`t we always taught all our children to do that. And besides, you know I have never allowed what people think or say dictate the way I live my life and I'm not going to start now.' She wants Agnes to travel with her to Dublin too as Seamstress, think of the experience that will be for the girl, would you deny her that.'

`I won`t go mam if it`s going to upset you` Agnes the ever- biddable daughter piped up.

`And what would you do then Agnes`, Thomas asked, `let her ladyship down and she after giving employment to you and half your family?`

`Oh no I wouldn`t want to do that either Da` the distraught Agnes replied.

Agnes had a heart of gold and never wanted to upset anyone so seeing her obvious distress Mary McDonald continued `Of course you will go with her ladyship Agnes and you too William she has been nothing but good to us, I am just anxious about the backlash that might come from this town, you know what they`re like, you will hear it on the street and in the public house William and the younger ones might even hear it in school, how their father and brother and sister went to Dublin to see the Queen.`

`William I am sure can look out for himself now Mary he`s a child no longer and the little ones will have to find their own way of dealing with snide comments and hurtful remarks they are part of life that we cannot shield them from forever. William, Agnes and myself are going to Dublin with our employer because she pays the wages that puts food on the table for everyone. We are not going to Dublin to see the Queen she just happens to be visiting there at the same time.`

Whether they went to see the seventy-two-year old Monarch or not, nothing prepared the McDonalds for the spectacular scenes they witnessed on the streets of their capital city.

Vinegar Hill had been massive two years before with forty thousand spectators in Enniscorthy but the Queens visit saw two hundred thousand, if not faithful subjects, at least curious ones, throng the streets of Dublin along with carriages, trams, horses, traps and the new- fangled automobiles of which the McDonalds had only ever seen one, belonging to the Roche family of Enniscorthy Castle.

Thomas, Agnes and William had never even imagined anything like the brilliancy and splendour of it all and indeed, albeit somewhat reluctantly, had to confess to feelings of sheer exhilaration despite their strong Wexford republican traditions.

The 4th April 1900 dawned as early morning Spring sunshine stole across the rooftops of a city dressed in all her best finery to receive a Queen. There were public decorations adorning the streets, private decorations embellishing houses not only all along the route but in almost every nook and cranny of the city.

Exquisitely uniformed sailors, soldiers and military bands lined the nine miles of road to the Viceregal Lodge and bunting of every description bedecked the highways and byways as the most distinguished personages of Ireland, mixed with ordinary city folk all eager to catch their first glimpse of the British Sovereign.

The ladies of Dublin were resplendent in their elegance and deportment, in dresses and hats of every hue and opulence, and gentlemen were dapper and smart of gait and bearing, indeed as Thomas relayed to Mary afterwards `even the ordinary folk, like you and me Moll, had a kind of nobility about them that day that made us all proud of ourselves, and proud of our city and the welcome it gave a Queen, even an English one.`

The scene in the Phoenix Park was one of indescribable gaiety and animation. Lady Gray looked majestic beside a group of ladies of the Viceregal party all on horseback, led by the Duchess of Connaught, who made an informal inspection of a line of troops just before the Queen's arrival.

Then at five minutes past four a murmur growing to a crescendo was heard coming from the direction of the city as the royal procession entered the park and amid the thunderous roar from two hundred thousand, all eyes were transfixed on the Queen, who sat in the fourth carriage looking very bright, her bonnet and parasol bedecked with shamrock, and facing her two daughters Princess Christian and Princess Henry of Battenburg.

The air was rent with cheers as the bands struck up God Save the Queen, and the multitude of military and naval groups filed past Her Royal Highness, dappled sunlight sparkling and glistening on helmets and bayonets, then to a hurricane of applause they were followed by the exquisitely attired cavalry on their trusted, well -groomed steeds and then, just before the Royal salute, a herd of about one hundred wild Irish deer trotted nonchalantly past, between the Queen and her armed defenders, with a collie dog herding them expertly, causing a ripple of laughter to erupt from the crowd and a smile to spread across the face of a Queen.

`Mary I`m not jokin ya` Thomas told his wife when they got home a week later ` it was the quarest thing ever, happening as it did at that exact moment, like the wild deer were our wild Irish ancestors filing past, acknowledging the presence of a foreign Monarch, but without homage or worship, just respectfully, making it known that she was very much a visitor to this land that was theirs long before her and her kind were ever heard of. It was extraordinary, and very funny and the crowds loved it. You know even though it didn't compare in any way to the pride I felt on Vinegar Hill two years ago, I would still have to say that I was proud of the way the Irish people conducted themselves in front of a Queen, we knew how to behave and that always impresses me, I suppose.`

`What was a wonderment to me`, William piped up, `was the obvious delight the ordinary Irish person had in the whole thing, we were like her Majesty`s royal subjects cheering and clapping and happy to do it, that`s what really surprised me Da, where was all our republicanism gone. How can we be pike carrying rebels one day and flag waving loyal subjects the next and seem to enjoy being both.`

`Ah, don`t read too much into that now Will` his father said quickly `the Irish love a good party and a day out, especially one with a bit of palaver and pageantry. We`re a complex people William with a complex history. What did you feel in Dublin, did you not feel proud to be Irish and proud of how we treated a Queen.`

`I did Da, and that's what's been bothering me ever since - how easily I could be caught up in all this monarchy malarkey. I felt pride in Dublin, but I felt shame too as though I was dancing on the graves of those who perished on Vinegar Hill.`

It was obvious that his son was confused and perplexed and Thomas McDonald didn't know what to say to him, because he felt much the same himself since his visit to the capital, glad to see it all but not quite comfortable being there.

`The Irish are a strange conundrum, there's no doubt about that` Thomas mused.

`And you Agnes, what did you think of it all?` her mother asked.

`I thought the Queen looked lonely and sad all the time Ma even though everyone was cheering and clapping for her she didn't look at all happy. I watched her as closely as I could, and her smile was only on her lips it never seemed to reach her eyes. I thought she was a bit of a tragic figure and I was so upset by all the really poor people I saw on the streets, I've never seen so many poor unfortunates in one place before.`

`But what about all the beautiful clothes and hats Agnes` her mother asked `did you love looking at all of them you that's so good with a needle and thread?`

`To tell you the truth Ma I didn't pay too much mind to them, it just didn't seem right to with all those poor people around.`

`The Queen of England and the cream of Irish Society and all my Agnes sees is the suffering and the hardship.` Mary McDonald worried about her sensitive daughter who was far too young to only see the pain and misery of others and wished her to be a bit more selfish and frivolous at a mere sixteen years old.

Mary would have worried even more, if she had known how much time the young Agnes had spent talking to one of the Indian party in the Queen`s entourage, about the poor on the streets in India.

`Any repercussions here in town while we were away?` Thomas inquired later before they went to sleep.

'Oh I heard a few whispers alright` Mary replied `you know the kind that`s said just when you`re passing and just loud enough for you to hear, like, who do they think they are heading off to Dublin to see the Queen and only two short years ago they were doing the big fellows on Vinegar Hill.`

`Oh is that all they had to say now` Thomas laughed.

`Please Thomas will you stop making fun of what I tell ya and take heed of me` Mary pleaded `there`s trouble brewing for ya, of that I`m certain`.

Chapter 5

Mary McDonald didn't know what to say when Agnes announced that she was going into the Convent. Most families prayed and hoped to have a son or daughter in the religious life but Mary had already lost two daughters to emigration and didn't like the idea at all of losing another one, even if it was to God.

Agnes hadn't been able to content herself since returning from the Queen's visit a couple of months before, her days and nights were tortured with the images of Dublin's poor, she just couldn't get them out of her mind, those unfortunate wretches that seemed to crawl the city's streets like some kind of human vermin, living in the shadows on scraps of rubbish and barely visible in the cracks and crevices of an unseeing and uncaring metropolis.

The McDonalds were by no means well off but they had a good home to live in, decent clothes on their backs and enough food in their stomachs so compared to Dublin's poor Agnes had felt like a Queen herself and instead of feeling grateful and privileged, Agnes felt nothing but guilt and shame and she didn't know what to do about it, until two Missionary nuns came to visit the Mercy Convent, Enniscorthy in August 1900.

The Sisters, Mother Teresa Cowley and Sr. Evanglist Glynn were part of a group of nuns who left the Convent of Mercy, Strabane in 1898, at the bequest of Bishop Anthony Gaughren, to establish a convent school for girls at Mafeking, South Africa.

The Sisters had arrived at Mafeking on 15th February 1898 and immediately began establishing a convent there. The following year the convent was ready to move into and the nuns set up school and had just begun to educate, when the Boer War erupted on 11th October 1899.

Agnes, who had planned to work with the poor of Dublin or the poor of India that she had heard about during her visit to Dublin, from some of the Indian servants in the entourage of Queen Victoria, was now completely enthralled by the stories from South Africa, especially about the dreadful seven month siege of Mafeking. Mother Teresa and Sr. Mary Evanglist told the Enniscorthy community how the nuns had remained in Mafeking to look after the dying and the wounded despite offers from Bishop Gaughren to get them out of it.

Their tales of bravery and endurance in the face of hardship and suffering struck a chord with Agnes, and she asked if she could return with them even as a lay person to help in whatever way she could.

Mother Teresa and Sr. Evanglist had come from London where they had received a donation of £2,000 from Lady Sarah Wilson, daughter of the Duke of Marlborough, who had been at the siege of Mafeking herself and had witnessed first-hand the many works of mercy performed by the sisters.

The convent had been almost destroyed during the siege and whatever was left had been swept away by a cyclone that followed, so Mother Teresa knew that they would need as much help as they could possibly get on return, and gratefully accepted Agnes's offer.

....

`Will we have anyone left at home here with us at all in our old age Thomas McDonald` Mary asked one sultry September evening as the two of them sat on the backstep drinking tea.

`Well now it`s far from old age we are woman, much too soon for you to be thinking like that` he laughed as he put his arm around her shoulders, knowing that her problem was not old age but the imminent prospect of saying goodbye to yet another daughter.

`I didn't mind Maryanne, she was going to do what she wanted to do, what was her vocation in life like, but poor Elizabeth only went to get

44

away from the shame and heartache and the awful prospect of seeing Richard Hatton and his wife somewhere around Enniscorthy, and now Agnes, can she really know what she wants that quickly, I don't know.`

`Agnes has always been a little bit different from the rest of them Mary both you and I know that, from the time she was a child` Thomas McDonald told his wife `sure she never wanted anything or asked for anything like the rest of them now did she, we always knew that she was special, we just didn't realise that it was special to God she was. Sure you said it yourself when we came home from Dublin that any other girl would have been going on about the dresses and the hats and the finery of it all and all our Agnes saw was the wretchedness of the poor. Sure, that should have been warning enough for us, and wouldn't any normal Irish mother and father be only delighted to have a nun for a daughter and here you and me are, nearly crying over it.`

`I only hope she knows what she's doing` Mary said sadly `South Africa is a long way away and she's heading straight into a war as well. I pray God will be enough for her when she's far away from her home and her family and I pray that he will keep her safe and out of harms way.`

Ten days later Agnes said goodbye to her family and Enniscorthy, and headed first for London with Mother Teresa and Sr. Mary Evanglist , who were received in audience by Queen Victoria on 24th September, to thank them and the Sisters of Mercy for what they had done during the Mafeking siege, and wish them well as they travelled on to Cape Town and eventually back to what was left of the convent at Mafeking.

Agnes would never see Enniscorthy or her parents again.

Three weeks later two letters arrived on the same day to the McDonald household at Court Street, Enniscorthy. One from Agnes to say that she had arrived in Cape Town safe and sound and one from Maryanne with a scribbled footnote from Elizabeth, saying that they would do their best to find Agnes and look out for her.

`Isn`t it a quare thing all the same, Mary McDonald` Thomas said that evening after they had read the letters for the fourth or fifth time `there`s you and me and all our people, McDonalds and Powers on Vinegar Hill in 1798 fighting the British and just over one hundred years later we have not one, but three daughters in South Africa where the British are fighting the Boers.`

`But they`re not fighting with the British Thomas` Mary said emphatically.

`I know that Moll but the three of them will be patching up British soldiers, maybe to fight against people like us, is all I`m saying` Thomas went on.

`Well I wouldn't be saying too much about that around this town` Mary warned ` better to keep stuff like that to ourselves`.

Chapter 6

On 21st December 1899 nurses from the Royal London Hospital sailed from Southhampton for Cape Town on the SS Dunotter Castle, as part of the Queen Alexandra Imperial Military Nursing Reserve, among them were two sisters from Enniscorthy.

`Well I never thought that we would be celebrating Christmas on the High Seas` Maryanne McDonald remarked to her sister Elizabeth on Christmas Eve 1899.

`Well that`s for sure Maryanne, I wonder what they`re all doing back in Enniscorthy tonight` Elizabeth said wistfully.

`Do you miss them as much as I do` Maryanne asked.

`I do and it breaks my heart to know that I won`t be going back there anytime soon, well not as long as there`s half a chance that I might run into Richard Saunders and his wife` Elizabeth replied.

Maryanne was both surprised and glad that she had mentioned his name, it was seldom that she spoke of him or of her own heartache. Elizabeth was like all the McDonalds, she shared her joy with everyone but her sorrow and pain were silent and private, and Maryanne felt privileged that she had opened up a little to her tonight. Perhaps it was something to do with it being Christmas Eve, she thought, as she put her arms around her sister and they clung to each other in an embrace that epitomised their terrible loneliness and longing for the warmth of their home and family and place of their birth.

....

Upon arrival at Cape Town, Maryanne was immediately recognised as a most caring and capable nurse and was snapped up by one of the surgeons, a Dr George Lindley, who was heading for the hospital at

Ladysmith. The sisters dreaded being separated, but good nurses were being frantically sought by the Cape Town surgeons, as it appeared there were a lot of inexperienced ladies passing themselves off as nurses in South Africa, when they were anything but.

These women known as "Society Butterflies" had come to South Africa more for adventure and excitement than to nurse the sick and the wounded and were causing quite a problem in many of the base hospitals around Cape Town. Doctors and surgeons were finding it extremely difficult to do anything about these "lady amateurs" as many of them were very well connected women indeed, so when "real nurses" arrived they barely had time to disembark before surgeons commandeered them as their own personal assistants.

Elizabeth was naturally intelligent and good at her job, but she didn't have the experience or caring concentration of her sister. There were many times when Elizabeth's mind strayed to the green fields and lush woods of County Wexford as she longed for their colour and coolness in this scorched, alien land, and most of all she longed for the chance to ride again and experience some kind of breeze, however feeble, in her hair, with the whiff of freedom on it.

She envied the "Society Ladies" the social butterflies of South Africa who wafted through the hospitals mopping brows, writing letters, and handing out cigarettes. These "frivolling women", who rode and danced and drove and raced and picnicked having a high old time of it, some seeking out potentially suitable husbands among the surgeons, officers and doctors, or more often, simply seeking out other women's husbands, while she, and nurses like her toiled from dawn until dusk in the intolerable heat and terrible suffering of the hospital tents.

Elizabeth watched them with envy, arriving either in their riding habits or in elaborate picnic dresses, heading to polo matches, afternoon tea parties or the races, a world she had gotten a flavour of during her time with Richard Hatton and without Maryanne to keep her in check she longed for the freedom and abandon of it.

Elizabeth craved freedom. Her mind was constantly crowded with memories that haunted her dreams and interrupted her daily thought patterns and she needed to shake them from her head and disperse them over this foreign soil before they drove her insane. She longed for the perfect recklessness of the "Society Butterflies" and thought that if she could just ride away into the wind some of those tormenting thoughts might just scatter on this barren earth and turn to dust.

`I notice you paying a lot of attention to our frivolous fillys`, Dr Peter Hargraves observed one morning as the "Sisters Frivol" glided through the wards like footless angels.

`Oh I am sorry Doctor Hargraves`, Elizabeth apologised, `my mind was miles away is there something you need or something that I haven`t attended to.`

`Not at all Nurse McDonald` Hargraves said with a smile `you are most hard working and efficient and I have no complaint at all about your work here, it was just an observation, I have seen you watching the "ladies" from time to time, not with the irritation and annoyance of many of our nurses, but with a kind of wistfulness and yes maybe even a wish to be among them. Would I be correct in saying that?`

`Well, God forgive me Doctor, but you would, I have to be honest. I do love my work here at the hospital, but it is hard sometimes to be constantly in the midst of pain and suffering and I envy the "ladies" their energy and gaiety and most of all I envy their freedom and carefree existence`, Elizabeth said, surprised that she was opening up so easily to a complete stranger.

`I don`t know that I would describe it as a carefree existence Elizabeth, a lot of these "ladies" have a great deal of wealth and lots of leisure time it`s true, but I`m not so sure their lives are as perfect as you seem to think. They seem rather shallow and without substance if you ask me, and they certainly should never have been allowed to come to South Africa to interrupt and interfere with good nursing practices.`

`I know that they have been described as "that plaque of women", and I know they have little or no nursing experience` Elizabeth said ` but some of them actually seem quite nice to the patients Doctor and I suppose there`s no harm in that, any little kindness bestowed on these poor unfortunates is surely welcome and can sometimes make our job a little easier.`

`You`re a kind person Elizabeth. Would you like me to introduce you to some of "the ladies" ?` Peter Hargraves asked.

`Oh no, not at all`, Elizabeth replied quite embarrassed, `I suppose I am just jealous of them and all the fun they have and the fact that they get to ride every day.`

`And do you ride Elizabeth?` Hargraves enquired with interest.

`Oh I do, well I mean I did, I rode as often as I could when I was at home Doctor, my father is a horse dealer and Stable Manager on an estate at home in Ireland, so we were taught to ride and look after horses as soon as we could walk.`

`And of course you must miss that terribly now.`

`Yes, I do, I miss it very much and long for the absolute freedom of galloping on the back of a horse and feeling the wind in my hair!` Elizabeth laughed at herself and blushed when she noticed Peter Hargraves smiling at her.

Elizabeth had paid little or no attention to any of the men, doctors, surgeons, officers, soldiers or orderlies since arriving in Cape Town, despite many of them openly expressing an interest in her. There was only one man for her and she had already left him behind in Ireland so she had gone to great pains to ignore all the overtures and innuendo directed at her and had opted to work under the very aloof and boring Dr Hargraves, who said little, worked hard and was over twice her age, at forty-five.

Little was known about him among the nursing staff, except that he was considerably wealthy and still single, so the general consensus in the nurses quarters was that there must be something terribly wrong with him if he hadn't been snapped up at this stage, after all he wasn't bad looking even if he was quite old.

`I can arrange for you to go riding if that is what you would like ` Peter Hargraves said.

`Oh please, could you?' Elizabeth gasped, her green eyes becoming almost luminous with a new excitement growing within.

`I certainly can, believe it or not I have some friends among the "Society Butterflies" and I can set it up for you to join them the next time you are free.`

`Oh but I would have nothing suitable to wear` Elizabeth stammered.

`Oh I'm sure I know someone who can sort that for you` Peter Hargraves replied amused.

....

Peter Hargraves had been hopelessly in love once with a society beauty Sarah Jane Chamberlain, who left him at the altar to run away with his best friend and best man, and in the twenty years since then, he had given women a wide berth preferring to concentrate on his work and career.

In the beginning women pursued and pestered him relentlessly finding his indifference to them strangely attractive, but of late he noticed this was beginning to wane and he was very happy to leave it at that.

He loved his work, having previously served in the Crimean War and he was most comfortable either alone or in male company. He had chosen Elizabeth as his assistant nurse because she seemed capable and quick to learn and totally oblivious to, and disinterested in, the attentions she evoked among the men.

He had been both surprised and amused at her longing to join "the ladies" finding her not all at frivolous or shallow, but perhaps it was only the horse riding she was interested in and he could easily arrange that for her.

Peter Hargraves cousin Beatrice Norwich-Beasley lived just outside Cape Town with her husband Randolf and the couple had been doing very well for themselves before war broke out. They had large stables and Peter availed of their horses regularly. Randolf was in the diamond mining business and Beatrice was quite the social butterfly herself and liked nothing better than to party with "the ladies" of Cape Town.

Beatrice took one look at Elizabeth McDonald and said she would be delighted to have her join them for their morning ride the following Thursday, under one condition, that Peter would join them as well.

`What an unusual beauty` Beatrice thought to herself and the first female that her cousin Peter had shown any interest in this twenty years.

And so began Elizabeth`s romance with South Africa. She rode as often as her work commitments would allow, and she began receiving invitations to polo matches, afternoon teas and even dinner parties and she accepted them all, because they helped her to forget.

Peter Hargraves couldn't believe the transformation in her. When she arrived she was a morose, attractive, mysterious, silent girl, now, especially on the back of a horse she was a wild, passionate beauty who was setting hearts aflutter all over Cape Town and even he had to admit, in the green riding habit given to her by cousin Beatrice, with her auburn hair flying wildly behind her, she certainly was a looker. The "Irish Warrior Queen" some of the soldiers had begun to call her, and on the back of a horse she certainly looked the part. She had already received several proposals of marriage, all of which she dismissed as kindly as she could, while the women around her envied and coveted her popularity.

Dr Hargraves had taken Elizabeth under his wing and was quite pleased with his prodigy, even if she was running with the ladies of South Africa, she was still improving her nursing skills daily, she rode and managed a horse with agility and expertise, she attended picnics, afternoon teas, dinners and dances and had even learned to drive an automobile, she was beautiful, intelligent, fearless and kind and women wanted to befriend her and men wanted to love her, but she would never be one of the "society butterflies". She had far too much substance and integrity for that. Besides she strangely had no interest in trapping a husband or taking a lover, quite a paradox in Cape Town.

One evening arriving late for duty having attended a rather elaborate afternoon tea Elizabeth had missed saying goodbye to one of her patients, a young soldier from Co. Kilkenny in Ireland who had lost a leg at Mafeking and was being shipped home that day. Elizabeth was disgusted with herself for staying longer than she needed to at the tea party instead of coming back to comfort and console the anxious, young man, who would never be able to go to war again, and who`s life would be particularly limited back in rural Ireland with only one leg and little money.

Before Peter Hargraves got a chance to chastise her for her tardiness, Elizabeth broke down and sobbed.

`It`s not that bad nurse`, Peter Hargraves consoled, `it`s the first time I`ve ever seen you late, some of them here are late all the time, is there something else bothering you Elizabeth?`

`Oh Doctor you have been so good to me and I have really enjoyed all the fun and excitement I`ve had for the past couple of months, but now, I`m not at all sure that I like the person I`ve become` Elizabeth said distressed. `I`ve just let that poor chap go home to Ireland without saying goodbye, and telling him that I would write keeping him up to date with all the happenings here. I`ve become selfish and unfeeling Doctor chasing after happiness and enjoyment, when many around me might never know them again.`

`But surely you have no need to be chasing happiness Elizabeth` Peter said perplexed `a girl as beautiful and intelligent as you could find that happiness with many a man here, and I do know that it`s not for lack of offers. From what I`ve heard you are one of the most popular girls in Cape Town.`

`But you see Doctor that`s just it, I don't want that happiness, I had it once and it was snatched away from me, and it took all the strength and courage I could muster to get over it and I never want to have to do that again.`

Elizabeth poured out her story and Peter Hargraves couldn`t believe how much her feelings mirrored his own. He had never spoken to anyone about Sarah Jane and his best friend Robert Lewis and now he found himself bearing his heart to a young twenty year old nurse in a hospital tent in South Africa.

People in the Cape Town circle were stunned when the announcement was made that the beautiful, young Irish nurse, Elizabeth McDonald had agreed to marry the austere and mature, Dr Peter Hargraves.

Of course he had money, it was said, but she could have had her pick of wealthy men, so that couldn't have been the motivation, nor could it have been his wooing of her, as he had never expressed a romantic interest in any woman, including Elizabeth, since coming to South Africa.

Elizabeth McDonald and Peter Hargraves had more in common than people realised, neither of them wanted a love match, and both recognised and respected the pain and hurt previously suffered by the other, giving them an understanding, compassion and kindness for one another, that many a more romantic relationship lacked. They wanted nothing of each other except trust, and to live and work together in peace and harmony, and to be left alone by all other would be suitors, male and female, and to never have to fall madly in love with anyone ever again.

`Are you quite sure Elizabeth` Peter Hargraves asked the day before they were to be married by the army Chaplain the Rev. Norman Cassells `after all you are only twenty years old, can you be certain that you won`t want more, even children at a later date?`

`I have told you already Doc...., I mean Peter that there were enough children in my home to last me a lifetime. If I want a child, all I have to do is send home for one of my younger brothers or sisters to come live with me....., I mean us. But I can`t see that happening as you have already said, we won`t be going back to England for quite a while yet.`

`Well we`ll see what happens here in South Africa when the war ends but we won`t be going back anytime soon, but you are so young, I want you to be sure and have no regrets.`

`All I know, is what any person can know on their wedding day, that it feels right for me to marry you. I have been running from something, or chasing something, since I left Ireland, here with your help I hopped on a merry go round of frivolity and thoughtlessness but since you asked me to marry you the world seems to have stopped spinning` Elizabeth laughed ` exactly the opposite of what most girls would want or expect, but your proposal has given me a calm and a serenity that I badly needed, without it I`m not quite sure where I was headed.`

`For the first time in twenty years I feel at peace, Elizabeth` Peter Hargraves said gratefully `my torment has finally ended.`

On 14th February 1901 Elizabeth McDonald from Enniscorthy, Co. Wexford married Dr Peter Hargraves of Berkeley Square, London in Cape Town, South Africa with the brides two sisters Maryanne and Agnes Mc Donald present as witnesses.

The significance of the date was lost on both the bride and the groom.

Chapter 7

By late 1901 Thomas McDonald and his eldest son William were operating a most successful business, trading horses to the British Government, thanks in the main to Elizabeth who had written from South Africa, relating how the British Army were finding their cavalry horses totally inadequate in the face of water obstacles, and suggesting that Thomas and William should exercise and train suitable replacements, and look to their influential contacts for the army contract.

Elizabeth also mentioned, as a footnote, that her wedding to Dr Peter Hargraves in February had been " ... a most pleasant occasion. I was delighted to have Maryanne and Agnes there with me. Peter is a good man, for an Englishman, and I think you would all be fond of him, Maryanne and Agnes have only good things to say about him and we are getting along very well".

William was now a valued member of the Bree Hunt and right hand man to its Master and founder John B. O`Neill, a horse trader from Tyrone who had come to reside at Carrigunane House, most likely, recognising both the quality of the Wexford bred horses and the close proximity of the Port.

John B. immediately became aware that the young William McDonald was a good judge of bloodstock, rode well and enjoyed hunting the Wexford countryside, along with which, himself and his horse dealing father, Thomas, knew all the local gentry and landowners.

John B. O`Neill was already horse trading in England, bringing about fifteen hunters to the English sales every year, trade was brisk and he realised that together with the McDonalds they could corner a most lucrative market and made up his mind to ask William to join him in business on a day when the Bree Hunt caused quite a stir in the town of Enniscorthy.

The Bree normally hunted foxes and hares but on this occasion they chased a stag through the streets of the town from Ballyorril through Greenville Lane, the Fairgreen and Duffry Gate, across Pig Market Hill, through Lymington Road, past St. John`s Workhouse and down Munster Hill, until William finally caught up with it at the Urrin River.

Not an easy task to hunt through a town but William handled himself and his mount well and John B. decided there and then to ask him to do the buying and selling for the English market.

Very few Irish farmers kept a horse for any length of time and were continually passing them on looking for the best possible price, and the British were always looking for good horses, in peace time for hunting and when at war requiring an even greater supply.

William and Thomas McDonald had begun buying up horses all over the county and beyond, training them to be of sufficient service to the British Army and William and John B had begun travelling back and forth to England on a regular basis.

That same year Lady Gray had made Thomas McDonald an offer to become a tenant farmer on the Brownswood Estate, and in light of the fact that William was well capable of looking after the business and recent Land League developments, Thomas felt that that the winds of change were begin to rise in Ireland and it would only be a matter of time before the law was altered with regard to ownership of land and he didn't want to miss the opportunity should it happen.

`What would you think about that now Moll`, he asked of his wife one evening, `if you and me were to turn into tenant farmers?`

`There you go now getting ahead of yourself again Thomas McDonald`, Mary scolded, `can ye never just be content with what you have, must you always be chasing rainbows searching for a pot of gold. Aren`t yourself and William making a fine job of the horse trading and aren't you more than happy running the stables for her Ladyship, why must you go now and bring more hardship on us.`

`Oh but you`re a quare one Mary` Thomas laughed `sure what hardship would it be to have a bit of land, her Ladyship has made the offer and all we have to do is take it and farm it, and who knows with all this land agitation we might even end up owning it someday, wouldn`t that be something to leave behind for our children, now wouldn't it.`

`Sure three of our children are on the other side of the world you might say` Mary replied `one of them even married and if what Maryanne writes is true, Elizabeth won`t be needing anything from us, she will have a very swanky house in London and a cottage, if you don't mind, in someplace called Somerset, sure why people would need two places to live I don't know. There`s something not quite right about that marriage Thomas McDonald mark my words, it was too soon after Richard Hatton, she couldn't have gotten over him that quickly sure she was devastated going away, that`s a marriage on the rebound, I`ll warrant.`

`Ah whist about all that Mary` Thomas said losing patience `our girl is not stupid, Elizabeth knows what she`s doing and by all accounts from Maryanne and Agnes he seems to be a fine man for an Englishman, older I know, but that doesn't mean there`s anything wrong with him.`

`Oh I`ve no problem at all with him being a good bit older than her` Mary McDonald agreed, `my grandmother always said that it was better to be an old man`s darling than a young man`s slave, only I`m just not so sure there`s too much darling in it, but then Maryanne says he treats Elizabeth very well, and sure that in itself is a blessing. Maryanne never talks about meeting anyone. Wouldn't you think now with all them fine soldiers that she`s nursing, that there`d be one of them at least to catch her eye. And as for our Agnes, she`s a lost cause, she`ll be depending on God to keep her in her old age, and he`s let down a good many as we know only too well.`

`Well Mary McDonald if that isn't blasphemy` her husband laughed `what`s gotten into ye at all.`

'Well to tell you the truth I`m worried about young Thomas` Mary confessed `that ould Fenian, Charlie Kearney is filling his head with stories, telling him all about the exploits of his Uncle James.`

'Well amn`t I quare glad that James Power is your side of the family and I can`t be blamed for him` Thomas laughed `but sure it`s not doing the lad any harm hearing about James now is it.`

'Sure it`s putting notions in his head that I`d rather wouldn`t be there ` Mary said concerned.

'Well now Moll he can hardly escape those notions living in the shadow of Vinegar Hill can he` Thomas asked.

'That`s just it Thomas` Mary replied obviously upset `maybe we should think about getting him out of the way of those Fenians and the like. He`s joined the Gaelic League you know, and always going to ould meetings, now what are they all about I ask ye, cos he surely doesn't tell me.`

'Well there`s nothing wrong with the Gaelic League now mind` Thomas stated adamantly `and sure he likes going to the ould meetings and keeping himself informed, there`s not too much else for a young fellow to do now is there until he finds a woman for himself.`

'He`s only fifteen, for God sake Thomas` Mary snapped.

'Old enough Mary mo croi, old enough` Thomas replied smiling.

....

Thomas McDonald, junior, was impressionable, and himself and his pals were a most attentive audience for the old Fenian Charlie Kearney who liked nothing better than filling their nights with colourful tales of the Fenians in their heyday, and although the Risings of 1848 and 1867 were neither military nor political triumphs, Charlie had a way of recalling them with fiery passion and romantic fervour that appealed to the young minds.

Thomas loved hearing about his mother's older brother, James Power, who it seemed was a bit of a character with strong republican beliefs and who liked being in the thick of things, so when the whiff of revolution reached him he headed straight for Dublin on the eve of the 5th March 1867, to strike his blow for Irish freedom.

But the ill-fated Rebellion was over before it began undermined by informers and spies. Hundreds were arrested in and around Tallaght, with others desperately trying to flee through the Dublin and Wicklow mountains. To avoid arrest James Power stopped briefly in Enniscorthy to say goodbye to his family and kin before boarding the first vessel out of New Ross bound for America.

Once in America James joined the Fenian Brotherhood and became involved with the invasion of Canada and the Fenian raids on that country in 1870 and 1871. Led by General John O` Neill, Irishmen who had fought on both sides during the American Civil War joined forces to invade the British Province of Canada, their object being to seize the territory, and then ransom it back to the British, in return for Ireland's independence.

A mammoth task, but a brave and romantic one that made the young Thomas McDonald nearly burst with pride for his relative.

`Can ye imagine that at all lads` Charlie Kearney said animatedly one evening `a group of Irishmen on foreign soil, brave enough, not just to take on the entire British Empire, but confident and bold enough to think that they could take on a country like Canada and hold her for ransom, now that's something lads. They were giants of men them Fenians I tell ya and they will be remembered forever, as long as Irish history is told around the world. Them Fenian boys will never be forgotten and your Uncle James was one of them` he said pointing at Thomas.
`Jaysus, I love to do something brave and bold like that ` Paddy Murphy said with a shine in his eye` ya know, something so wonderful and fearless that we would be remembered forever for it.`

`But sure what could you do around here, there`s no Rising planned for starters, and we just spend all our time sitting around talking like this about what the ould Fenians did, what can we do, that`s what I want to know` Sean Whelan asked.

`Oh there`s plenty of ways of striking a blow for Irish freedom lads` the old Fenian almost whispered, making them all sit up and listen intently.

When he was certain he had their full attention, he continued in hushed tones` Who is the symbol of the British Empire right here in Enniscorthy, right on our very doorstep`.

The lads looked at each other blankly, then Jimmy Devereux said `The Constabulary there in the Barracks, don't they uphold the law for the Brits?` and the lads all nodded.

`Not a bit of it` Charlie Kearney sneered `sure them fellows below in the Barracks are only there for the few bob, it` s just a job for them, now I don't hold with them mind you, but in fairness they don`t really care tuppence for the Empire. I`ll tell ya who the symbol of the British Empire is here in Enniscorthy, it`s her Ladyship now isn`t it, sitting off high and mighty down there in her big house, with her servants and her stables and her tenant farmers and her insisting on being called Lady Gray. She`s the symbol of the British Empire in this town, I`m telling ya, sure isn't she ninth in line for the British throne, you won`t get much closer than that here in Ireland.`

`Don`t you work for her` Johnny Doyle accusingly asked of Thomas McDonald.

`Ah……. I`ve done odd jobs down there in the stables ` Thomas said embarrassed.

`Ya surely have, lots of times` Johnny Doyle insisted ` and sure don't your father and brother work for her too`.

`Well it`s better than your father and brother`, Thomas retorted angrily, ` they don't work at all`.

61

`Ah you`re quare funny now aren't ye` Johnny said `but at least mine are not traitors.`

Thomas McDonald, wiry and agile took a leap from where he was sitting and landed on top of a surprised Johnny Doyle knocking him to the floor and began pounding him with his fists, until Jimmy Devereux and Paddy Murphy pulled him up.

`Will ya stop all this nonsense immediately now lads` Charlie Kearney roared ` amn't I always telling ye, that is Ireland`s downfall always fighting between ourselves. Thomas can`t help what his father and brother do no more than any of us can, it`s what he does himself that matters, isn`t that right now Thomas.`

Thomas nodded in silence, feeling a mixture of shame for his father and brother along with a very strong loyalty to them and the desire to defend his family. But he knew he had to redeem himself and his standing among his peers, so he asked of Charlie ` Well what can we do about Lady Gray anyway, even if she is the symbol of British authority, sure there`s not much the five of us can do now is there.`

`All the blows for Irish freedom don`t have to be big rebellions Thomas `Charlie Kearney replied conspiratorially `there`s many a small strike that we can land to make Lady Gray`s life here in Enniscorthy a lot less comfortable.`

....

`Where is he, I`m going to fucking kill him!` William McDonald burst into the kitchen at Court Street, Enniscorthy as Mary and Thomas were just about to head to bed.

`Where is who? ` Mary asked, about to chastise her son for using foul language in the house but there was something wild in William`s eyes that stopped her in her tracks.

`That fucking idiot of a brother, I'm going to fucking kill him I'm telling ya Ma and ya won't stop me`. William was heading up the stairs when his father caught him.

`What is it William, what's the matter can't you calm down and tell us what you are so upset about`.

`Ask him, ask that fucking stupid son of yours what he and his imbecile friends have done and then tell me to calm down`, William roared.

All of the McDonald family were now out of their beds and standing on the landing staring at William, all except Thomas.

William burst into the room he shared with Thomas before his father could stop him and pulled his younger brother out of his bed, shaking him and shouting ` What were you thinking of you stupid little bollicks.`

`Let your brother go this instant William` Thomas McDonald yelled `and tell us what this is all about, you're frightening the little ones.`

JohnJoe the baby had begun to cry, and little Mary had started to shake. The McDonald children were not used to these kind of violent outbursts.

`Let him tell you then before I fucking kill him` William said red with rage, words spitting from his mouth like nails.

`What's he talking about Thomas, tell us what you've done, it can't be that bad sure you're a good chap, so come on out with it now`, Thomas McDonald said to his third son.

`He better be quick about it` William interjected `cos the RIC will be here any minute looking for him and his stupid Fenian pals.`

Thomas seemed to have been struck dumb and continued standing there looking at his feet saying nothing.

`You're not too brave and bold now are you` William roared at him.

`Well at least I'm not afraid to strike a blow against the Brits instead of being a lackey for them`, Thomas retorted, suddenly finding his voice.

It took all the strength that Thomas McDonald Snr. could muster to keep his first born from physically attacking his brother and his patience was growing thin. `For the last and final time Thomas what have you done` he roared still holding William at arm's length.

`Him and his Fenian comrades set fire to the Brownswood stables earlier this evening causing major damage to the stables and the death of one of our horses that got trapped inside` William screamed, losing his patience with his mute brother.

Mary McDonald had never before seen such a murderous look on her husband's face in all the years she knew him, and began to fear for the safety of her second son, just as the sound of frantic knocking was heard on the front door.

`That'll be the Peelers now` William said, releasing himself from his father's grip and going to answer it.

But it wasn't the Peelers it was the Devereux's from down the road, Paddy and Ann with Jimmy in tow. `Holy Mary, Mother of God`, Ann Devereux was crossing herself as she entered the house, `what have these two yahoos landed us in at all, the Peelers will be on top of us in no time what are we to do.`

Thomas McDonald still bore the murderous scowl and was directing it at his second son in disbelief. `It is bad enough what you've have brought upon us ` he said through clenched teeth to his son `but to target defenceless animals, how could ye Thomas .... Jimmy`, he said looking from one to the other, `you've helped myself and William look after those very horses Thomas you have played and ran around those stables since you were a young fella, what in God's name were you thinking of?`

`A blow for Ireland how are ya, a blow of insanity more like it` Paddy Devereux uttered `but what are we going to do about it? Would you be able to have a word with herself Thomas, her Ladyship like, and ask her to show lenience to the chaps, that they were put up to it by men who were old enough to know better.`

`I`m not too sure that`s going to work` William interrupted `the horse that got trapped was Star, Da, her Ladyship`s favourite hunter.`

······································

It was one of the hardest things that Thomas McDonald ever had to do, to plead for compassion for his third son when he was totally disgusted by what the boy had done and found it difficult to even look at him, but out of deference to her trusted Stable Manager of many years and William who had promised to find her the best hunter in the country, as a replacement for Star, Lady Gray said that she wouldn't press charges, on one proviso that both boys Thomas and Jimmy Devereux would be sent away from Enniscorthy, and as far away as possible from the influence of the Fenians.

It was the Devereux`s who came up with the solution. Young Jimmy`s grandfather, James Devereux, Grocer, and Tobacconist at Market Square, Enniscorthy was also agent for the Allen Brothers who had been operating a trade and passenger line to Savannah, Georgia in America since the 1850s.

Almost half of the Irish population of Savannah were from Wexford, due in the main to the nonstop shore to shore sailings from Wexford town and New Ross directly to Savannah, and to the Kehoe family from the Mount Howard area of the county who had emigrated there in 1851, establishing a thriving Iron Works in the city and employing a large force of Wexford emigrants.

The Kehoe family had sailed with the Allen Brothers booking their passage with their agent, Jimmy`s grandfather, James Devereux, and had remained in contact with him over the years. Many members of the

Devereux family had already emigrated to Savannah finding employment in the Kehoe Iron Works and Paddy Devereux intended to send Jimmy and Thomas out to his cousin Martin who was a foreman at the very successful plant.

`It`s the best thing for them` Paddy comforted his wife Ann and Mary McDonald `they can begin again in a new city and a new country, and if they`re any good at all they`ll make brand new lives for themselves and sure they`ll be among their own, there`s so many from Wexford in Savannah it won`t feel like they`ve gone away at all.`

`But it will for us, they`ll be gone away from us and we won`t have brand new lives we`ll just have the same old ones but without them` Mary McDonald said despondently `there`s just going to be another empty part in my heart, where my son Thomas used to be.`

Chapter 8

By Christmas 1901 there were four members missing from the McDonald household at Court Street, Enniscorthy, leaving Mary McDonald with the feeling that her life blood was ebbing from her drop by harrowing drop.

Thomas and Jimmy Devereux had arrived safely in Savannah after a pleasant enough voyage and were met at the Docks by Martin Devereux who had arranged lodgings for them in the predominately Irish neighbourhood of Old Fort and jobs for them at the Iron Works.

An exuberant Thomas had written home at Christmas, in good spirits, saying how nice everyone was and how good they were to him " … this city is teeming with all kinds of life and with people from all over Ireland and there`s so many from Wexford here it`s just like being at home except for missing all of ye".

The tension between father and son had been palpable up to the day before the sailing when Mary McDonald could stick it no longer.

`Please Thomas for my sake will ya make it up with your son before he leaves for the other side of the world tomorrow` she asked of her husband on the eve of the departure.

`I dearly wish I could woman, but every time I look at him, I think of what he did and I just can`t get past it` Thomas said obviously distraught.

`I know he did a terrible thing Thomas` Mary said with compassion `but he is your son and we might never see him again and sure we can`t blame him for having republican blood in his veins now can we.`

`For God sake Mary, this has nothing to do with republican blood` Thomas replied irritated, `I can surely understand that, but like a bad dog he bit the hand that fed him. Lady Gray was good to him and to all of us and that`s how he showed his thanks and gratitude. He was too weak to stand up to his peers and just went along with what he knew to be wrong. We raised to be better than that. And then there are the animals, Mary. You know how I feel about horses, I thought that I had brought my children up to be decent people showing respect where it was deserved and providing kindness and protection to defenceless animals. I am just so disappointed that I can`t even look at him.`

`But please Thomas just for my sake`, Mary pleaded, `can you bring yourself to shaking his hand and wishing him well tomorrow before he leaves us forever.`

`I do wish him well Mary, surely to God, you know that, I wish the very best kind of life for him and I hope and pray that he will do wonderful things in Savannah and that he will be very happy there, but I am afraid to look at him in case he sees the disappointment in my eyes`, Thomas said with a heavy heart.

Mary McDonald clung to her third son on the Wexford Quay the following day and refused to let him go until himself and his father and his brother William had all made their peace with each other. In the end love and family loyalty reigned, as the brothers hugged each other in forgiveness and father and son embraced.

`I know I haven`t turned out the way you wanted me too Da but I will make you proud of me I promise, even though it be on the other side of the world` Thomas McDonald said looking straight into his father`s eyes for the first time in days.

Thomas Senior returned the gaze saying `You are a McDonald, from Enniscorthy in the county of Wexford and you are my son. Always remember who you are and where you came from and don`t be swayed by others, be true to yourself and your kind.`

Mary McDonald stood on the Wexford Quay until the ship and her son were out of sight, knowing in her heart of hearts that it was the last time that she would ever see him.

Kate had not wished to add to her family's misery leading up to Christmas so she kept her secret to herself, in the knowledge that her plans would only bring more heartache to her already struggling mother.

Earlier that year Victoria, Queen of the British Empire for sixty-four years, passed to her eternal reward, at the ripe old age of eighty-one years, at Osborne on the Isle of Wight, and her funeral took place eleven days later on 2nd February at Windsor.

Lady Gray being ninth in line to the throne, felt it her duty to attend and included the young Kate McDonald among her staff making the trip to London for the solemn event.

Kate was delighted with the chance to travel and to see London even if it was for a funeral. They would be away for nearly two months as Lady Gray intended taking up residence at her Kensington home and spending time with her daughter Eileen, who had been a student of Fine Art at the London Slade School for almost a year.

`London for two months` Kate hugged the notion to herself, `how lovely would that be.' She loved being with her brothers and sisters of course, but at a very grown up sixteen she had outgrown the younger ones and the older ones had all gone away, apart from William who might as well have left, he was at home so seldom, between trips around the country buying horses, and trips back and forth to England selling them. William was hardly ever there.

`Oh yes` Kate thought to herself, she was going to love London, she got on well with her Ladyship and with the house staff at Brownswood especially Bridie Murphy, her best friend, they would have the time of it together in London.

Eveleen Gray was looking forward to the trip herself even if there would be no grand parties or afternoon teas or social gatherings of any kind, as the entire country would be in mourning for their beloved

Monarch, but she did miss her daughter Eileen and would welcome the chance to be with her for a while, away from the responsibilities of Brownswood.

She had spoken to Thomas McDonald about taking Kate with her, the girl was only sixteen but had been working as a maid in the Gray household for the past two years. She wasn't at all like her mother and sisters, having little or no vocation to care for the sick and elderly, she knew exactly what to do but had no great inclination to do it, but she was capable and intelligent and indeed a beauty with her black curls and ice blue eyes. 'Kate hadn't quite found her niche', Lady Gray mused, but when she did, her Ladyship had no doubt that she would make a most excellent job of whatever it was.

Like all the McDonald girls Kate had beauty, a quick wit and an air of capability accompanied by a ready, sparkling smile. 'Yes Kate McDonald had the potential to go a very long way indeed.'

....

London was thronged: everyone wanting to pay their last respects to the longest reigning Monarch Britain had ever had and with rumours of planned assassination plots to kill her grandson Kaiser William and Leopold, King of the Belgians during the funeral procession, Scotland Yard security was everywhere.

The Queen had left instructions that she wanted a full military funeral, her coffin paraded through the streets of London on a gun carriage pulled by eight white horses, to arrive at St. Georges Chapel in Windsor for the final ceremony.

Kate McDonald and Bridie Murphy were standing on their tippy-toes at the end of Windsor Street, packed liked sardines in the massive crowd trying desperately to catch a glimpse of the solemn cortege, when the horses kicked and broke loose from their traces almost toppling the coffin to the ground. All hell ensued as the eight horses terrified by the screams and cries from the crowd darted and reared seeking an escape route.

Naval and army personnel franticly tried to bring the animals under control, while Scotland Yard scanned the crowd in case it was a diversion, part of an assassination plot. In the mayhem Kate was knocked to the ground and tried in vain to get back on her feet, as Bridie screamed at people walking all over her in their rush to get away from the increasingly panicked animals.

`Dear God someone help us please`, Bridie roared, `my friend is being trampled to death.`

Suddenly, two men appeared and while one kept the crowd from walking on her, the other lifted Kate into his arms and began carrying her down the street.

`Stay close beside me` the other man said to Bridie as they headed down the street in the direction of the Castle Hotel. Bridie, recognising the Wexford accent, felt an immediate sense of calm and security amid the chaos.

The Hotel Reception was crammed with people trying to get off the crazed streets but the man holding Kate in his arms seemed to know where he was going and opened a door to a small room behind the Reception Desk where he laid Kate down gently on a chaise longue.

Kate had fainted and looked bruised and bloodied. `Jack, get a basin and some water and see if we can get her cleaned up a bit to see what injuries she has', Kate's rescuer said to his companion, and again Bridie recognised the Wexford accent.

`I think I know you` Bridie said almost in disbelief to the man now kneeling in front of her friend in the middle of a hotel in Windsor, England.

`You most likely do` he replied `I'm Harry and that's Jack, we're Staffords from the Castleboro Estate just outside Enniscorthy, and you two are most definitely from Enniscorthy or thereabouts: I knew it as soon as I heard you screaming for help.`

Just then Kate mumbled `What happened, where am I`.

`You`re in good hands, Enniscorthy hands even` Harry said marvelling at her unusual blue eyes as he looked down at her.

`Oh Enniscorthy` Kate muttered confused `are we still in London?

`You are in the Castle Hotel, Windsor, do you remember waiting to see the Queen`s funeral and the horses breaking loose` Harry asked.

Kate nodded as it began to come back to her.

....

The Stafford brothers, Harry and Jack had come to London some six years before as part of the staff of Lord and Lady Carew of Castleboro, who came to take up their annual six monthly residence at their home at 28 Belgrade Square.

Harry and Jack had recognised immediately the opportunities available to them in the vibrant and expanding city, opportunities that they would never have in Enniscorthy. And so, when it came time for the Carews to return home the Stafford brothers had already secured positions for themselves at the Windsor Castle Hotel with the assistance of Lord Carew, who was well acquainted with the Hotel Concierge, Henry Gilbert.

Although Harry and Jack had no prior experience they were fine looking men: standing six feet four in their stocking feet, with honest, open countenances and warm, wholesome smiles. `They will look good in uniform` Henry Gilbert mused `and it`s all about first impressions` he thought, wisely deciding to give the Stafford brothers the position of doormen at the prestigious hotel, and besides which, Lord and Lady Carew were valued customers having stayed on several occasions when attending functions at the Castle.

Little did Henry Gilbert know then that only six short years later he would be replaced as Concierge by one of those doormen.

Harry Stafford was affable, and an extremely quick learner, he had the kind of face that people like, attractive but not overly handsome, he was observant and knew instinctively what made people tick, he could anticipate what you wanted almost before you knew you wanted it, which moved him rapidly up through the hotel ranks until one day when Henry Gilbert fell ill and knew that he would never return to work Harry Stafford was his obvious replacement.

It had been a wise move for the hotel, Harry had gained the respect of some very wealthy and influential customers in his six years and had an excellent reputation around Windsor and London, but more than that, he handled his staff superbly, instilling a sense of responsibility and making them feel that they were a very important part of a large family, rather than an employee. He ran his hotel on much the same style as the big house at Castleboro, with staff taking a pride in everything they did and in anticipating every need of those they looked after.

Working as hard as he did Harry Stafford had little time left for personal activity of any kind and certainly not of the romantic kind. Many women, from maids to grand ladies, had shown an interest in him but he had not felt the need to pursue any of them, so he was quite taken aback with his reaction to the young Irish woman he had rescued at the Queen`s funeral.

Harry and Jack had come out onto the Windsor streets, even though their view from the hotel would have been greatly superior, but they wanted the experience of being part of the crowd and had been watching with amusement the two young girls bobbing up and down to get a first glimpse of the Queen`s cortege, they looked so young and so excited that their curiosity and enthusiasm was almost infectious.

When the eight white horses pulling the gun carriage carrying the Queen`s coffin bolted, Harry and Jack were about to lend a hand getting them under control when above all the din they heard a Wexford accent screaming for help.

The brothers immediate and automatic reaction was to run in the direction of the voice from home, like will always find like, and the whole of Windsor could have toppled around them as they searched for that Wexford voice in the crowd.

When Kate McDonald opened her eyes and looked up at the man gazing down at her, she worried that she might be in trouble. He was so authoritative and stern, watching her intently, that she felt that she was going to be scolded for something she had done and became quite nervous.

She wanted to get to her feet to regain some semblance of dignity and composure, for some strange reason it was important to her that this man, bending over her, didn't see her as the frail damsel in distress, she wanted him to know that she was quite capable of looking after herself, but when she tried to get up the room went into a spin and blood trickled from her forehead.

Laying her back down on the chaise longue Harry Stafford was taken quite unawares by a surge of wanting to care for this young woman with the dark hair, pale skin and piercing blue eyes, that he could have easily passed over to one of his staff, but instead he ordered a cup of tea to be brought to the room for her and asked Jack if he would summon Mrs. Lennon, the hotel housekeeper to come and take a look at her injuries, there being no point at all in looking for a doctor on the crowded streets.

`I'm okay really` Kate said again trying to raise herself up and get her feet under her but Harry Stafford was having none of it until she had been seen by Mrs. Lennon and imbibed her sweet tea.

Bridie had been relaying their story to Jack with Harry catching snips of it. He knew they were staying in Kensington with Lady Gray and he knew that they both worked for her Ladyship at home in Enniscorthy on the Brownswood Estate.

Mrs. Lennon couldn't find anything broken or sprained and the gash on Kate's forehead didn't appear too deep, but the girl had had a shock and seemed quite unsteady, so she felt it might be better not to move her too quickly and besides it was still mayhem on the streets and it would take strength and fortitude for the girls to make their way back to Kensington.

`You must stay here and rest awhile and when you feel up to it I will get a carriage to take you back to Kensington` Harry told Kate.

`Oh but they will be worried about us` Kate said eager to leave this embarrassment behind her as quickly as she could `they will have heard about the commotion here in Windsor today and they will be concerned.`

`I'm sure they will` Harry said with authority `but you are going to remain here until Mrs. Lennon is happy for you to leave`. Kate looked pleadingly at Bridie who just shrugged her shoulders and that was that.

Bridie seemed to be enjoying chatting to Jack and not at all perturbed either by the apparent unease of her friend or the delay in returning to Kensington.

By the time Mrs. Lennon was satisfied that Kate was sufficiently recovered to make the journey Harry Stafford knew that he wanted to see this slip of an Enniscorthy girl again.

There was something about her that appealed to the very core of him that he couldn't quite understand or put a description to.

From the time he lifted her off the street into his arms something just felt right. When he caught her hand as she tried to rise from the chaise longue he experienced a connection, like a shock running up the length of his arm, through the network of veins and arteries all the way down to his Irish soul, a feeling of knowing, of recognition from a vague and ageless past, and looking into those ice blue eyes, he knew that she had felt it too, and was just as much afraid of it as he was.

This was beyond them both, almost as though they already knew each other in a far away time, in a distant, ancient place.

As Harry helped Kate into the hotel carriage that would take her back to Lady Gray`s residence in Kensington, he knew with certainty and an amazing clarity that this chance encounter on the streets of Windsor was his destiny.

Chapter 9

In the two months that followed Kate and Bridie had the very best time of their lives. London was a wonderment to them, another world from the one they knew in Enniscorthy, everything was so big, so bright and so busy and Harry and Jack made as much time available to them as possible.

Lady Gray and Eileen required little looking after, leaving the girls with lots of free time to explore and enjoy.

Harry and Kate didn't fall in love, they had been in love from the moment of touch and beyond.

But Kate was only sixteen and would have to return to Enniscorthy, at least until after her seventeenth birthday which fell on 4th November, and so they planned for Harry to return to the Stafford household in Clonroche for Christmas 1901, and Kate to travel back to London with him in the New Year to take up a position as maid in the Windsor Castle Hotel, along with her friend Bridie.

Kate thought the time would never pass, missing Harry was like losing a limb, like part of her being had been cut off leaving her in some way disabled without it.

They wrote to each other every week and Bridie and Kate had told Thomas and Mary all about the two Stafford brothers who had saved Kate`s life and treated them so well in London.

Indeed, Lady Gray had spoken warmly about the two young men from Clonroche and how well they were doing for themselves in Windsor `in particular the oldest of them` she said to Thomas McDonald on one occasion `he is a fine looking man with an air of subdued confidence about him, when one knows ones worth, there is no need for flamboyance or arrogance, in the fullness of time people will always recognise ability`.

Kate never alluded to a love interest between herself and Harry, thinking better of it due to her youth and the age difference between them and because her parents seemed to be having enough trouble at the time with Thomas, but she thought Christmas 1901 would never come, it was like being a little girl again waiting for the enchantment of Christmas Eve.

....

As long as Kate lived, and she lived to be a very old lady, she never forgot that Christmas morning in 1901 when Jack Stafford knocked her door to tell her that her soulmate was gone from her forever.

Two days before, on 23rd December, the Stafford brothers had boarded a ship to have them home in Wexford on Christmas Eve. Harry had been looking forward to it for months. It had been difficult to take time off, he hadn't had an Irish Christmas for years and the excitement of coming home and seeing Kate again made his heart pound in his chest every time he thought about it.

The months without her had been torture, how could this one person mean so much to him, he failed to understand it, he had never felt like this before about anyone. Yet he wanted to tread carefully because of her youth. He didn't want to rush her into anything that she might not be ready for, so by giving her a position of employment at the Windsor they could spend time together and take things nice and easy. Besides, it might be a lot more acceptable to her parents that she was going to London to work, as her siblings before her, rather than because she had fallen in love with a man in two short months, who was almost ten years her senior, and had decided that she wanted to leave home and family to spend the rest of her life with him.

Yes, they had both agreed that it would be easier on Thomas and Mary to think that Kate and Bridie were heading to London to take up employment at the Windsor Castle Hotel that the Stafford brothers from Clonroche had secured for them, after all Kate had always said that she wanted to work in a big hotel in London, and they would be happy that her dream was coming true for her.

Kate stared into Jack Stafford`s face on that Christmas morn in 1901 knowing that she would never enjoy Christmas again.

....

Harry and Jack had been standing on deck together reminiscing on Christmas past in the Stafford household, when the alarm was raised, a man had fallen overboard.

`There he is Jack` Harry shouted grabbing Jack`s arm `I can see him there in the water` he said beginning to take off his heavy overcoat.

`What are you doing Harry?` Jack asked in rising dread already knowing the answer to his question.

`Sure I can see him just there below us Jack` Harry replied jumping up on the edge.

`Well let someone else go in after him, can`t you` Jack Stafford pleaded with his brother, all the while knowing it was pointless.

`He`ll be swept away if I don't go now Jack, you know I`m a strong swimmer, now run and throw me a buoy as soon as I`m in the water`, and with that he was gone.

Jack grabbed the buoy and swung it with force into the sea and got to the side just as others were coming to help. He saw Harry put the buoy over the man`s head as some of the crew threw a rope and a ladder over the side. Harry tied the rope around the man`s chest and guided him to the ladder hoisting him up on the first rung. As he began to climb the ship seemed to roll slightly causing him to lose his balance and kick out frantically catching Harry in the side of the head.

Within seconds Harry Stafford had disappeared from sight.

Jack screamed his name as men restrained him, preventing him from going over the side after his brother.

Several members of the crew were already in the water, but Harry Stafford had vanished into the deep never to be seen again.

....

No-one understood why Kate was so upset except her friend Bridie. Thomas and Mary McDonald were concerned for their daughter who hadn't touched a morsel of food in days and it was only when Jack Stafford called to see her a week later that they began to realise that Harry had been a very important person to their young girl.

Lifeboats had launched searches on both sides of the Irish Sea but Harry Stafford`s body hadn't been found. There had been a funeral service in the packed Church in Cloughbawn. The Staffords were a very popular and well known family in the area and the terrible tragedy and sentimental time of the year brought people from miles around to express their sympathies for the fine young man cut down in his prime, but Kate had been too upset and too weak to attend.

It was Jack who eventually jolted her out of the unforgiving, grey fog that engulfed her, when he called to see if herself and Bridie were taking up the positions waiting for them at the Windsor, or would he let the hotel know that they weren't coming.

Kate had completely forgotten that they had planned to return to London with Harry and Jack, and she didn't know what to do.

How could she carry on with life without Harry, it was impossible, and no-one understood. She had known him for just a couple of months, how could anyone understand that they had found each other through the mists of time, each part of the others preordained destiny.

Finally, she made the decision to leave with Jack and Bridie, they were the only two people in the world who had any idea how she was feeling and she couldn't be separated from them, besides London was the only place she had known Harry, the only memories she would ever have of him were there on the streets of the city where they had shared a lifetime together.

On 10th January 1902 a tearful Kate McDonald stood on deck staring into the Irish Sea with her friend Bridie Murphy on one side of her and Jack Stafford on the other, and scattered snowdrops, the first of the year on the Castleboro Estate, into the dark waters for her beloved Harry.

Mary McDonald was at a loss to know why her sorrowful seventeen-year- old daughter Kate felt the need to return to London with Bridie Murphy and Jack Stafford.

`I know the three of them are friends` she said to her husband Thomas when Kate told them of her plans `but we're her family.`

`I know Moll ` Thomas said sharing his wife's confusion ` but I suppose they have shared a tragedy the three of them and that can bring people close together, you know.`

`I do know,` Mary replied `and he seems to have been such a fine young man by all accounts I'm really sorry that we never got the chance to meet him but sure Kate didn't know him all that well, sure she spent time with him in London but that was months ago and he was good enough to organise positions for herself and Bridie but it's not like they were seeing each other or anything and yet she seems so sad and lost since his death.`

`I think there was more to it than we know`, her astute husband said, `maybe London and a new job are the best thing for Kate at the present time, she needs something to keep her busy and God knows something to bring the life back into those beautiful eyes and she won't find it in Enniscorthy I'm afraid.`

`That`s five now Thomas McDonald `, Mary whispered sadly, ` five children gone from us and Ireland. Will it stop there, I wonder, or is that to be the destiny of all Irish mothers forever.

Chapter 10

Kate began working in the Windsor Castle Hotel in a veil of sorrow but, as Lady Gray had long ago remarked, she was a clever girl and almost in spite of herself she learned quickly and excelled at everything she did.

In a way it was her tribute to Harry, he loved the Windsor and was so proud of his position there. Kate understood that and made it her mission to live her best possible life there in his memory.

On her free afternoon each week she combed the streets of London desperately seeking his face among the indifferent crowds. His body had never been found and she never gave up hope that somehow, somewhere they would meet again, in this world, or another.

Kate was on the London streets on 31st May 1902 when news came that the South African war was finally over, and watched with envy the utter joy of those who knew their loved ones would be returning home to them soon, and felt the pain and anguish of those who knew their loved ones would never be coming home again.

Kate wouldn't see her sisters Maryanne and Elizabeth or Elizabeth's husband Peter for quite a long time yet. Maryanne had written to say that although the war had ended, there was still terrible turmoil and suffering in its aftermath, and many of the wounded were too ill to be moved.

Maryanne, Elizabeth and Dr Hargraves had volunteered to remain until all the wounded had either passed to their eternal reward or were sufficiently recovered to be able to make the journey home, it could be another six months or more before Kate would be reunited with her siblings.

....

Agnes was staying behind with the nuns in the convent at Mafeking there was so much hardship in the wake of the war for those who were left behind that she wanted to stay and help them in any way she could. The British policy of `scorched earth` had left vast areas of the country devastated and it could take years for them to return to full production.

She would miss Maryanne, who had been like a mother to her and a connection to the family she had been born into, but she had another family now and the Sisters were all very kind and caring, nevertheless, when the time came for Maryanne to leave for Cape Town a deep and unexpected sorrow came over Agnes. She somehow knew that her goodbye to Maryanne had a finality about it, she didn't know where her new life would take her but she had a feeling that she wouldn`t see Maryanne or the rest of her family ever again and it both frightened and saddened her.

Maryanne hadn`t seen Elizabeth and Peter since the day they were married, and indeed hadn't had much of a chance to talk to Elizabeth that day either, but she had picked up on the fact that both parties seemed to have entered into an mutually beneficial agreement rather than a love match, and she hoped, with reservations, that her sister would be happy and that this wasn't just a hasty decision on the rebound from Richard Saunders.

But seeing Peter and Elizabeth together now, over eighteen months later, Maryanne was pleasantly surprised to see the love that had blossomed between them.

`Oh Elizabeth I`m so pleased to see you both so happy and so much in love, I thought Richard Saunders had destroyed that capacity in you forever` she said as the sisters were preparing the last of the recovering wounded for the journey home.

`Whatever do you mean Maryanne?` Elizabeth asked looking perplexed. `Peter and I have been very happy together in our work here in Cape Town, but we`re not in love, we respect and admire each other greatly and Peter is the kindest and most gentle man I have ever known and I suppose you could say that we both have love for the other but we are not in love Maryanne, there is a difference`.

`Oh is there?` Maryanne asked feigning ignorance. `I wasn't aware, but then what would I know, I see the way Peter looks at you when you are about your duties administering to the men here in the hospital, it's with the greatest of admiration and yes even gentleness, and I see you watching him perform surgery with a look akin to adulation, and I see you both searching for each other in crowded spaces and I see the smiles that light up your faces when you turn a corner and your eyes meet, I'm sorry, but I did mistake that for you being in love with each other, was I wrong?'

`Maryanne`, Elizabeth began determinedly, `both Peter and I have had previous experiences of being "in love" which neither of us want to re-visit ever again. Yes, we are very happy together and yes, we are kind and gentle to each other and have the greatest of respect one for the other and that is quite enough for both of us, we don't want the awful highs and lows of being "in love" and the despair of it all, we just want to partner each other in a fruitful and contented life, is that so difficult to understand?`

`Well no, of course it isn't` Maryanne replied `but are you quite sure Elizabeth that is all it is?'

Elizabeth shook her head but didn't reply.

If Elizabeth was honest, she would have to recognise that there was a smidgeon of truth to what Maryanne was saying, but she was reluctant to admit it to herself let alone to anyone else. It wasn't what she had signed up to, and Peter had been quite clear what the arrangement between them was, and besides it was working so well, they had both been extremely happy in the past year perhaps the happiest either of them had ever been, with the exception of that first three months with Richard Saunders, and she really didn't want to upset the apple cart in anyway. But she did have reservations about going back to London and was worried what life might be like for them there.

Peter was an only child and his parents were both deceased. He had kept pretty much to himself over the years since his failed love affair so there weren't many friends in his life either. Sometimes he envied Elizabeth with her large family and loved to hear stories about them, hoping someday to meet them all.

Indeed, Peter Hargraves could spend hours listening to his new wife, and found, in the months since their nuptials, that he wanted to spend more and more time with her.

The arrangement had been quite clear between them: it was most definitely a marriage of convenience, both of them looking only for life partners, so they would never have to go through the whole romantic process and run the risk of being hurt again. They would be kind and respectful to one another, but there would be neither romantic nor physical involvement.

Life, despite the war, had taken on a peaceful contentment for both of them, they worked well together, lived and laughed together, enjoyed the same leisure pursuits in their spare time, reading and horse riding, laughed at the others jokes and constantly sought out the others company and as they had agreed, there was nothing physical between them to spoil the pleasant ambience of it all.

And they were happy.

But as their first year together drew to a close, Peter Hargraves began more and more to want to put his arm around his wife when they were walking, or touch her when she handed him a scalpel during surgery, or brush a stray wisp of red hair back from her face when they went riding and he found himself watching her more and more as she moved gracefully and efficiently around the ward stopping with a kind word and a smile at each bedside.

Peter Hargraves was becoming deeply concerned that he was falling in love with his wife and was terrified that he was about to spoil the beautiful relationship they had, and above all else, he was petrified that he would lose her, so he would just have to go on pretending that all was fine, but secretly, he knew that he wanted her with every fibre of his being.

Lately he had begun to dream about taking her in his arms and making long and lingering love to her, it was all that he could do at night to keep his hands away from her and frequently paced up and down outdoors, until he was sure she had fallen asleep.

What was to be done, he wondered, she seemed quite happy apart from being worried about returning to London and the life they might have there, and he wished to put her mind at ease.

`I'm not a lady Peter, and wasn't brought up to be one. As your wife in London I would be expected to stay in your home in Berkeley Square and do nothing, and that would be extremely difficult for me, but I do understand that as a doctor's wife I couldn't return to nursing, well not in London anyway. So, what will I do, you and Maryanne will both be going back to your work, but what will there be for me to do?` Elizabeth asked with growing concern as their departure loomed.

`You know I've been thinking a lot about it Elizabeth and I want you to be happy and I know that you will need to be doing something and eh…… with no possibility of family between us.` Elizabeth looked up rather expectantly, but Peter having missed the look continued `I have given it a great deal of thought and perhaps London is not the right place for us at the moment.`

The war had been over for well over a year, all the wounded had either passed to their eternal reward or were finally well enough to make the journey home and still, Maryanne, Elizabeth and Peter had remained.

`So are we not going back tomorrow then?` Elizabeth asked.

A ship was leaving for England the following morning with passages booked for the last of the British Medical Personnel, including Elizabeth, Maryanne and Peter.

`Well, we do have to go back, as there are a great many things to sort out legally, now that we are married, but I was thinking, we`ve been happy here in Africa and there is a great need for doctors and nurses here so maybe when things are sorted we could come back, what would you think about that, or we could try India or anywhere that you would be happy Elizabeth` Peter said with tremendous feeling.

Forgetting herself, in her relief and gratitude, Elizabeth rushed into his arms and kissed him on the lips. It was like a bolt of lightning shot through his being, every nerve ending in his body tingled, causing him to involuntarily spring back. The look of shock, disappointment and rejection on Elizabeth`s face propelled him into immediate action, grabbing her before she had a chance to turn and run, he took her in his arms and he kissed her long and passionately.

Both of them were surprised and a little horrified by the intensity of feeling between them, never breaking eye contact they both frantically sought the others mouth and kissed again and again.

`Oh my God Elizabeth, I want you so badly I think I`m going to explode` Peter exclaimed breathlessly.

`Peter, if you don't take me right here, right now, I think I will die` Elizabeth said lifting her skirts.

They came together in a frenzy that shook them both. As Peter penetrated his wife her body moulded itself around him in a perfect fit, becoming difficult to know where one ended and the other began, the two becoming part of the whole, as spasm after spasm of raw passion and ecstasy engulfed them, swelling to a crescendo and exploding as Peter spilled himself into the very depths of Elizabeth and she cried out his name again and again in absolute abandonment until they collapsed against each other in total exhaustion and fulfilment.

`Elizabeth` Peter whispered `please tell me that you wanted that to happen just as much as I did.'
`Was that not obvious Peter Hargraves!` Elizabeth laughed, giving him a wicked smile, as she smoothed down her skirts just in time, as

Maryanne burst through the door to tell them that the transportation would be ready at 3am to take the three of them to the harbour where a ship would be waiting to take them to England.

Peter`s heart swelled with a love that he had hardly thought possible as he gazed at the flushed and happy countenance of his young wife, vowing to himself that he would spend the rest of his life endeavouring to recreate that look of utter joy and fulfilment currently lighting up her face.

As he sprang joyfully into the front seat of the transportation, Peter Hargraves was not to know that he would never see that look on his beautiful wife`s face again.

Maryanne was observing with interest the happy and satisfied face of her sister Elizabeth, when something exploded on the road directly in front of their truck, killing two and seriously maiming the rest.

Chapter 11

Bridget McDonald was the only fair-haired child of Mary and Thomas McDonald and stood out like a sore thumb among her dark and auburn haired siblings.

That wasn't the only reason Bridget McDonald stood out.

All the McDonald girls were handsome, tall and willowy with good skin and hair and striking eyes `They are of fine people ` Thomas McDonald used to say proudly `in the olden days my father told me the women of the McDonald Clan were as tall as the men and often as not fought side by side with them.`

`Oh and indeed` Mary McDonald would say puffing herself up to her full height `the Power women weren't dwarfs either I`ll have ya know and could hold their own in any argument.`

`Oh and don't I only know it` her husband would say with a grin.

But in truth both Mary and Thomas often asked themselves where their stunning daughter Bridget had come from. She had the face of an angel with large almond shaped brown eyes framed by long curling lashes and arched half moon brows, a perfect pink pouting mouth concealing a dazzling smile and all surrounded by cascading golden tresses.

And she wasn't blandly beautiful either, if there be such a thing, her eyes twinkled with intelligence and a joie de vivre, and her mouth sparkled with mirth and merriment.

Bridget, and Mary insisted on her being called Bridget not Bridie or Bruge or Brid, hungered for knowledge and was a delight for the nuns at the Convent of Mercy in Enniscorthy.

She loved to read and was a talented singer with a heavenly voice making her an automatic choice for the School and Church choir. Indeed, looking at Bridget on a Christmas Eve, singing Silent Night, one could be forgiven for mistaking the crib at St. Senan's Church for a stable in Bethlehem.

But Bridget was a mimic too and could keep her family entertained long into the night taking off well known town characters, copying their mannerisms and gestures to perfection.

However, Bridget's real passion was Shakespeare.

Whenever she got the chance she pleaded with her parents to let her attend the Shakespearean performances in the newly built theatre on Castle Street, the Athenaeum. Named for the Greek Goddess of learning Athena, the Athenaeum was the pride and joy of the townspeople of Enniscorthy who had raised the funds to have it built in 1892 and delighted in the many events regularly held there, dances, concerts, feiseanna, and theatrical performances by the many dramatic groups touring Ireland at the time.

The touring group would come to town for an entire week, sometimes two, staging different Shakespearean plays each night along with matinees at the weekends and would cause such excitement and anticipation that the town would be in a flurry for the duration of their stay.

Convent Schoolgirls could be seen almost swooning, if they happened to cross paths with the leading man on the town streets and it wasn't just schoolgirls either, many a respectable married woman in the town would question the banality of her own wedded bliss when listening in rapture to the eloquence and passion before her on the Athenaeum stage, and schoolboys of a certain age could be seen outside their front doors attacking each other with make believe daggers and swaggering and swashbuckling in the Market Square with make believe swords challenging each other to duels and the like.

It appeared that only the men were immune to the Athenaeum's theatrical charm, partially amused and partially embarrassed by it all, until one evening, as a regular feature of the performance, a member of the audience was called upon to give a party piece and lo and behold Bridget McDonald gets to her feet and volunteers to play Juliet to the leading man's Romeo.

The sixteen year old's performance was nothing short of magical. She was the perfect Juliet in every possible way, she looked the part with her slim silhouette and long golden locks and she was the part with her silken voice, perfect accent and expert delivery and men, young and old, all around the Athenaeum auditorium suddenly sat up in their seats and began to take notice.

Bridget's complete command of the stage and the audience was awesome making every man in the place fall immediately in love with her and becoming the envy of every woman present, even the suave leading man Charles Blake appeared to be smitten by her youthful charms and captivated by her natural ability.

Her timing was perfect, her diction flawless, her acting powerful, her stage presence natural and hypnotic, the young Bridget McDonald brought the house down and returned to her seat beside her friend Kitty O'Brien fully convinced that she had fallen madly in love with Romeo.

That was the thing about Bridget, she loved so easily, as her father Thomas had once remarked to his wife Mary "Bridget will love you quickly and forever if you just let her, that's just who she is".

'It is', Mary replied despondently, 'and it will bring trouble a plenty for her and us, mark my words Thomas McDonald.'

And they didn't have to wait very long for her prophesy to be fulfilled.

Bridget attended every performance from that night on and played the beautiful Juliet each evening falling more and more in love with the twenty-eight year old Romeo and by the end of the week had made up her mind that she was going to elope with him and they would marry and live happily ever after on stages all over Ireland, England, Scotland and Wales.

The experienced Charles Blake knew exactly what he was doing. Bridget was going to be a marvellous asset to the touring group, as his leading lady she would help spiral the Black Horse Touring Company to great heights, along with his own career, he was sure of it. She was young and impressionable and he had spent the entire week filling her head with happy ever afters, Shakespearean love quotes and the promise of the glamourous and exciting life of the Shakespearean actress.

It had been all too easy, Bridget gobbled his every word. She was in love, and not just with him, she was in love with the life and the excitement and the glamour he promised, and she wanted more than anything in the world to be onstage.

This was her destiny.

When she stood out there in front of an audience a metamorphosis occurred, allowing Bridget to become anyone she wanted to be. No longer was she just the pretty daughter of Mary and Thomas McDonald from the small town of Enniscorthy, she could be Cleopatra, Ophelia, Dessdemona, Rosalind, Juliet and much, much more.

Bridget told the attractive Mr. Blake that she was eighteen and he asked her if she would elope with him to England when the theatre company finished their Irish run. Bridget almost swooned in his arms. Charles Blake was debonair and handsome, sophisticated, and eloquent and not like any of the boys Bridget knew in Enniscorthy.

Her life was taking on a Shakespearean element of its own. It never occurred to the infatuated Bridget that it could be a Shakespearean tragedy.

The couple pledged their plighted troth to one another and planned that Bridget would meet Charles in Dublin when the company finished its final week in Kilkenny. Bridget would take the 4pm train from Enniscorthy and meet the Company at Kingstown before they sailed for England.

Bridget was to tell no-one.

But sure, what good was it heading off on the adventure of a lifetime with the love of your life, if you couldn't tell your best friend all about it.

Bridget took Kitty O`Brien into her confidence.

`Can you keep a secret Kitty O` Brien`, Bridget asked of her friend one day as they made their way home from Choir practice.

`You know I can Bridget sure who else would I be talking to except yourself, who would I tell, sure I don't have any other friends` Kitty said matter of factly.

`Yes but this is a really big secret, one that could not be told to my parents or even Constable Halley` Bridget whispered.

`What in God`s name is it Bridget you`re making me nervous. Now, don't tell me if it`s something very serious I will just worry about it` Kitty said concerned.

`But I have to tell someone, or I`ll burst with the keeping of it`, Bridget continued, `and you are my best friend.`

Bridget knew quite well that she could tell Kitty anything, if she confessed to murder, Kitty would assume that the victim had driven her to it and that Bridget was the injured party rather than the other way round. She was the best friend anyone could have.

`Well you know I`ve been on stage every night with Charles Blake at the Athenaeum and you know that since that first night I`ve been backstage with him every night too.`

`Of course I know that ya eejit. Sure haven't you gotten the free seat for me every night to go and haven't I waited for you at the side door every night to walk home with you Bridget. What are you talking about sure don't I know all that already.`

`Well the thing is`, Bridget went on nonplussed, `Charles Blake and I are in love and we are going to elope together when the Theatre Company leaves Ireland next Wednesday and we are going to be married in England and spend our lives performing Shakespeare all over England, Wales, Scotland and Ireland and Charles says maybe even America who knows the world is our oyster.`

The simple Kitty was horrified, elated, happy, sad, excited, and terrified all at once and just stood there in front of Bridget with her mouth open and no words coming out.

'Well say something for God`s sake Kitty`, Bridget roared grabbing her friend by the shoulders, `aren't you happy for me, this is my dream come true, and Charles Blake is very handsome and we are going to become the most celebrated couple on the British stage. You know I`ve dreamed about this since I was eight years old and now it`s finally coming true are ye not delighted for me Kitty?`

Kitty O`Brien began to sob. `But what about me, I`m going to lose my best friend. You will be gone from me forever`.

Kitty didn't mean to be selfish, but she was at pains to know what she would do without her animated friend who brightened up her darkest days, and God knows she had plenty of them.

....

Kitty`s father was a drunkard, with a big mouth, who spent a lot of his day in the local public houses either causing a row there or causing one when he eventually got home much the worse for wear.

His poor wife Lizzie and his seven children were terrified of him and walked on eggshells whenever he was around. Because of his drinking they were always short of money and Mary McDonald did what she could for them although it wasn't much, by the time she had her own brood fed and clothed, but anything she had to give away she gave to Lizzie O` Brien who was a decent, God fearing, intelligent woman who had just made the wrong decision when choosing who to fall in love with, and now herself and her children were paying the price everyday of their lives.

Every time she thought of Lizzie, Mary McDonald thanked God for the good man she had herself and the good life he was providing for her and their children, but she wouldn't tell him that of course just in case he would get carried away with himself.

Mary was also pleased to see her daughter Bridget befriending the rather shy and awkward Kitty. Bridget was a popular girl and could have had many best friends, most of them better off and probably a lot more fun than Kitty but Bridget had sat beside Kitty their very first day at school and they had remained close friends ever since.

`That was the thing about Bridget` Mary thought, just as her father said, `she would love you completely and forever if you just let her.`

Mary knew that Bridget was often ostracized by other friends because of her relationship with Kitty but the girl was steadfast in her love and loyalty and stood by her friend even when she had no clean clothes to wear to school or when she arrived with cuts and bruises that she said came from tussles with her brothers or falls she had when chasing the chickens.

No one believed her of course and many made fun of her but Bridget was always there ready to stand up for her and stand beside her and that was all that mattered to Kitty, but what was she to do now, who would be her friend and her champion now?

She wished Bridget had kept her secret to herself. It was all Kitty could think about. If she said nothing the best friend she ever had would go to England and she would never see her again, if she told on her she would get her best friend into trouble and she might never speak to her again.

Kitty was distraught with worry and plagued by indecision.

....

As her day of departure drew near Bridget could hardly contain her excitement. Instead of attending choir practice on Wednesday after school she would be catching the 4pm Dublin train getting off at Kingstown where she would meet Charles Blake and the theatre company before they all sailed off into the sunset and a life of fame, fortune, love and Shakespeare.

Bridget had smuggled some of her personal belongings out of the house and herself and Kitty had hidden them in a field near the bridge where they could be picked up on the way to the train.

Neither Bridget nor Kitty could sleep the night before. Both tossed and turned, Bridget wishing for it to be time to get up and begin her adventure and Kitty for a very different reason, as the sounds of her inebriated father hurling abuse at her poor unfortunate mother went on through the night, finally causing her to make a decision.

The following day Bridget was as skittish as a newborn lamb, indeed Sr. Gabriel had to curb her enthusiasm several times remarking that she would have to tie her to her seat to keep her from flying out the window.

After school both girls made excuses to Sr. Josephine for choir practice saying that they were needed at home and instead headed in the direction of Enniscorthy train station, picking up Bridget`s hidden belongings in the field along the way.

`You`re very quiet` Bridget said to Kitty who simply shrugged her shoulders.

`Was it a bad night in your house last night` Bridget asked, well used to Kitty`s silences in the aftermath of her father`s rage.

`Yeah it wasn't good`, Kitty replied beginning to cry.

Bridget`s generous heart went out to her friend and she said `As soon as I am settled in England Kitty O`Brien I am going to send money for you to follow me, do you hear me now and as soon as you get it you`re to get out of that terrible house once and for all.`

`But what about my mother Bridget I couldn't leave her and the rest of them on their own with him.`

`I know Kitty your poor mother is a saint, but you have to make a life for yourself and if you did well in England you could send money home to help her and your brothers and sisters.`

`I`m not talented like you Bridget, how would I make money in England.`

`Sure lots of Irish people do Kitty, don't we know lots of families who get letters with money in them and parcels from England and America all the time, the Murphy`s down the road are always wearing clothes from America.`

`I`m not a dreamer like you Bridget` Kitty said despondently `I am never able to see a future like you do.`

`Well I have enough dreams for the two of us Kitty O`Brien `her generous friend said `I`m going to make a future for both of us in England and that's that.`

Kitty hung her head and sobbed.

Kitty had thought about it long and hard it had kept her awake for nights on end since Bridget told her of her plans.

Kitty's life was dreadful enough but without her happy, bubbly friend it just wouldn't be worth living. Bridget gave Kitty a reason to get up every day. She loved meeting her on the way to school each morning and listening to what the McDonalds had been up to the night before. She loved to hear all of Bridget's madcap schemes and ideas and her fantastic dreams for the future.

Where would she be without Bridget to stand up for her, she would be bullied and laughed at in school and she would have no-one to walk home with in the evenings after choir practice and the local lads would torment and jeer her, and most of all, she would have no-one to talk to when things got really bad at home.

She simply couldn't be without her best friend, her life would just be over.

She had to stop Bridget from leaving Enniscorthy one way or another.

Chapter 12

Michael McDonald`s love affair with sport began at the annual Enniscorthy Sports Day on the last Sunday in July in the summer of 1899.

Michael was already an able horseman and a fine cut of a chap. At six foot he was muscular, broad shouldered and athletic, his pace being matched by his strength, his determination, and his natural ability.

At the Gala Sports Day he was going to try his hand at the Show Jumping Competition and had also been persuaded by his friends Paddy Kavanagh and Jimmy Leacy to register for the cycling races, the running races and the jumping events. `You can win `em all` Jimmy Leacy assured him confidently.

The annual Enniscorthy Sports Day was always a gala event attracting huge crowds, along with townspeople and those from the surrounding areas, many travelled from afar due to the special excursion rates with the new Dublin Wicklow and Wexford Railway Company.

At a field at Bellefield a cycle track had been laid, fences erected and even a spacious stand built for spectators. This was a big day on the Enniscorthy calendar.

The arrangements for the prestigious Sports Day brought the many factions and divides in Enniscorthy together as all clubs in the town united to organise the event.

And indeed, the divides were many at the time in Enniscorthy. Not just the obvious Catholic, Protestant divide, the landed gentry, tenant farmer, labourer divide, the shop keeper, professional, industrial worker divide, not to mention, the many and varied political divides, there were also divides all over town sometimes coming down to street by street divide, hence the formation of no less than five different GAA Clubs when the much larger town of Wexford had only one.

But sport it seemed was the great leveller, uniting all factions, as Walter Hanrahan, a leading GAA official from Wexford town and a member of the IRB, with responsibility for handicapping, took his place on the Organising Committee, alongside Robert Westley Hall-Dare and Sir John Talbot Power, judges of the show jumping competition.

Michael already knew both Hall-Dare and Talbot Power through hunting circles, with both his father and his brother William buying and selling horses for them, the two being very prominent members of the Wexford Hunt, and he had come across Walter Hanrahan through his association with the GAA.

In fact Michael was due to play with the Vinegar Hill ` 98s in the closing stages of the Wexford Senior Football Championship the following weekend and had already been warned not to get himself injured at the Sports Day, but as Michael commented to one of the team selectors `all the lads are competing in the Sports Day not just me`.

`We know that`, Billy Mernagh replied, `but all the lads are not our star player, now are they.`

Michael`s talent had been spotted by the local GAA from an early age when he was observed kicking football on the street. He had a natural aptitude for the game, great ball control, strength, pace, and an ability to always be in the right place at the right time. Michael had a footballers brain, he read the game well, he had a passion for winning and being from a family of thirteen, he knew how to look after himself, so it came as no surprise that there was a scramble among the many GAA Clubs in the town to sign him up.

The Enniscorthy Gaelic Athletic Club, the Vinegar Hill `98s, the Slaney Football Club, the Irish Street Old Campaigners, the William O` Briens and the Duffry Hill Club all wanted the young gifted footballer to play for them.

It was unusual for a small town to have so many GAA Clubs and it presented Michael, who liked to keep things simple, with a dilemma. All he really wanted to do was kick football.

`What club would you join Da?` he asked Thomas McDonald who had always been too busy making a living for his large family to have the time to engage in any kind of sport, except horse riding which was his livelihood.

`I'll let that be your decision Michael`, Thomas said wisely, `but choose carefully.`

`What do you mean? All I want to do is kick football. Surely it doesn't really matter what club I join, does it?` Michael asked confused.

`Michael you know as well as I do that it's not just about football, there's a political element to all the GAA Clubs in town so just be sure you are comfortable with the one you choose that's all I'm saying. You're a good footballer and all of them would be glad to have you.`

`Well then`, Michael said decisively, `because it's the 100th Anniversary of the Battle of Vinegar Hill, I guess it will have to be the Vinegar Hill `98s.

`Well sure that makes sense` his mother interjected `weren't you born in the shadow of the hill and hardly a stone's throw from it.`

`A good choice son` his father said proudly.

And in truth Michael had been a huge asset to the team and it could be said that he was one of the main elements responsible for getting them to the final stages of the competition the following year.

His ability to win possession, turn his opponent, and accurately take his score made him a key element of the team despite his inexperience and youth.

Sunday morning dawned bright, bold and beautiful as Michael and the rest of his family prepared for the 1899 Enniscorthy Sports Day.

Thomas McDonald was proud of his son, not least because of his ability, but because of his eagerness to participate and always compete. Michael didn't always have to win but he certainly always did his best to, and that's what his father loved about him most.

Michael McDonald enjoyed the contest, winning was a bonus.

'Well Mick are you looking forward to the battle today?' his father asked.

'What battle would that be now Da', Michael said smiling, 'sure this is only a bit of fun now isn't it.'

'Don't you want to win Michael?' his sister Sarah asked.

'He better win', his younger brother Thomas said, 'I told all the lads that he was going to beat the lard out of everyone else, don't go making a liar of me now Michael.'

'It seems all our battles were not fought on Vinegar Hill then' Michael said amused.

Michael McDonald was that special breed of sportsman who competed mainly with himself, and had an admiration and respect for all those taking part, that is not to say though, that when it came down to it that he wouldn't pull out all the stops to get over the line.

That Sunday in 1899 he excelled, and won every event he entered, winning well with a quiet and dignified confidence and accepting his prizes graciously from Lady Power, wife of Sir John Talbot Power.

Before leaving the field at Bellefield that day Michael had been approached to join the cycling club, he was asked to play polo and bicycle polo, Sir John Talbot Power had asked him to join the Wexford Hunt and the Vinegar Hill '98s were very proud that he was going to line out for them the following week, against the Wexford town team, St. John's Volunteers, in the county final.

In Enniscorthy it seemed to Thomas McDonald that sporting talent was the great equaliser transcending all the divides, making him a very proud but cautious father, who worried that his son's sporting prowess had the potential to bring him as much grief as joy.

....

At Ballinagore, near Blackwater the following week, the Vinegar Hill ` 98s were a point behind the St. John` s Volunteers in the closing stages of the game, when the young Michael McDonald who had been outstanding throughout, and responsible for most of their scores, rose high in the air to make a catch over the full backs head, turned quickly on landing and was bearing down on goal when he was viciously knocked to the ground by no less than three Volunteer players.

In seconds all hell broke loose in Ballinagore with players running from every corner of the field to enter the fray, mentors coming in from the sidelines to throw punches at each other and spectators from both sides engaging in pitched battles all over the field brandishing sticks and stones and anything else they could lay their hands on.

The game was abandoned as the battle continued down into the village of Blackwater with the more plentiful Enniscorthy supporters driving the Wexford supporters and team back into the covered lorry belonging to Whites Hotel which had brought many of them to the match.

Michael thankfully was unhurt, the game was unfinished and the County title was later awarded to the St. John's Volunteers by the Wexford County Board on the basis that they were ahead when the fracas broke out.

The Committee and players of the Vinegar Hill `98s were fuming at being denied a County title but Michael McDonald appeared unperturbed, his youth affording him the luxury of time, and besides Walter Hanrahan had already been in touch with him about joining the County football team which indeed was a great honour at only sixteen years of age, and Sir John Talbot Power 3rd Baronet of Edermine had

104

sent him an invitation to ride with the Wexford Hunt at the September meet.

Michael very quickly proved himself to be a major addition to the Wexford Hunt, being a most excellent horseman and fearless over fences he gained the respect and admiration of many of the local gentry including Charles Beatty and Robert Hall Dare, both officers in the British army, along with many of the "gentlemen farmers" of the area.

He was modest, mannerly, and unassuming, yet confident, intelligent, and able, his swarthy, dark looks and athletic shape endearing him to many of the female hunt members, including Sir John Talbot Power's only daughter Eileen Mareli.

His popularity grew as he enjoyed games of polo at Lymington, cycled with the Slaney Cyclers and played tennis and croquet on the lawns of Enniscorthy Tennis, Club, Sir John Talbot Power being Vice President, and all the while indoctrinating himself in the ethos of the republicanism of the IRB through Walter Hanrahan and the GAA.

Michael McDonald was an enigma.

Everyone thought they knew him, yet no-one really did.

`It will all land you in trouble one day my son` Mary McDonald would warn `you can`t juggle all those balls forever no matter how clever you think you are.`

`But sure I`m not juggling anything Ma` her attractive son would say sweeping her up into his arms and spinning her round and round `I just love to play games.`

`Well mind you know the game you`re playing Michael`, his father often advised, `there`s something brewing here in Ireland, what it is I`m not exactly sure, there`s them that want to remain under Britain, there`s them that want Home Rule and there`s them that will settle for nothing less than a Republic, and you are friendly with all of them, so mind how you go, and don't get caught between the stools.`

`Ya worry too much about me`, Michael said, `I`ll be grand`.

Michael McDonald went to work for Sir John Talbot Power at his John`s Lane Distillery in 1901. It was ideal employment for the young sportsman. Sir John Talbot Power was a very generous and forward thinking employer and land owner, with a passion for Irish agriculture and dedicated to improving the lives of those who worked the land and indeed the waterways, and invested heavily in building a village of model houses for his employees at Oylegate.

The cot fishermen of the River Slaney were employed by him on a seasonal basis allowing them to fish the river in summer whilst working in his John`s Lane Distillery in winter when the distilling began. It was an arrangement that suited everyone.

`What do you think Da?` Michael asked. `I can do the same as the cot men, work in the Distillery in the winter and work with you on the land for the summer along with playing football, tennis, croquet, polo and a bit of hunting, the best of all worlds.`

`Well Michael that couldn't be better son. Sir John has certainly set you up nicely and you will be a great help to me on the land during the summer now that I have become a tenant farmer.` Thomas McDonald was delighted with the way things were working out for Michael and indeed for himself having just acquired his tenant farm from Lady Gray.

When the Slaney cotmen went to Dublin in the winter of 1901 Michael McDonald went with them and learned many a new skill at the John`s Lane Distillery and had many a new experience in his country` s capital city.

The cotmen were hard and conscientious workers doing a minimum of carousing in the city, preferring to use the time wisely and to the advantage of their families at home in Wexford and besides many of the workingmen`s pubs in Dublin were tough, raw establishments, providing an escape for many from the terrible poverty of the city and at the same time increasing it.

Once again sport provided an outlet and opened doors for Michael McDonald in Dublin just as it had done in Enniscorthy. When he wasn't working he went along to cycling and athletic meetings held in fields at Jones Road where he was introduced to the game of hurling as well as playing a bit of football. It was at Jones Road that he met Paddy Farrell, a soccer player with Bohemians Soccer Club, who convinced Michael to "give the soccer a go, it`s a skilful game and becoming very popular and you`d be good at it".

And he was, with perfect co-ordination, agility and speed Michael was a natural.

On a trip home that winter Michael noticed he was getting a bit of stick from his friends Paddy Kavanagh and Jimmy Lacey and even from his Vinegar Hill `98 teammates about joining Bohemians and playing soccer, in fact Walter Hanrahan had appeared decidedly unhappy about it and told him out straight ` I don't know why you`d even bother playing that foreign game I can`t see any skill at all in it.`

`It is quite skilful Walter once you get into it ` Michael tried to explain, but Hanrahan made it clear he didn't want to hear `an English game like soccer has no place in Ireland haven't we got our own lovely games` he said vehemently `are they not skilful enough for you Michael McDonald.`

Michael had no wish to argue with his friend and simply replied `Ah sure for me it`s just another game to play and something to pass the time when I`m away from home`.

But he was perplexed by the incident and later mentioned it to his father. `I`m on your side Michael` Thomas McDonald said `I don't think sport should be used to further anyone`s political persuasions or aspirations and I believe we should be free to play whatever sport we want or whatever sport we are good at, you, Michael, are unfortunately good at them all, which should be a wonderful enhancement of your life but in this complex and sometimes bizarre country we live in it could be a major drawback, so tread carefully my son.`

Another thing that perplexed Michael in the winter of 1901 was the invitation from Eileen Mareli Talbot Power, to join her at the Wexford Hunt Ball at the Athenaeum on 30th November.
Eileen Mareli Talbot Power was promised in marriage to Durham Simpson Matthews of Thorp Arch Hall with the wedding planned for April 1902, and her friend and bridesmaid Charlotte Tottenham had been staying with her since the September Meeting of the Wexford Hunt where she had been quite taken with the young horseman Michael McDonald.

His dark wavy locks, large deep blue, almost violet eyes and ready smile tormented her dreams and tantalised her daydreams and if she cared to admit it, which of course she didn't, his muscular back and the image of his well-shaped rear as he cleared fences was constantly in her mind`s eye.

Her intended, Sydney Lancaster was a close friend of Durham Matthews, and was indeed a fine cut of a man himself, ADC to Lieutenant General Sir Barker Russell of the 17th Lancers, he was tall and rather pleasant looking but he lacked that indescribable something, that made young ladies hearts go pitter, patter, whereas Michael McDonald had it in abundance. It was that indefinable quality, that almost raw, animalistic element that made you just look at someone and want them, totally and immediately, without bond or consequences. Sydney Lancaster would never have that.

Charlotte Tottenham felt that when Michael McDonald looked at her he could see her without her clothes and neither he nor she were embarrassed by it. They had spoken little, apart from formalities, but she had watched his banter with others and admired, and was attracted by the ease with which he spoke to all, from her host Sir John, to the stable boy. Sure, he was little more than a stable boy himself, but it didn't seem to faze him, he treated all with dignity and respect, which was immediately reciprocated.

Neither Durham Matthews nor Sydney Lancaster would be attending the Wexford Hunt Ball so Charlotte asked her friend Eileen Mareli to suggest to her father that it might be nice to invite Michael McDonald, who possibly wouldn't otherwise attend unless by personal invitation.

`By all means, my girl, invite him` Sir John replied enthusiastically ` he will add to the enjoyment of the evening, I`ve no doubt.`

Eileen Mareli had little doubt, but that he would, knowing her friend Charlotte Tottenham.

....

`Will you go Michael` Mary McDonald asked with concern.

`Of course I will Ma` her young son replied excited `sure why wouldn't I now?'

`Well for one you have nothing that you could wear to something like that and for two I don't even know where you might buy something for it or how much it would cost and wouldn't it be a pure waste of money, sure where would you wear it again` his ever practical mother replied.

`Sure maybe I`ll get asked to lots of Balls Ma`, Michael laughed, but what to wear was indeed a dilemma.

His father came to his assistance with the help of Lady Gray, who`s own son Lonsdale Richard Douglas Gray had died the year before at only thirty years of age, leaving a full and varied wardrobe including lots of evening and dinner wear that Lady Gray didn't quite know what to do with, so, she was delighted to be able to give Michael his full attire for the forthcoming Ball.

Adjustments would have to be made but Mary McDonald was adept with a needle and thread and soon had the perfect outfit for her son.

`I`m not sure at all about this Ball, Thomas` she said to her husband one evening while working on Michael`s dinner jacket ` he`s getting beyond himself altogether, he`s only just gone eighteen, he doesn't see the consequences at all. I`m worried about him.`

`Sure Mary mo chroi he will go as far as he can, or as far as he is let` Thomas said wisely `and he will have to deal with the disappointment and consequence of either, but it wouldn't be right to stop him and I`m not sure that we could, all we can do is comfort him when his star dims, and maybe that won`t be for a long while yet so let him enjoy it all love, because when the end comes all he might have left is memories.`

Michael McDonald looked dashing in Lonsdale Gray`s evening wear and every head in the Athenaeum turned when he made his entrance, and he met each with a broad charming smile. Michael was here to enjoy the evening and wasn't going to be put off by anything, he was wise enough to know what he didn't know, and only offered opinions on subjects he was familiar with, like horses and sport, he steered well clear of politics, having to bite his tongue, many times, to stop himself from reacting, but somehow he managed to curb his IRB tendencies and mix and mingle and exchange pleasantries.

`Getting bored Michael?` Charlotte Tottenham asked appearing at his elbow.

`Oh not at all Miss Tottenham`, Michael replied, `I am really enjoying myself very much, sure how could one be bored in such elegant company.`

`Well come and dance with me then, you do dance don't you.`

`Badly I would say` Michael grinned `and as you can imagine I`ve had very little practice.`

`Don`t worry I will direct you` Charlotte said with confidence, as she took his hand and led him on to the Athenaeum dancefloor.

Charlotte Tottenham was petite, and attractive if not a beauty, and looked delightful in a cornflower blue evening gown that matched the colour of her eyes and even though she was twenty-three years old and Michael just gone eighteen they looked like the perfect pair as they turned and twirled around the floor, Michael taking her lead easily, being as natural a dancer as he was a footballer.

Charlotte knew that she was to be married within three months but tonight at the Wexford Hunt Ball she felt careless and free and yes, even a bit reckless, as she glided around the room with the most handsome man in the Athenaeum, possibly even in the town.

There were of course several pairs of eyes watching them, but she was ignoring the disapproving glances, tonight was going to be her night and she was going to enjoy every moment of it and remember it forever.

Besides there was no harm in it, everyone knew that she wasn't going to jeopardise her future and her reputation for an employee of her host and yet....... and yet....... there was a pure magnetism about the young Michael McDonald that was almost hypnotic causing her to forget everything else as they whirled around the floor.

At the end of the third dance together Charlotte said she needed some air and asked Michael to take her outside.

`Aren`t you going to kiss me?` she asked coquettishly leaning against the Athenaeum wall.

`Do you want me to?` Michael asked looking down at her, and he didn't have to wait for the reply as she closed her eyes and raised her pretty, pink mouth to his.

Chapter 13

When they got to the station Bridget noticed that Kitty was hanging back and looking around her anxiously, but she put it down to Kitty's naturally nervous disposition.

She knew her friend would be worried for her and terrified that something would go wrong with their plan.

Bridget thought Mr. Doyle the station master asked rather a lot of questions when she was buying her ticket.

Bridget was buying a ticket for Dublin even though she was going to get off in Kingstown.

`And where might you be going now Bridget McDonald?` Jack Doyle asked inquisitively.

`I'm going to see my aunt Mai Power she's a nurse in Dublin` Bridget replied cheerily well used to acting a part.

`And why might you be going up to Dublin to see her now in the middle of a school week?` Jack Doyle pried some more.

`Well she's been feeling a bit poorly and has no-one in Dublin to look after her.`

`Has she no family now?` Jack Doyle kept probing.

`No she never married so there's only her and we're her closest relatives she's my mother's sister you know.`

`And what hospital would she be in now?` Jack Doyle continued.

`She's a midwife in the Coombe and a very good one I believe.`

'Is she now, and are you going to follow in the family footsteps and become a midwife yourself Bridget.`

Bridget had to almost swallow her tongue to stop herself from saying `Oh no I`m going to be a famous Shakespearean actress.`

Instead she replied `Well I might now so I might, Mr. Doyle, I haven't made my mind up yet`.

'And would you be heading over to England like your two sisters Maryanne and Elizabeth do you think?` Jack Doyle asked continuing his interrogation.

'Oh I don't know about that Mr. Doyle but you`ll be the first to know if I do, sure I`ll be getting the train from here wont I` Bridget said haughtily walking off with her ticket.

As calm and cool as Bridget was, she had never seen her friend Kitty so agitated.

'Anyone would think it was her that was eloping and not me` Bridget thought to herself. Kitty was a paler shade of white than she had ever seen her, and she was wringing her hands and glancing to and fro fretfully and hopping from one foot to the other like she needed to go to the lavatory.

'What`s the matter with you Kitty, sure I`m the one who should be nervous not you` Bridget said with a smile trying to cheer her up `don`t be worrying about me I`ll be grand and don't forget now as soon as I am set up I`m going to send for you and you better be ready to come or I`ll come back here and drag you over myself kicking and screaming if I have to. You and me Kitty, we`re going to make a good life for ourselves in England, make no mistake about it.`

Kitty forced a weak watery smile but in truth she was sick to her stomach. She had betrayed her friend out of pure selfishness and now she was terrified that if things went wrong she would lose her forever.

As the train pulled into the platform a sense of anticipation and excitement engulfed Bridget, the same time a spasm of terror gripped Kitty.

`Come here Kitty and give me a hug` Bridget said as she placed her foot onboard and couldn't understand the look of utter torment that came over Kitty`s face, tears were welling up in her eyes and she had such a look of misery about her that Bridget alighted from the train and was about to take her friend in her arms to comfort her when she felt a hand on her shoulder and her father`s voice in her ear

`And where might you be going now Bridget McDonald?`

Bridget froze and took one look at the crumbling Kitty and knew the game was up.

All Bridget`s dreams for the future came tumbling down on top of her, and in that moment with her father holding her arms and Jack Doyle sneering at her from the ticket office the normally kind, charitable friend was transformed into a vengeful vixen.

`Some friend you are Kitty O`Brien you rotten little informer you`ve destroyed my whole future and your own, I hope you know that. We will never be friends again, you keep away from me do you hear, I will never speak to you again` Bridget roared as her father frog marched her off the platform as the devasted Kitty sank to the ground wailing.

....

`What in God`s name were you thinking of Bridget McDonald` her mother asked when they arrived home `that Charles Blake most likely has a girl in every town they perform in, I hope you didn't do anything with him that you will regret my girl`.

`We did not, Charles is a gentleman. Bridget defended him vehemently, `We were going to be married when we got to England`.

114

'A clever gentleman then I'll warrant` Mary McDonald went on `was going to seduce you far away from home where you would have no-one to fall back on, where do you think you would have ended up then?`

'We were going to be stars together on the London stage and play Shakespeare all over England, Scotland and Wales` Bridget went on defiantly `and who knows maybe even America. Charles says I have talent you know and I could go a long way and if it hadn't been for little Miss Busy Body O`Brien you could have been reading about me in the London Times.`

'We have no doubt but you have talent Bridget, everyone in town says you have, but that was no way of doing things, running away from everyone you love with someone we have never met. Surely you have more respect for your mother and me and yourself than that, I thought we had done a better job of bring you up` her father said sadly.

This seemed to bring Bridget to her senses and she began to calm down `You`ve done everything you could for me Da, it was time for me to do something for myself and I thought this was my opportunity, maybe I didn't think it through as well as I should have but I do love Charles and he does love me.`

'Well if that is the case Bridget he will wait for you` her father said wisely `sure maybe he won`t leave Ireland without you, maybe when you don't arrive in Kingstown he will come back down here looking for you, shall we wait and see Bridget just how much he loves you.`

Bridget was distraught and sank into bed that night in a vale of tears, the lively Bridget had never been as unhappy in her life, she had lost her love, she had lost her dream and she had lost her best friend.

Things couldn't get any worse .... Or so she thought as she fell asleep exhausted.

....

Bridget awoke startled by the frantic knocking on the front door and a voice calling her mother's name. It was Kitty's mother, Lizzie and she appeared to be distressed.

`Kitty's gone` she cried `and we've looked everywhere and we can't find her. God in Heaven what are we going to do.`

Mary McDonald tried to calm her and get the story out of her. ` Sit down there now Lizzie and tell us what happened. What do you mean Kitty is gone.`

`She's gone I tell you, and God only knows where, or what she might have done to herself` Lizzie sobbed as Bridget's heart began to pound in her chest.

`She told me all about your plan Bridget and how you were going to send for her when you were set up in England, and how you were the best and only friend she ever had, and how she had betrayed you and now you were never going to talk to her ever again`. Lizzie gulped back the tears ` I tried to comfort her telling her that she had done the right thing and that when you had time to think about it you would see that and not blame her, and I thought I had her pacified when himself arrived home from the pub with too much drink in him and began slapping her around and calling her "a snivelling little bitch" . I tried to stop him hitting her and Kitty managed to get away and as she ran out the door she said "I'm never coming back to this God awful house again, I've lost the only person who could have saved me from all this, my life is not worth living" and she was gone.`

`Myself and Sean and Larry the eldest two boys have been searching for her for the past two hours and we can't find her anywhere I don't know what to do Mary McDonald what if she is gone into the river Slaney, my poor, poor Kitty she has put up with so much.`

Bridget began to shake and weep. `It's all my fault` she sobbed `if I hadn't said mean things to her she would be at home in her bed now.`

'Stop that now immediately Bridget' Mary McDonald said taking command 'there's no time now for the likes of that, pull yourself together, get dressed and we will all begin to look for her. God is good Lizzie, you have enough hardship, he surely wouldn't expect you to carry this cross as well, we'll find her Lizzie. Now everyone get dressed Sarah you stay with the smaller ones and the rest of us will look for Kitty.'

It was the longest night that Bridget could ever remember. They searched the banks of the Slaney, up and down both sides of the bridge, her mother and father, Lizzie her brothers William and Michael, Kitty's brothers Sean and Larry, her sister Jane and herself and as dawn broke over Vinegar Hill there was still no sign of Kitty.

Every now and then Bridget would stare into the dark waters of the Slaney and say a silent prayer that her friend wasn't lost forever in its depths. How would she live with herself if she had caused Kitty to end her own life, how would she cope with life without her friend, how would she cope with her best friend's death on her conscience. She had said those horrible things in a moment of despair, as she saw all her dreams come crashing down to earth she wanted to lash out and hurt Kitty but she never meant for any of this to happen.

'Dear God don't let her be dead, please I beg of you, don't take my friend this night, she's had such a miserable life please don't let it end this way, give me a chance to make it up to her and to you, please' Bridget begged.

As the first rays of morning light came sliding up the Slaney the desolate group on the riverbank caught sight of one of the Enniscorthy cot men coming from the direction of Edermine and waving his arms frantically. All hearts sank, thinking the worst, that he had seen something in the river and he was coming up to Enniscorthy to report it.

Bridget almost fainted.

As he drew close to them he shouted ` Are ye searching for a young girl?`

`We are`, Thomas McDonald called back, the only one able to find his voice, `have you seen her?` he asked in trepidation, terrified of the reply.

`I have,` the cot man called back, `there`s a young slip of a girl standing like a statue on the bank down at Edermine House she looks as though she`s thinking about going into the water. I called to her several times but she didn't show any sign of hearing me. I thought maybe she`s deaf or something. I couldn't get the boat in close enough to her so I thought I`d come up the river and get some help.`

`Oh thanks be to Jesus and his Blessed Mother` Lizzie O` Brien cried falling to her knees `she`s alive.`

`Well she was when I saw her Mrs ` the cot man said quickly `but you`d want to hurry to her, I`m not sure how long she`ll stay standing there. I can take two in the boat here with me and head back up stream.`

William and Thomas McDonald climbed into the boat and Michael being the fastest runner took off at a gallop along the bank with Sean and Larry trailing behind him.

When Michael reached Edermine he could see no sign of Kitty and was about to take off his shoes thinking that she must have gone into the water when he saw Sir John Talbot Power walking towards Edermine House carrying something lifeless in his arms.

Michael knew immediately it was Kitty and his heart sank.

Michael reached Sir John Talbot Power at the steps of Edermine House panting, fearfully he glanced at the lifeless form in Sir John`s arms.

`She`s not dead` Sir John said quickly, noticing the grief on the young man`s face, `I saw her through the mist when I was walking my dog she was just standing on the bank staring into the river I thought she was a ghost, when I called out to her there was no reaction. When I eventually reached her she just fell into my arms in a faint. I think it`s exhaustion. She seems to have been there all night. She is frozen through and through. If we don't get her warmed up quickly I fear she will die from exposure. Do you know her?`

`I do` Michael replied a little relieved `she`s my sister`s friend, her name is Kitty O`Brien, we`ve been searching for her all through the night.`

Sir John carried Kitty into the drawingroom placing her on a large couch in front of the big Italian marble fireplace and rang for a maid to come quickly to light the fire.

Sir John began rubbing Kitty`s hands and feet as blankets were brought to wrap around her pitiful little form.

And still she lay there lifeless.

Michael ran back to the river to tell the others, while Sir John sent a man servant to fetch Dr Daniel Levingstone.

Bridget McDonald ran to her friend once inside Edermine House, thanking God and all the saints in Heaven that she wasn't at the bottom of the Slaney.

`Kitty it`s me, it`s Bridget and I`m so, so sorry for the hurtful things I said to you. I didn't mean them, you`re my best friend now and always` she sobbed.

Kitty`s eyelids fluttered at the sound of her friend`s voice and her lips spread in a little smile, she raised a small, cold hand and Bridget took it between hers and held it tightly.

`I tried to do it Bridget, I really did, I tried to go into the water, all night I tried to do it but I was just too much of a coward, I was too afraid of being damned forever in the hereafter` Kitty spoke softly.

`Oh God Kitty I am so glad you didn't, what would I have done without my best pal` Bridget sobbed in relief.

`But I wanted to Bridget, with all my heart I wanted to, I just didn't have the courage. How lame is that.`

`It's not lame at all Kitty, it's made me the happiest and luckiest person on earth to still have my friend, we will be friends forever Kitty O'Brien and we will never fall out, ever again.`

`But what about London and Charles Blake and Shakespeare` Kitty asked feebly.

`Oh to hell with them all Kitty, it's you and me from now on, and don't you forget it, as soon as you're up and about we'll make new plans just for the two of us` Bridget said with conviction.

`Bridget will you get up this minute and let Mrs. O'Brien in near her daughter for God sake ` Mary McDonald scolded `and don't be going on with your silly notions` she could see that Kitty was a lot sicker than anyone knew and it would be a miracle if she didn't develop pneumonia standing in the cold all night.

Kitty O'Brien could have a long road off illness ahead of her and it might be a very long time before she and Bridget were out and about in Enniscorthy again.

Chapter 14

Elizabeth had not thought it possible for her to love anyone after Richard Hatton. He had been her first love, her soulmate and she believed she would go to her grave loving him.

She had thought that she would die in the weeks and even months after their relationship ended. She didn't want to eat, she found it difficult to sleep and indeed all she really found comfort in was work, and she had thrown herself into it hook line and sinker. The Boer War, in a strange way, had been a God send for her, she was so busy she hardly had time to think and amidst the misery of those wounded and dying her heartache paled into insignificance.

Her arrangement and marriage to Peter Hargraves had been ideal, they were compatible and worked well together. They both understood the heartache of being in love and had made the decision to steer well clear of it.

And they were happy, they were having a good life without the demands and the physical ordeals of the "being in love" state of mind.

And now, in a couple of fleeting moments they had well and truly destroyed the pack they had agreed, and Elizabeth worried how things would work from here. What exactly was this that they had just experienced, was it love, was it simply lust, had it been a hunger of the flesh that just needed to be sated.

Elizabeth was confused, she still had feelings for Richard Hatton and would never forget him, but she had to admit the moments with Peter Hargraves had been magical, even now as they trundled down the dirt road on their way to the harbour and England, she felt herself tingle in the afterglow.

She couldn't help noticing that Peter looked the picture of happiness as he assisted her up into the back of the transportation truck and whispered into her hair `I can`t wait to get you home and have you all to myself, my love that was exquisite, I don't want us to waste another moment, we have squandered enough time already you and I.`

So obviously he wasn't having any misgivings about their actions, so why was she, and if she wanted to be absolutely honest, she had felt something wild and wonderful in their coming together, it felt right and natural, like it was meant to be, there had been no awkwardness between them and she was certain that she wanted it to happen again.

Maryanne saw a warm, secret smile pass between her sister and Peter Hargraves just before the flash, then darkness and nothing.

....

Maryanne had a broken arm, cracked ribs and a head injury, Elizabeth who came round screaming Peter's name sustained a head injury and a broken leg. Two other nurses who were also on their way home had died in the blast along with the ambulance driver, and Dr Peter Hargraves was paralysed from the waist down.

Elizabeth woke up to someone screaming Peter's name, it took a while for it to register with her that it was her own voice ringing in her ears.

And as always it was Maryanne who came to her to comfort her.

`What happened, where are we, where's Peter, are you alright?` All the questions in her mind came tumbling out together.

`We hit an old buried shell on the dirt track, injuring everyone on board and killing poor Annie Gilpin, Patricia Jones, and the driver Andrew Foyle. Peter is in another ward and is lucky to be alive. I've just got a broken arm and some other minor injuries. They must have been praying for us back in Ireland as always, cos I don't know what else could have saved us` Maryanne explained.

`Oh thanks be to God and his holy Mother Mary` Elizabeth exclaimed, `can I see Peter?`

`They think one of your legs is broken Elizabeth you won't be moving around for a while`.

`I could if I had something to lean on` Elizabeth said, as her voice trailed off and she fell back into a drug induced sleep.

....

Peter Hargraves had been mumbling her name day and night for over two days before he finally came round, between flashes of their love making, interrupted by white flashes in his head.

When his immediate questions about Elizabeth and what had happened had been answered by Dr Michael Winter, he noticed with dread the absence of feeling in his lower body ` How bad is the paralysis? ` he asked his colleague.

`I can't hide anything from you Peter, you know too much and at the moment we don't know enough, except that your injury appears to have damaged the spinal cord, how badly we have no idea, will you recover, we have no way of knowing, you know as much about this type of injury as we do, you have seen lots of young men go home in wheelchairs since this damned war began, and you know all the implications.`

`By that you mean that the paralysis affects every organ from the waist down I presume` Peter said harshly. `Oh yes, I know the full implications only too well, thank you Michael.`

`I didn't mean to be that blunt with you Peter but I know better than to try to conceal anything, you would very soon find me out` Michael Winters said sympathetically ` the best we can do for you now is make you comfortable and get you ready for the journey home as quickly as possible. The sooner some of our eminent people in London see you the better.`

Peter Hargraves knew only too well all the implications of a damaged spinal cord, resulting in paralysis of all motor and sensory activity accompanied by complete loss of control of the bladder, bowel and sexual functions and in approximately 80% of cases, eventually fatal due to renal infection.

Having enjoyed exquisite pleasure with his beautiful, young wife just before the accident Peter found it almost unbearable to think that he might never experience the same physical bliss with her again.

She was such a beautiful woman, tall and slender, lithe and well proportioned, athletic and graceful with almost gazelle like movements, a lovely face, alluring green eyes and a mane of auburn hair that looked sometimes on fire when the sunlight caught it flickering like a flame behind her, as she galloped her horse with abandon. When she wasn't around his world was darker and when he turned a corner and she came into view, greeting him with her charming smile, his heart soared, and his world became immediately brighter.

More and more, Peter Hargraves had begun to notice, just how beautiful Elizabeth was, and it wasn't just his heart that she was affecting. Peter was both shocked and pleasantly surprised that, at forty-five, he was experiencing sexual arousal akin to a man half his age.

But he refrained, and restrained himself from making any hasty moves, lest he spoiled it all, and now, lying helpless in his hospital bed he agonised over his self- control, Elizabeth having proven herself more than a willing lovemate, her passion and hunger matching his in intensity and fervour and their lovemaking greater than anything he had ever imagined.

Almost, unwittingly, Peter Hargraves had stumbled upon his perfect life partner and as quickly as that realisation dawned, it was snubbed out.

....

Maryanne had tried to prepare her, and yet Elizabeth got a shock when she was wheeled into see Peter, he looked so pale and troubled and sad, she wanted to run to him and wrap him in her arms.

Peter turned to look at her and tears immediately welled up in his eyes thinking of all that could have been between them and now might never be.

She saw his distress and immediately tried to banish it with a smile and good spirits. `Well will you look at the two of us Peter Hargraves what a dreadful pair of old crocks we are`, she said with a watery smile.

`Some of us a little more crocked than others Elizabeth` he replied weakly, and she pushed herself forward and put her hand on his, sobbing `Oh my poor darling` as she bent her head and kissed his hand.

`Elizabeth my love I am so glad it`s me, and not you or Maryanne, so don't feel sorry for me, we are all lucky to be alive and besides we don't know the extent of the injuries yet so the paralysis may not be permanent` he said, rather more confident than he actually was.

`When we get back to London I will consult some of the most reputed specialists in the field and see what they have to tell me, so in the meantime all we can do is hope.`

`Oh and pray` Elizabeth said `don't you know us Irish Catholics are great believers in the power of prayer, regardless of what all your renowned physicians may tell you Peter, we believe that God has the final say, so I will write to my mother immediately and ask her to begin her Novenas and beseech all the Saints in Heaven until you are well again.`

`Well Elizabeth you know I`m a more practical man and believe only in science, it can`t do any harm, but try not to get your hopes up too high I don't want you to be disappointed.`

`No Peter it can`t do any harm and besides I was writing to my mother anyway, to tell her that we are returning to England alive, and to ask my sister Bridget if she would come to London to look after Maryanne and myself until we are sufficiently recovered to begin taking care of you.`

`We can employ a nurse to take care of me` Peter replied a little too quickly, conscious that he didn't want his wife performing some of the rather distasteful caring duties that he might be requiring in the future.

`But you forget, I am a nurse Peter and as soon as I am on my feet I will be the one nursing you, make no mistake about that, do you know how fine you are to me Peter Hargraves` Elizabeth said with all the love that swelled in her heart.

But Peter didn't reply.

....

Michael McDonald had limited experience when it came to women, only just gone eighteen and a busy sportsman he had had little time to form relationships, but he did have some pretty definite ideas about them.

Lots of girls had shown an interest in him since he had come to their notice at the 1899 Enniscorthy Sports Day and certain ladies at the Polo Club and Lawn Tennis Club were prone to giving him admiring glances and passing complimentary remarks as he went past, but apart from the odd kiss and a bit of a fondle Michael had had no previous sexual encounters and was taken completely unawares by the attentions of Ms. Charlotte Tottenham.

She, on the other hand had confided to her friend Eileen Mareli that she was quite certain that the handsome Michael was still a virgin, and she was determined to have him, and as he inclined his head and brushed her lips outside the Athenaeum the gentleness of the kiss and the sweetness of his innocence only served to increase her resolve.

Charlotte Tottenham had enjoyed several liaisons in her twenty-three years and instinctively knew that there was a natural passion and ardour in Michael that she desperately wanted to be the one to unleash.

She knew enough about men to know that her love life with Sydney would be somewhat pedestrian and he would not in any way appreciate her rather wanton enjoyment of the sex act, seeing it mainly as a necessary regular release and a means of continuing the Lancaster line.

Eileen had been a little horrified by her friend`s rather blunt and callous declaration. `So are you saying that you are just going to use Michael McDonald the night of the Ball for some personal pleasure and then discard him and never see or think about him again?` she asked Charlotte, incredulously.

`Well I certainly might want to see him again depending on how well he satisfies my needs` Charlotte laughed seeing the shocked look on her friends face `and I can assure you that I definitely will think about him again most likely every time I make love to Sydney.`

`But don't you think that`s all a bit cruel?` Eileen Mareli asked, `I mean you are not really being fair to either Sydney or Michael, I don't really know Sydney, but Michael is really terribly nice.`

`Oh you are so very archaic Eileen dear` Charlotte said dismissively `this sort of thing happens all the time in London. It`s got nothing to do with being fair and besides don't you think he`ll enjoy it? I haven't met a man yet who has refused me or my attentions, and why would they?`

`Well they might if they knew they were being used for just em............sexual pleasure` Eileen Mareli said a little embarrassed.

`Oh really Eileen you are so naive, there`s no man alive going to pass up a sexual encounter with no obligations or consequences ` Charlotte scoffed.

`But what if there were consequences Charlotte?` Eileen Mareli asked.

`Well there won`t be now will there. I am getting married in approximately two months, aren't I and children can always arrive early now can`t they` Charlotte said matter of factly.

`But that would be the ultimate deception Charlotte` Eileen Mareli said somewhat aghast `have you no feeling at all for either Sydney or Michael McDonald.`

Charlotte Tottenham simply shrugged her shoulders and laughed ` Oh you are such a prude Eileen Mareli you need to live a little before your own wedding in April or you`ll be sorry, if you wish, I will let you know what Michael McDonald is like and you might make a play for him yourself when I am finished with him.`

`Oh that`s simply disgusting` Eileen Mareli said beginning to have second thoughts about her choice of bridesmaid `I know very little about the high life of London but here in Wexford we have some regard for peoples` feelings. Michael McDonald comes from a good, decent, well respected family here in Enniscorthy and as you say he might well be a virgin and eager to experience physical pleasure but perhaps he thinks more of himself than you give him credit for.`

`Don`t be ridiculous Eileen Mareli` Charlotte said with disdain ` the likes of Michael McDonald isn`t likely to refuse the chance of sexual pleasure with someone like me, that would be simply ludicrous.`

Chapter 15

`Won't you be missed inside at the Ball` Michael asked, as Charlotte led him 'round the corner and into a dark alleyway between Enniscorthy Castle and the Athenaeum.

`Oh not at all, the Ball will go on for ages yet and no-one will look for me until the end` Charlotte replied.

`But what about Miss Talbot Power wont she miss you and come looking for you.`

`Oh Eileen Mareli knows where I am, she won't come looking for me she'd be afraid of what she might discover` Charlotte laughed.

`What do you mean she knows where you are` Michael asked perplexed `you mean you told her you were going to be outside here with me?'

`Oh Michael do stop talking and put that lovely mouth of yours to better use` Charlotte insisted reaching up to bend his head to hers.

As he kissed her Michael felt himself harden as she flicked her tongue in and out of his mouth, and when she guided his large hand over her pert little breast he moaned involuntarily which seemed to excite her as she pressed herself against his swelling.

Reaching down she grabbed his throbbing member `Oh my Lord, Michael how very well developed you are for an eighteen year old, aren't the girls in Enniscorthy very lucky.`

`No girl in Enniscorthy has ever done that to me` Michael said panting, his obvious arousal causing intense excitement in Charlotte Tottenham, as her erect nipples pressed against her flimsy dress, Michael shot his tongue deep into her throat as a current of pleasure passed through her body creating a tingling sensation between her legs.

How could this inexperienced country virgin bring her to the brink so very quickly she mused, but she knew she was ready, and could hardly wait to have him inside her emptying him manhood into her.

Charlotte began rubbing and stroking Michael's pulsating part until he thought he could bear it no longer, and when she began unbuttoning his pants it was with mammoth resolve and discipline that he stood back and removed her hand ` What are you doing Miss Tottenham?` he asked between gasps of breath.

`Well what the hell do you think I'm doing` Charlotte said slightly irritated at having been interrupted `I want you to enter me, to put your manhood inside me and release yourself into me, surely you know what to do Michael, you must have seen the mares being serviced.`

`Of course I know what to do` Michael said calmer now that he had moved away from her pleasurable stroking `but how can we Miss Tottenham aren't you promised to someone and due to be wed shortly.`

`Oh yes of course I am` Charlotte said dismissively` but that's nothing for you to worry about, now come and give me pleasure before the Ball is over and they come out and spoil our fun.`

`But Miss Tottenham` Michael said now in full control of himself again `how could I possibly take what rightfully belongs to another man.`

`Oh for God's sake Michael` Charlotte said harshly `what do you mean take what belongs to another man.`

Charlotte was becoming increasingly agitated. She hadn't realised how badly she wanted this young man to take her, and it was becoming a great source of annoyance to her that her plan was back firing on her. She was supposed to be the experienced, sophisticated seductress in control of the situation, and he was supposed to be the lust crazed virgin so mad for her that he wouldn't be able to contain himself long enough to pleasure her.

`Well if I was marrying the woman I loved, I certainly wouldn't want her to have given her virtue to another she hardly knew, in a back alley in Enniscorthy, under cover of darkness` Michael said with poise and just the right amount of emotion to cause the London sophisticate to feel about as belittled and degraded as she ever had.

It was as if Michael McDonald had slapped her across the face, but he had done it in such a dignified and noble way that even the callous and calculating Charlotte Tottenham had no recourse except to smooth out her skirts and rush up the steps of the Athenaeum and back into the Ball, completely deflated.

When Eileen Mareli saw the countenance of her friend Charlotte, she knew her plan had worked, it wasn't the face of arrogant satisfaction but rather self-effacing shame, causing Eileen to feel justified in taking Michael McDonald into her confidence and making him aware of Charlotte`s rather base intentions for him.

Michael McDonald was a full blooded eighteen year old eager to experience all the pleasures of the flesh, but when Miss Talbot Power told him that he was about to be used like a stallion put to stud, by someone who thought so little of him, he summoned up all the pride and dignity of his race to resist her advances at a critical stage in proceedings, leaving Miss Charlotte both red faced and disappointed.

Mind you it took all his resolve, several times, not to ejaculate in his trousers, Miss Charlotte Tottenham was after all a most attractive temptress and Michael knew that he would have to make a stop in a field on the way home to purge his ever increasing bulge and expel the build-up of pulsating pleasure still throbbing, in his loins.

....

All in all it had been a rather successful evening Eileen Mareli mused, her arrogant and conceited friend was a little easier to deal with in its aftermath, and if possible, was even showing a little more regard for Eileen's opinions and values, despite them being terribly archaic and outdated.

Michael McDonald was walking a little taller, proud that he hadn't succumbed to the wiles of a most dangerous and manipulative woman.

`Well what kind of an evening was it Michael` his mother asked when he rose the following day.

`Oh sure it was grand Ma` Michael said with a grin thinking to himself: 'if only she knew.'

....

But someone did know.

Michael McDonald had been seen by a member of the Vinegar Hill `98s, cavorting with an English woman and attending a dance organised by Wexford Hunt members Robert Westley Hall Dare and Major Charles Beatty both Officers in the British Army.

`I'm telling ye lads he was at it, I saw him with my own two eyes coming out of the Athenaeum all dickied up in one of them fancy suits looking every bit the English gent with an English wan on his arm, with a swanky accent and her nose cocked in the air and I could tell ya more too` Spider Dwyer told the Vinegar Hill `98 Committee conspiratorially.

He was called Spider because he crawled around the town, sidling in and out of every nook and cranny until he came up with snippets of information that he would delight in passing on to the most suitable sources to blacken a person's good name.

The GAA had introduced a set of rules to erect barriers between "native Irish games" and "foreign games" such as soccer, polo and cricket. The new rules prohibited a GAA member from promoting or attending "foreign games" or attending at dances organised by the

British security forces or by "foreign games clubs". Anyone found to be in breach of the new rules could be suspended from the GAA.

`Well now Michael McDonald is a very good footballer and comes from a very decent family` Martin Doyle a member of the `98 Committee said. `You'd want to be very sure of your facts before you go accusing him now Spider.`

`I am sure. It was him and I saw him kissing the quare wan in the alley way and doing a whole lot more too` Spider said delighting in taking Michael's good name.

`What he did with that lady is his own business Spider and nothing to do with this investigation` Pat Hall pointed out.

`She was no lady I can tell ye that for sure and certain` Spider went on determined to release the information whether it was required or not.

`Well sure don't we know from the cot men that he has played that soccer in Dublin, sure isn't that enough to suspend him under the rules` Paddy Kavanagh interjected.

`Oh I thought you were a friend of his Paddy` Martin Doyle said with a degree of sarcasm.

`Well I am, but rules is rules, lads` Paddy replied quickly.

`And of course it would have nothing to do with the fact that if Michael doesn't play on Sunday you are his obvious replacement, now would it` Martin Doyle retorted cynically.

`I propose that we don't suspend him until after the game on Sunday` Larry Byrne said `it's a very important game that we don't want to lose to them shaggers from Wexford, and what difference is another couple of days going to make, have a bit of sense now lads.`

'I agree with Larry, I don't want to suspend him at all, the Vinegar Hill '98s won't be the same team without him that's for sure, but I know we have to set an example with him' Jamsie Nolan added

'We have I'm afraid Jamsie', Martin Doyle said solemnly, 'my only hope is that we don't lose the likes of him to Gaelic football forever, he's an all-round sportsman not a political activist.'

'Yes but he's either Irish or he's not' Jim Walsh piped up.

'As I've often said, there are a great many shades of Irishness, I wonder how many of us held up for scrutiny would incorporate them all', Martin Doyle spoke with sadness as he put the vote to the floor.

....

Michael McDonald came in from the game on Sunday evening and threw his football boots in the corner with a determined finality that made his father stop what he was doing and ask: 'You look angry Michael, did ye lose the match or what.'

'Na we won it.'

'Well did something happen then, what has you in such a foul mood' Thomas McDonald inquired sensing something was definitely out of kilter with his usually good-natured son who normally took winning and losing in his stride.

'Something happened alright. I'm suspended from playing GAA', Michael said angrily.

'Did you hurt someone badly or what?' his father asked incredulously.

'I did not, but I certainly would like to hurt them, all of them', Michael said harshly.

'That's not like you Michael tell me what happened.'

134

`I`m suspended from playing football because I attended the Hunt Ball the other night and because I`ve played soccer and cricket and polo. It seems now you can only play "native games" and nothing else, and if you do play the "foreign games" then you can`t be a member of the GAA.`

`But what has the Hunt Ball to do with it?` Thomas McDonald asked.

`Well it appears I was reported for attending a dance organised by members of the British forces namely Major Charles Beatty and Robert Westley Hall Dare.`

`Sure the McDonalds have been associated with the Hall Dares and the Beattys for years through the horses, they would surely have known that` Thomas said dubiously.

`I know Da, but it seems they are beginning to introduce and implement these new rules with rigour now` Michael replied.

`Well I suppose every organisation has to have rules, even if we don't agree with them, and if you break them then you have to pay the penalty` the ever practical and fair Thomas mused.

`It`s not that Da, in my opinion the rules are stupid ones. Sure they`re all just games, and supposed to be for a bit of fun and recreation so who cares who plays what, but I can accept that if I break the rules, like you say, I have to pay the penalty but they let me win the game for them today and get them into the County semi-final and then they told me on the middle of the pitch afterwards that I was suspended from all GAA activity until further notice, and as I left the field at Bellefield my friends and teammates were lined up and waiting and threw stones at me as I headed down the town, shouting things at me and calling me a traitor to the cause. I couldn't believe it Da. Fellows that I`d have given my life for on the field, threw stones at me, even my two lifelong pals Jimmy Leacy and Paddy Kavanagh` Michael related close to tears.

`Oh son, I'm so sorry` Thomas Mc Donald said sadly `you of all people didn't deserve to be treated like that`.

`I didn't Da, I've been more than fair to many of those fellows, always giving the pass to some of the weaker ones so that they could take the score and get the credit and I was forever encouraging them and driving them on to be better during a game, but I'm finished with them and the GAA now Da, that's the end of it now I tell ya .`

`Ah no Michael, don't let them take that from you, you're a great footballer and you love the game, don't give them the satisfaction of denying you that pleasure ` Thomas said trying to prevent his son from making a decision he would regret forever.

`When lads that you called friend and neighbour and teammate turn on you like a pack of hungry wolves in the name of sport it's time to say goodbye to them and the activity shielding their prejudices`, Michael retorted disappearing out the door.

....

Bridget McDonald did all that she could to make retribution to her friend Kitty O'Brien, partly from a deep concern for her fragile wellbeing but largely due to the fact that she felt she owed a debt to God who had spared her friend and saved her from the lifelong shame and guilt that might have been her lot, had Kitty actually gone into the dark waters of the Slaney on that fateful night.

She was kind and caring and visited Kitty everyday, but in truth it would have to be said, that things were never quite the same between them again.

That long night on the banks of the Slaney had taken its toll on Kitty who never fully recovered from her ordeal.

She did develop pneumonia as Mary McDonald had feared, but thanks to the tending and nurture of the Sisters of Mercy who took the frail girl into their Convent and into their care she pulled through but remained delicate.

Bridget went to see her every day bringing all the news of the town, but Kitty O`Brien had changed. She no longer hung on Bridget`s every word, that long night staring deep into the dark waters of her soul would set her apart forever. Kitty had no wish to return to her home and family nor indeed did she seem to have any more than a passing interest in the happenings of the McDonald household, she listened only vaguely, to Bridget`s many stories about her siblings, those at home and away, always appearing aloof and distant.

Part of her did disappear into the shadowy depths on that bleak night and never returned. From then on, she was brittle of mind and body and easily broken.

Bridget did her best to fix her, she brought her flowers, she read to her from Shakespeare, she stroked her hair and sang her songs, but nothing worked. Kitty O`Brien was gone, maybe not into the Slaney but gone nevertheless into another world and in her place was a shell that used to surround the friend that Bridget knew and loved and longed for.

`What am I to do Mary McDonald`, Lizzie O`Brien, Kitty`s mother asked perplexed, `I miss her so much at home but she has no wish to ever come home to us: I think she feels safe and protected in that Convent and is afraid to venture outside it.`

`She does for sure Lizzie and sure who could blame her, she`s had it hard and she`s only yet seventeen and the nuns are very good to her` Mary McDonald said `Bridget has tried everything but so far nothing has worked. She doesn't want to leave that Convent and it wouldn't surprise me at all Lizzie if she never did.`

Sir John Talbot Power called several times to see the girl he had thought was a vision in the mist that night, and even offered her a job at the big house at Edermine. `We will make sure Kitty that it isn't too taxing, only light duties until you`re stronger` he said kindly, but as polite and grateful as she was in her thanks she was as definite in her refusal, even though Sir John told her to take her time and think about it.

`But you should take time and think it over`, Bridget said trying to encourage her.

`I have no need to Bridget`, Kitty said calmly yet explicitly, `I won`t be leaving the Convent.`

`You mean not right now you won`t, but in the future Kitty you`ll be leaving it sometime in the future won`t you, sure how are we to have all the adventures and dreams waiting for us if you`re not going to leave the bloody Convent` Bridget said emotionally.

`You may have them all without me Bridget` Kitty replied smiling.

`What are you talking about Kitty, what about all the great times ahead of us, we`re only seventeen, you can`t lock yourself away in this Convent forever, don't be daft, what about the lives we were going to have`, Bridget cried.

`This is the life I want now Bridget` Kitty said softly `and don't be cross with me now I don't want us to fall out but I`ve had enough of the life outside these walls, it`s harsh and unkind and I have no need of it. I`m happy here Bridget and I would like you to be happy for me too.`

`But Kitty you are so young, I know you didn't have a great life at home and I certainly didn't do anything to improve it` Bridget admitted with tears in her eyes `but that`s not the only life you can have.`

`Bridget you have been my one and only friend and the only good parts of my life were with you and because of you` Kitty said warmly.

`But I said those terrible things to you Kitty and I`ll never forgive myself now for ruining everything for us.`

`Bridget you`ve forgiven me for telling your secret, and I`ve forgiven you for saying those things to me, so now can you just forgive yourself and try to understand that I am happy with God and the nuns. This is my destiny and in a strange way you brought me to it.`

At Mass the following Sunday morning Fr. John Murphy announced proudly from the pulpit that the Sisters of Mercy were to have another Sister soon, Kitty O` Brien was to become a Postulant.

As the congregation gave thanks to God for the vocation, Bridget McDonald wept bitter tears.

Chapter 16

William McDonald's star had been rising rapidly in equestrian circles on both sides of the Irish Sea. By 1902 he was buying and training horses for local gentry like Major Charles Beatty who had taken second place at the Aintree Grand National only five years previous and the Mahers of Ballinkeele who owned and trained Frigate the first filly ever to win the Grand National.

He was making a name for himself as an excellent judge of horse flesh and in January of that year the young William had been approached and asked to buy horses for the newly formed South of Ireland Imperial Yeomanry, a Special Reserve cavalry regiment of the British Army.

'Oh Jesus, Mary and Joseph Thomas McDonald what are we to do if the local yahoos find out that William is buying and training horses for the British Army, and the Yeomanry no less' Mary McDonald was agitated, and if she cared to admit, more than a little afraid. Yeoman still echoed menacingly around the slopes of Vinegar Hill.

'Sure what of it Moll' Thomas replied in his calm, diffusing way 'he's making his name and a good living at what he does best, now what's so wrong with that. You should be proud of him woman, he's a good son and a hard worker with a natural flair for horses and if that puts him in the way of those grander than himself well so be it. He's an intelligent man and can carry himself in any company and in any conversation, I've seen the way he deals with people and the regard they have for him.'

'You know I am proud of him Thomas, he could be lying around Enniscorthy doing nothing of any worth, like many a young scoundrel we know, but I do fear for him, I do. There's them that are fiercely jealous of anyone who tries to make something of themselves in this town and they use republicanism and our past to hold the person back or to give them a bad name, sure look what they did to Michael and they'll do the same to William given a chance.'

`I know there`s truth in what you say Mary and it broke my heart to see Michael banned from playing GAA, he is a gifted footballer and it is their loss I`m afraid, sure look what he`s up to now playing for that Bohemians Soccer Club in Dublin every weekend and loving it. I would far prefer to see him at the Gaelic but he seems happy and that's really what counts.`

`I know it is, but we don't get to see him anymore because he has matches every time he`s off, that`s what saddens me, I would far rather have him kicking football for Wexford and the 98`s` Mary went on `but don't you worry about them at all Thomas?'

`They`re men now Moll and they must make their own way and live with the consequences, whatever they might be` Thomas said matter of factly `we`ve done what we could for them and they are good, honest, hard working chaps and we can`t ask them to be any more than that and we can`t hold them back in any way from being who, and what they want to be.`

`I know they`re fine lads I just want them to be safe that`s all, and away from all the ould bigotry and prejudice that lurk in the shadows of this town, to do what they want and become who they want without fear or favour.`

....

Elizabeth wouldn't hear of employing a nurse to look after Peter when he got out of hospital but neither herself or Maryanne could manage it. She was still on crutches and would be for some time and Maryanne had only limited use of one of her arms. They could just about manage to look after themselves, and if the truth be known, needed help with that.

Kate was too busy in her job at the Windsor Castle Hotel to be able to take enough time off and really didn't want to leave her employment even though Elizabeth told her that they could pay her handsomely. Kate loved what she was doing and it was the only place she really felt close to Harry so she declined, leaving Elizabeth no option but to send home for Bridget.

It was exactly what Bridget needed. Charles Blake hadn't come looking for her when she didn't turn up at Kingstown, but he had replied to her letter when she wrote to explain the reason for her nonappearance. He was still smitten, he wrote, quoting Shakespeare and Byron and others, to illustrate just how much, and he reminded her of her duty to herself to develop her amazing talent and promised that both he and the London stage would be waiting for her should she ever get to England.

But by that time Bridget had quite gotten over the Black Horse Touring Company's leading man and wasn't sure if she wanted to renew her acquaintance with him.

The nightmare with Kitty had put paid to any romantic notions she might have had about them as a couple, but she did desperately need to get away.

Kitty was gone from her for ever, ironic Bridget mused, the whole tragic episode stemmed from Kitty's fear of losing her, and instead in a strange twist of fate it was she, who had lost Kitty. The nuns were Kitty's family and friends now and she was only politely interested in Bridget's dreams and plans and indeed Bridget could hardly blame her, those hopes and aspirations had paled significantly in the wake of all that had happened, with Bridget finding herself at a crossroads and not knowing which way to turn.

Elizabeth's request was a timely godsend and the only thing she had looked forward to in weeks but she knew her parents were reluctant to let her go in light of her past misdemeanours and were actually contemplating sending the twins, Sarah and Jane her younger siblings instead.

'Over my dead body', Bridget thought to herself, 'there's nothing in Enniscorthy for me now and Kitty doesn't need me to make a life for her anymore, this is my chance and I'm not letting it pass me.'

But she wasn't at all sure how she could bring her parents round to her way of thinking when Michael wrote from Dublin, to say that Paddy Farrell's Uncle Jim, who was doing quite well for himself in the building trade in England, had seen him play for Bohemians when he was home for a family funeral and had offered him a job and a chance to play for West Ham, a soccer club he was involved with in London.

`He thinks I'm quite good and is offering me employment, food and accommodation if I decide to go` Michael wrote ` this could be my one and only chance so I've made up my mind to take it. I'm sorry about the land Da, I know that you will miss me giving you a hand but sure you're still hail and hearty and it's no bother to you to work the farm yourself, and sure if this soccer thing doesn't work out I'll be back soon enough.`

`I suppose Mary if Michael is taking his chance we better let Bridget take hers what do you think now ` Thomas McDonald said to his wife `she'll be with Elizabeth and Maryanne and now Michael will be there in London too, surely to God between the three of them they should be able to keep an eye on her and keep her from getting too carried away with herself.`

`Oh sure, I suppose it wouldn't be right to stop her, she's gotten a lot more sensible I have to say since the whole Kitty thing, but that's not to say that our Bridget won't fall in love with the first man she meets in England` Mary laughed `will we have nothing only English in laws Thomas McDonald, do ya think.`

`Well God between us and all harm, I hope not, but sure if they're good people and treat our children well, we won't have much cause for complaint now will we Moll` Thomas replied.

`But what about us in our old age?  Will they look after us I wonder`, Mary McDonald asked.

`Well blessed be to God and his holy Mother we're far from needing looking after yet' her husband said smiling and leaned over to kiss her

143

'and who knows we might have even stranger in- laws with William going to Belgium soon to buy horses. At least we'd know what the English ones are saying.........well some of it anyway.'

'Ah sure our William is too interested in his ould horses to think of girls, but I suppose that could change very quickly if the right one came along' Mary McDonald said thoughtfully.

....

The British Army had seen how valuable horses were in the Boer War and were anxious to increase the National Stable exploring strong breeds that could be used to pull supplies and heavy artillery.

The Belgian breeds Brabant and Ardennes were thought to be some of the best war horses in the world. The Brabant, shorter and stockier than the English Clydesdales from the Brabant region of Belgium had broad backs, strong shoulders and kind and gentle dispositions. The Ardennes was one of the oldest breeds of draft horse in the world used since the 11th Century as war horses in the Crusades, known to be docile and patient with heavy bodies and short legs and used both as cavalry mounts and to draw artillery.

William was commissioned to leave for Belgium in June 1903 and spend six months examining the two breeds, travelling around the country exploring the best and most competitive purchasing options and arranging transportation back to England.

It was an exciting time for the young horseman and he was looking forward to the valuable experience it would give him. William loved horses, he always had, and liked nothing better than working with them, in fact he preferred them to people and often remarked to his family 'the more I see of people, the better I like horses.'

To be given the opportunity to witness and work with two breeds that he had never seen before in their natural habitat would give him a greater understanding of them and their needs which would prove extremely useful back in England.

Leaning over the bridge in Enniscorthy as the setting sun glistened like twinkling diamonds on the surface waters of the River Slaney, Thomas McDonald sighed with contentment as he contemplated all that himself and his family had achieved in the last few years.

William was in Belgium buying horses for the British Army, Michael was making a name for himself playing soccer for West Ham in London, Kate was now House Keeper of the Windsor Castle Hotel, Elizabeth and Maryanne had recovered completely from their injuries, Maryanne had returned to work at the Royal Hospital and Elizabeth was nursing her husband Peter at their home in Berkeley Square, Bridget was living with them and running the household in her theatrical way, young Thomas had become a foreman at the Kehoe Ironworks in Savannah, Georgia and Agnes was happy among the nuns at the Mercy Convent, Mafeking, South Africa and Thomas himself was now a farmer, farming his own land.

The Wyndham Land Purchase Act had been passed on 14th August 1903, allowing the sale of estates to the occupying tenant farmers who received government grants in advance to purchase the land, which would be repaid in annual instalments over a period of years.

Thomas McDonald was one of the first to approach Lady Evelyn Gray to buy out his tenancy at Brownswood.

Yes, life was good for Thomas McDonald and his wife Mary and their remaining five children. The older ones, the twins Jane and Sarah were showing an aptitude for learning and had both professed a wish to become teachers and Thomas McDonald now had the means to allow them to further their education, and besides, William, Michael, Maryanne, Elizabeth, Thomas and Kate were all in a position to help them in their quest, as well.

Thomas smiled to himself enjoying the sultry September evening and his good fortune and thanking God for all that he had as he gazed lazily over the town he loved.

`Do you know what`, Thomas mused, `I think I`ll have a drink to celebrate all that is good about my life, before I head for home` and Thomas McDonald did something that he very rarely did, he went into Murphy`s Public House at the bottom of Slaney Street and ordered a ball of malt.

`Well what has you looking so pleased with yourself Thomas McDonald` the proprietor Martin Murphy asked.

`Well to tell ya the truth Martin, not wanting to brag or boast or anything like it, but life is going kinda well for me and mine` Thomas replied `and I thank God and his Blessed Mother for it.`

`And how is that now?` the curious barman enquired.

`Well sure I`ve only gone and bought my own bit of land on the Brownswood Estate under the new Land Act and become a farmer` Thomas said proudly.

`Well, have you indeed` Martin Murphy mused `and sure we all thought that you were a horse dealer, didn't we now lads` he said to the group sitting in the corner, who were showing interest in what was being said.

`Well I am, well I mean I will always have horses but my eldest son William is really the horse dealer of the family now` Thomas said a little uneasy with all the attention he was getting as the four men in the corner stood up and moved closer to him.

`More than a horse dealer now I would say` Tommy Moorehouse piped up `sure didn't I hear he was buying horses for the British Army, in Belgium no less, I suppose Irish horses are not good enough for him now.`

'William is looking at a particular type of horse in Belgium, his expertise with horses has grown and is recognised on this Island and beyond' Thomas said defensively.

'Oh so we hear' Eddie O'Brien said coming up to stand closer to Thomas, who didn't back away. Eddie was Kitty's father and had resented Thomas and all the McDonalds since the episode with his daughter. He was a menacing man, always bordering on aggression but Thomas McDonald had no fear of him and stood his ground.

'Yes' he said 'my son William is doing very well for himself. Thanks be to God.'

'Well now I would think God had very little to do with it', Seanie Casey said under his breath and then louder, 'and what about that other lad of yours, the one that left the GAA to play soccer in England, we hear he's doing well for himself too.'

'My son Michael didn't leave the GAA', Thomas said emphatically, 'he was banned from playing and was stoned leaving the pitch at Bellefield by his friends and teammates and people he had known in this town all his life.'

'Oh yeah, because he was playing all them foreign games polo and tennis and croquet and took a swankey English wan to the Wexford Hunt Ball at the Athenaeum run by them two British Officers, with the quare names, Hall Dare and Beatty' Seanie went on.

'He did, he did' Spider Dwyer butt in 'and I could tell ya a whole lot more about that too if ya want to know' he cackled almost dancing around Thomas.

'You have no need to tell me anything about my sons', Thomas McDonald said with pride, 'I know that they are fine, honest men making good and decent lives for themselves.'

'Sure ye got rid of the only one that was any good at all, shipped him off to Savannah I hear, in case he'd cause any more trouble for your very good friend, her Ladyship down there in Brownswood`, Eddie O`Brien said accusingly.

`What my family do is no concern of yours Eddie O`Brien`, Thomas said regretting with all his worth his decision to have a drink that evening, but reluctant to be seen to back off in any way, `it might serve you better to look after your own.`

Eddie made a great play of rushing at Thomas but was held back by Tommy Moorehouse and Seanie Casey. `What do ya mean by that ya blaggard` Eddie O` Brien roared `sure if it wasn't for that slut of a daughter of yours planning to elope with that English actor my poor Kitty would still be at home with her mother and me.`

`I think we all know why Kitty doesn't want to live at home with you now Eddie, and it has very little to do with our Bridget, so don't ask me to spell it out for you` Thomas McDonald said through gritted teeth making a tremendous effort to hold his temper.

`Take it easy there now lads, we`ll have none of that in here, can`t you lave Mr. McDonald alone to have a well deserved celebratory drop now can`t ye` Martin Murphy said a little disparagingly.

And still Thomas McDonald couldn't just drink up and leave, it was as if he was stuck in a hole, continuing to dig him further in rather than be seen scrambling out of it.

`And what about your other girls now Thomas aren't some of them away too and how are they doing `the ingratiating proprietor asked.

`Oh sure they`re all in England too`, Spider Dwyer jumped in before Thomas had time to answer, `I hear one of them even went and married an Englishman and a Protestant too I`ll bet`.

Ignoring him Thomas ordered another drink even though he had no stomach for it but nor had he a wish to let them see that he was in any way intimidated or fearful of them.

`My girls are doing well`, Thomas said deciding in a moment of madness that he was watering nothing down to suit these good for nothing blaggards. `Elizabeth lives with her English husband at their very grand home on Berkeley Square, Maryanne nurses at the Royal Hospital, Ormonde Street and Kate is head housekeeper at the Windsor Castle Hotel. I suppose you`re only interested in the ones in England but I have a girl, a nun, in South Africa too. Agnes is a Sister of Mercy at the Convent at Mafeking and is helping to educate and feed young African children, and I am as proud of my girls and the women they have become as I am of my sons. God has blessed Mary and me with fine children and there`s not a day passes that I don't give thanks for them.`

Well now isn't that all lovely for you and your Mrs., I suppose they send home lots of money too, sure no wonder you could buy that bit of land` Martin Murphy said cynically.

`They do indeed send money home, because they can afford to and because they want to help educate their siblings at home but I didn't use any of their money to buy the land`, Thomas McDonald replied, `I got a grant from the Government to do that.`

`A grant from the Government, I ask ya, now just how did you manage that, was it because of all your Brit connections` Seanie Casey scoffed.

`If ye had any aspirations to ever owning land and bettering yourselves ye would know that the grant is available to all tenant farmers` Thomas said `and can be paid back over a period of years.`

`Well I don't see why we should have to buy our own bloody land back anyway` Tommy Moorehouse muttered `it's giving it back to us they should be, sure wasn't it them that stole it from us in the first place.`

`Well, you`ll get no argument from me on that one ` Thomas agreed, thankful that the conversation had turned away from his family `but we are where we are now and if you want to get on you just have to work within the system.`

`Well not for long more, I can tell ya,` Eddie O` Brien said puffing out his chest, `the day is fast approaching when we will be taking back Ireland for the Irish and running the likes of your friend Lady Gray and others like her out of our country once and for all. Where will you and your precious family be then Thomas McDonald with all your fine airs and graces and your fancy connections. And that son of yours working for the British Army tell him he better be looking over his shoulder when he comes back from Belgium.`

`I would strongly advise you not to threaten me or mine Eddie O` Brien` Thomas Mc Donald said angrily `I`ll have you know that neither myself or my sons are in any way fearful of a man who to raises a fist to women and children.`

This time when Eddie O` Brien lunged at Thomas McDonald, his three comrades did nothing to stop him, instead they grabbed Thomas from behind pinning his arms to his side preventing him from defending himself as the brave Eddie landed punch after punch.

`Take it outside lads` Martin Murphy roared `it`s none of my business what ye do but not in here.`

Seanie Casey grabbed a glass of whiskey from the bar counter and poured it down Thomas McDonald`s throat as the others held him gagging and struggling `Give me another one quick` he shouted at Martin Murphy and did the same with that.

As Thomas Mc Donald was dragged semiconscious, from punches and alcohol, out on to Slaney Street and down towards the river, he looked, for the last time, on his horses grazing unwittingly on the Island, and heard the voice of his beloved wife warning him time and again `Mind how you go now Thomas McDonald and don't be getting too far ahead of yourself and others, because there`s them in this town riddled with bitterness and begrudery, just waiting in the shadows for the chance to take you unawares and knock you back down to size, reminding you of who you are and where you came from.`

The Shadow of the Hill

Part II

Chapter 17

The dark waters of the River Slaney refused to render the body of Thomas McDonald to the town and family he loved so well, even though his life partner and soulmate Mary McDonald patrolled its banks night after freezing night in one of the coldest winters on record until she collapsed with exhaustion, grief and pneumonia and died two months to the day after her beloved Thomas.

She had never believed the accounts of the eye witnesses to Thomas`s last movements, the publican Martin Murphy and his four best customers Eddie O` Brien, Tommy Moorehouse, Seanie Casey and Spider Dwyer, not exactly Enniscorthy`s finest and her body recoiled involuntarily any time they came into close proximity.

Martin Murphy told Constable Halley that Thomas McDonald had been in his pub the evening that he disappeared saying that he had come in to celebrate purchasing his tenancy from Lady Gray.

`Oh and very proud he was altogether`, Martin Murphy whispered to the Constable, `and probably had a few too many boasting to the lads how well he was doing to be able to own his own farm. You can ask them yourself, they will all tell you the same. He wasn't a drinking man and was lowering whiskey to beat the band and bragging about his children in England and how well they were all doing for themselves over there.`

`And would you say that he was very much under the influence leaving here` Constable Halley asked.

'Oh well and truly under the influence' Martin Murphy was happy to confirm 'sure ask any of the lads there he was hardly able to stand. I kept telling him to go home but he kept ordering another drink and saying that he had every right to celebrate, that it wasn't every day in Ireland that a man like him got to own land.'

'Well that's the truth now Constable Halley, it surely is' Spider Dwyer said 'me and the lads offered to see him home but he was having none of it. Asked us to leave him alone at the bridge and stood there looking into the river as he often did, sure we thought he was waiting to sober up a little before heading home to the Mrs, if you know what I mean.'

'And that's the last you saw of him then', Constable Halley looked around at the four sitting at the table in the corner.

'Oh it is, it is' they all nodded in agreement.

'And ye all headed to your own homes then, did ye' the Constable asked.

'Well no sure we all came back in here' Seanie Casey said entering the conversation.

'And you heard nothing and didn't go out later to check that Thomas McDonald was gone off the bridge' Halley asked.

'Sure why would we now, don't people go out of here drunk every night of the week and nothing at all happens to them' Seanie stated.

'Well it's just that you said he was in a bad state I thought you might have taken a look later to see if he was still there' Constable Halley replied.

'He wasn't exactly a friend of ours Constable, much like yourself now' Eddie O'Brien said with venom, 'why would we care whether the likes of Thomas McDonald made his way home or not, it was nothing to us.'

`Well he was very well liked by many, Mr. O` Brien, and his death is a great loss to the town, never mind to his poor wife and family, Thomas McDonald was an honest, hardworking, well respected man` Constable Halley replied ` and it seems alien to his nature and contrary to his habits to be in here drinking a lot of whiskey of an evening. His wife tells me that he seldom took a drink and she can`t remember the last time she saw him drink whiskey.`

`Well that`s what he was drinking all the same` Martin Murphy interjected `and everyone here can verify it.`

`Mmmm` Constable John Halley murmured his eyes scanning the four, not entirely convincing witnesses.

....

Mary McDonald couldn't understand what had possessed Thomas to go into Martin Murphy`s pub that evening. He wasn't a drinking man often referring to the habit as "the Irish plaque" and whiskey "the poison of the Irish". "We`d have been among the great Nations of the earth only for it`" he told his children regularly, and Mary just couldn't get her mind round him lowering whiskey after whiskey, especially in the company of the four blaggards reputed to have been in the pub at the time.

Thomas McDonald would have nothing in common with any of them and would have had very little time indeed for them, especially Eddie O` Brien. Mary couldn't quite understand if he did go in for a celebratory drink after buying the land why didn't he just drink up and come out when he saw the quality of the clientele on the premises.

They said he was boasting about buying the land and bragging about his children in England. Thomas McDonald wasn't a man to boast or brag either about himself or his family. He was proud of all his children and proud of himself and what he had achieved and he was thankful for his good fortune but he wasn't the kind of man to rub anyone`s nose in it, certainly not those less fortunate.

No, she really couldn't understand any of it and the more she thought about it the more her mind pained her. She couldn't eat, she couldn't sleep, she couldn't rest, her children couldn't reach her, even the needs of little JohnJoe, who was only four years old, were oblivious to her. All she wanted to do was pace the banks of the Slaney talking to and goading her beloved Thomas, asking over and over again `Why Thomas, why did you go in there that evening instead of coming home to celebrate in the bosom of your family, hadn't I warned you often enough to be careful. Oh God Thomas why didn't you listen to me.`

Mary McDonald knew in her heart of hearts that her husband's disappearance was no accident and it pained her that she hadn't done enough to save him. Hadn't she always told him to be careful, not to be getting ahead of himself and rising the shackles of jealousy, resentment and begrudgery among his peers. Had she not advised him strongly enough, had she not alerted him often enough to the dangers lurking in the spiteful suspicious shadows of the town waiting, waiting........always waiting for their moment to bounce and strangle and trample anything and anyone that raised his head above their permitted lowly level.

But her laughing, trusting husband heard nor heeded none of it, constantly driving himself onwards to provide a better life for her and their children, and she always knowing that his drive and ambition would eventually be the death of him.

`I told you it would happen Thomas McDonald and so it did. Why could you not be happy with what we had instead of always and forever hankering after more` she wailed night after bitter night.

But she got no answer from the harsh winter wind or the stark Slaney waters and no relief from the torment and anguish that gripped and froze her mind, body and soul.

Maybe if some of her older children had been able to make it home it might have been different for her, but Europe was under heavy snow preventing William from returning from Belgium and Kate from returning from Lausanne in Switzerland, where she had been enrolled in the Ecole Hoteliere de Lausanne by the management of the Windsor Castle Hotel.

Peter Hargraves had passed to his eternal reward, his death veiled in a cloud of ambiguity leaving his wife Elizabeth in a similar state as her mother and rendering her completely unable to cope, without her sister Bridget to care for her.

Michael McDonald was bound by contract to West Ham Football Club and would owe them a lot of money that he didn't have, if he failed to fulfil his obligation to them.

It was too far for Thomas McDonald Junior to travel from Savannah and for Sister Mary Agnes to come from Mafeking, South Africa.

And Maryanne McDonald had contracted scarlet fever from a child she had been nursing in the Royal and was too ill to travel home to be at her mother's side.

It was something that they would all regret for the rest of their lives when the news came to each of them that she was dead.

Chapter 18

By the time William was able to make it home to Enniscorthy, both his parents were gone. Their house at Court Street had been gone through with a fine tooth comb by concerned relatives, McDonalds and Powers, and anything of any value, of which there was little, had somehow mysteriously vanished.

His twin sisters Sarah and Jane, only just managing to get their hands on enough cash, prior to their home being ransacked, to buy their passage to England and make their way to Elizabeth and Bridget.

His sister, Margaret, who was ten years of age, had been taken by his mother's brother James Power to help with work on his farm in County Wicklow, his six year old sister Mary had gone to his mother's sister Mai Power, a retired matron in Dublin who had never married and lived alone, and wanted someone to keep her company and do and fetch for her, and the baby of the family JohnJoe ,was taken by his father's childless brother Jack and his wife Mag, who ran the Station House at Palace, Clonroche.

William was beside himself with grief. In six short months he had lost his entire family. He couldn't fathom what had happened to his father. No body had ever been found and the details of the night he disappeared were ambiguous to say the very least. According to Constable Halley his father had been drinking in Murphy's Pub on Slaney Street, a thing his father very rarely did, and appeared to get quite drunk, something that William couldn't even visualise, having never seen his father under the influence, and yet somehow he seems to have fallen drunkenly into the River Slaney and drowned and the body carried out to sea.

`A most tragic and unfortunate accident` Constable Halley had told him unconvincingly, William getting the feeling that the Constable didn't quite believe what he was saying himself ` and sure your poor mother never quite recovered from the shock, drove her a little bit insane I'm sorry to say, walking the riverbank day and night talking, always talking to him, your father that is, until she met her own tragic end and went to join him.`

`We have no witnesses to the actual death`, the Constable went on, `but all Murphy's customers tell the same story, that he was celebrating the buying of his tenancy from Lady Gray and drinking quite a lot of whiskey. I didn't know your father well but I wouldn't have taken him to be a drinking man and certainly not the type to drink so much as to cause him to fall in to the river, but what else are we to presume happened. I have no other lines of enquiry and no reason to believe anything other than what I`ve been told.`

William got a strong sense of being told something by the Constable but he couldn't be exactly sure what it was, and in truth, had so much on his mind that he couldn't find the time or energy to devote to it.

William was gravely concerned for his younger siblings and very much wanted to gather them all back under the one roof, however, he was a single man who's livelihood took him away from home quite frequently. But he did have the house at Court Street to maintain and needed to discuss with Lady Gray, the land at Brownswood.

Lady Eveleen Gray had been devastated by the disappearance of her trusted Stable Manager and long-time friend Thomas McDonald. She too, like Mary, had difficulty swallowing the story of Thomas`s last movements and couldn't reconcile herself to the fact that he had entered a public house to celebrate the purchase of his tenancy.

It was true, she told William, that he had been elated the day she signed the farm over to him, unable to conceal his excitement and pleasure from her he said ` You have no idea what this means to me and mine Lady Eveleen, you and your people have always owned property and land, you couldn't know what it means to someone like me who has never really owned anything. It was a great day when the Land Act was passed and saving your presence, but I am certain that there was rejoicing among the Angels in Heaven to see even, a small bit of Ireland going back to the ordinary Irish people, like myself`.

`Well now Thomas McDonald are we seeing your true colours after all these years` Eveleen Gray said smiling, amused at his excited outburst.

`Well sure now I suppose you are, and meaning no offence to you and yours, but there is a great satisfaction in my heart today knowing that I have in some way honoured and vindicated those who went before me, those who lost the land of Ireland, today I have taken one, albeit small, piece back and there are others like me around the country doing the same thing, someday, maybe things will be different here in this country and I am happy and proud to be part of that beginning.`

`Well Thomas do you know in a strange way so am I,` Lady Eveleen Gray said, surprising even herself.

William wept for his father and his dreams for himself and Ireland but knew that he wouldn't have time to work the farm at Brownswood, and yet he very much wanted to fulfil his father's aspirations of owning land, and was in a dilemma as to what to do, when a decision was forced upon him following the tragic accident of his friend, partner and mentor John O'Neill.

On the afternoon of Monday 7th March 1904, while hunting with the Wexford Hunt at Carrigbyrne, John O'Neill was thrown from his horse and fatally injured. John had been to the forefront of the riders on the day, oblivious to all else save the excitement and exhilaration of the chase, and while jumping a difficult stone ditch between Bartholomew Curtis' s land and that of Philip Doyle, his mount struck it's forefeet against the obstacle throwing him head first into a large boulder.

William was first on the scene and knew immediately that things were serious for his friend and colleague, while he did his best to make John comfortable and keep him conscious, Robert Hall Dare rode for the local doctor, Dr Clarke and the very Rev. James Canon O' Brien, Parish Priest at Newbawn, with both arriving swiftly at the scene.

Unconscious and failing, John O' Neill was removed to Dr Clarke's surgery where he passed away a short while later, leaving a wife and three children, the youngest only a week old.

William was devastated by the loss of his friend and mentor and whilst feeling a deep responsibility towards his own siblings, he now felt an obligation to the wife and children of John O' Neill, deeming it necessary to continue to work the very lucrative equine business they had nurtured and built together.

Michael was still on contract to West Ham, so William wrote to Thomas in Savannah and asked him if he would consider returning home and farming the land his father had purchased.

....

Since arriving in Savannah Thomas McDonald Junior, had made a good life for himself in the picturesque city that he soon began to call home. He liked his job at the Kehoe Iron Works and worked diligently and well, quickly bringing him to the attention of the owner William Kehoe, a fair and decent man who made sure all his employees were fed, clothed and educated, and a man quick to spot talent and ability.

The young Thomas was eager to learn and worked hard, traits that William Kehoe was happy to acknowledge and reward, and in no time the young Enniscorthy man found himself elevated to the position of Foreman at the Iron Foundry.

Thomas loved his new job and in particular the financial increase that came with it. Many times, as Thomas roamed the beautiful avenues and squares of Savannah, he would find himself in front of the magnificent Kehoe family home on Habersham Street on Columbia Square, and standing there admiring its wonderful architectural style and exquisite iron terraces and balconies he would vow to himself that one day, he, Thomas McDonald from Enniscorthy would own something similar in Savannah, after all if one Wexford man could do it so could another.

159

`What part of Wexford do you come from Thomas` William Kehoe asked him one afternoon on one of his regular visits to the factory floor.

`My hometown is Enniscorthy, in the shadow of Vinegar Hill` Thomas said proudly.

`Is it indeed` William Kehoe replied amused and pleased by the Vinegar Hill reference. Although leaving Wexford at the tender age of ten with his mother, father and siblings, William Kehoe was raised on the lore of Rebellion and had been baptized in the church at Boolavogue, the parish of Fr. John Murphy the 1798 martyr and was well aware of the significance of Vinegar Hill in the struggle for Irish freedom.

`And what, pray tell, are you doing all the way over here in Savannah then` William inquired of his tall, handsome Foreman.

`Well it`s a bit of a long story Mr. Kehoe and probably one that you are better off not knowing` Thomas said honestly. `Suffice it to say that some of the history and tragedy of The Hill has rubbed off on me.`

`On us all Thomas`, William Kehoe said shaking his head, `even though thousands of fathoms of water separate us, it`s never deep enough or wide enough to wash away the pain or the memory.`

The young man not long passed his eighteenth year, looked at his sixty year old employer, and as their eyes met, both knew they had found a kindred spirit.

....

In 1902 William Kehoe was Chairman of the Renaming Committee of Irish Green, one of the largest parks in Savannah and encouraged the young Thomas McDonald to join him on the committee. The young man very quickly proving himself to be intelligent, capable and a fine speaker.

'That young McDonald lad has a way about him`, John Flannery, friend, fellow Irishman and committee colleague remarked to William Kehoe one evening after a meeting of the Renaming Committee, `in fact I would go so far as to say he has charisma, he could be a good crowd puller, has he any interest at all, in politics.`

'Well from what I can deduce he seemed to have been interested enough in them back home in Wexford, one of the reasons he ended up here in Savannah I wager` William Kehoe replied.

'Indeed` was all John Flannery said but William Kehoe could see that he was already formulating plans that included the enthusiastic Enniscorthy man.

John Flannery was one of the leading lights of Savannah, and an example to all Irish emigrants, having arrived there in 1851 from his hometown of Nenagh in County Tipperary. He was elevated to the position of Captain of the Irish Jasper Greens during the Civil War, he became President of the Southern Bank of the State of Georgia, owned his own company the John Flannery Company: was a director of the South Bound Railway Company and the Georgia & Alabama Railroad Company, a member of the Hibernian Society and a staunch supporter of the Democratic Party and its principles. John Flannery was an exemplary citizen of Savannah and one of the honoured and loyal subjects of the state of his adoption.

He had suffered much in his personal life, meeting and marrying Mary Norton in 1867. Only two of the six children born to the union survived beyond three years, a daughter, Kate, who was now married, and his son John McMahon Flannery, who had passed away at only twenty-eight years of age in 1900, a year after his mother had gone to her eternal reward.

John Flannery was alone, but he had money, influence, and ideas, all he needed was a focus.

Following a most successful campaign Irish Green was renamed Emmet Park after the United Irish hero, Robert Emmet in 1903, to celebrate the centenary of his death.

The delighted William Kehoe invited a gathering of friends and acquaintances to his home to celebrate the occasion, and it was here that Thomas McDonald had two encounters that would change his life forever.

Chapter 19

It didn't take the McDonald twins, Sarah and Jane, long to realise that the world that they knew was slipping away from them like sand between their toes.

Their poor mother's body was barely cold before well-meaning neighbours and relatives began to arrive to their home at Court Street.

Through the dark clouds of despair and grief the girls noticed that callers concern and sympathy was tinged with small town curiosity and the materialism of those who had never had enough. The abject misery of the Famine was only a short memory ago, and people still lived on the verge of poverty and the poor house, and with both mother and father gone, many were vigilant, as to what could be removed from the reasonably comfortable home of the late Thomas and Mary McDonald, without serious consequence.

Sarah and Jane watched and observed as many discreetly pocketed treasured trinkets, and relatives carved their family up like pieces of cake, deciding that little JohnJoe should go to the childless Mag and Jack McDonald of Palace, Clonroche, who had no offspring of their own and would make a good home for the little lad.

Mary, their six year old sister, would be sent to Dublin to live with their mother's sister Mai Power, a retired matron and spinster, who had no-one to look after her as she got on in years. Mai, was rigid in her ways and wanted one of the youngest girls so that she could mould her to her liking. Poor little Mary was petrified, all she wanted was her mother and sat in her Ma's favourite chair for the duration of the Wake, perhaps feeling closer there, to the mother she knew than to the cold, motionless woman lying in the bed with candles burning all around her and rosary beads intertwined through her stagnant fingers.

James Power, their mother's brother, had a farm in Wicklow, near Avoca, he had two strong sons who helped him on the land and with the stock, but his wife Monica had passed away in childbirth only three months previous, leaving a small baby in need of looking after. James had employed one of the local women to look after little Sean, but now he had the opportunity to have one of his own kin doing the job, for a roof over their head and a bite to eat.

He took stock of the twins, 'Two good looking girls, no doubt about that`, he thought to himself, `but way too skinny and flighty for the wilds of Wicklow. Now that Margaret one could be exactly what's needed, well built for a ten year old, strong, athletic limbs, good looking but in a sensible sort of a way, yes, and her head not yet turned with the nonsense of boys, she could be the one alright.`

And so it was settled. Margaret would go to Wicklow, Mary to Dublin and JohnJoe to Palace, but what of the twins.

`Oh we'll be alright`, Sarah told the gathered clan, `we can look after ourselves until William gets home, and he will take care of us then.` But in truth the twins had their own plans and had been clever enough to go to their mother's secret hiding place, a hollow in the much-revered statue of St. Anthony that stood in the landing window. The girls remembered their mother laughingly saying: `the safest place ever to hide money, sure haven't I got St. Anthony on the job, you couldn't get a better minder of your few bob than that.`

They had been at the bottom of the stairs when Mrs. Byrne from down the road had lifted the statue up to admire it: `Oh poor Mary had a great devotion to St. Anthony` she told Mrs. Kelly, who owned the local shop on Castle Street .`She did indeed`, Mrs. Kelly replied, `and I hope and pray the holy Saint is remembering all that to her now for she surely deserves it, God knows.`

Mrs. Byrne was still holding the statue as Sarah and Jane held their breath, both hoping that she wouldn't turn it upside down and find their mother's secret. They were only fourteen years old, but both had decided that they would fight the two older women for their birth right if it came to it. But as easily as she picked it up Mrs. Byrne laid St. Anthony back down again on the landing window, still doing his job, protecting Mary McDonald's secret stash.

There were of course questions about the burial and who would pay for it and both girls were interrogated as to whether their mother had any money in the house, but they held fast and said nothing. As relatives pondered the selling of some of Thomas and Williams horses to cover the funeral expenses and maybe give a few bob to those taking the children, word arrived from Lady Eveleen Gray, through Constable Halley, that all bills accruing to the burial of Mary McDonald should be forwarded to her.

The twins were free to put their plan in action.

Their pleas to relatives to leave the family together had fallen on deaf ears. No-one had heard anything much from William, and weren't aware when, or if, he would return to Enniscorthy, Maryanne was still suffering from scarlet fever, Kate was still in Switzerland, and the correspondence received from Bridget, expressed grave concern for Elizabeth, who wasn't sleeping or eating or reacting since Peter's tragic death.

The twins had made their decision after overhearing themselves being discussed in a conversation between their fathers sister Annie Quinn and the local Priest Fr. Michael Murphy `You think now that's the best thing for them then Father do ya, only those two are bright as buttons and I know they were doing very well with the nuns and had high hopes of going on to do something a lot better than that.`

`Now, now, Annie you know as well as I do, that all those notions went out the window with the disappearance of your good brother Thomas. Those two will have to get any grand ideas they might have out of their heads and be thankful that they have people like you and me looking out for them, and besides they could do an awful lot worse than service you know.`

`Oh I do, I do Father,` Annie Quinn said quickly, in case he would change his mind, `but they won`t like being separated those two, they`re thick as thieves you know the pair of them, but of course you`re right they are only fourteen and having your good self in the Manse above and Fr. John out there in Davidstown keeping an eye on them would surely be the best thing of all and will no doubt make their mother and father happy up there in Heaven.`

`Well it`s almost like it was meant to be, orchestrated surely from on High, Mrs. O`Connor our present housekeeper is pushing on a bit and needs help keeping both the Manse and the Church in pristine condition and Fr. John has just lost his housekeeper of twenty years, Mrs. O`Reilly, who passed away, as you know a few weeks ago and hasn't yet been replaced. They are two young lasses and it should be no bother to them, and you`re right Thomas and Mary must surely be looking down from Above on them, sure it's a job for life for them, I will have a word in the Bishop`s ear and I`m certain it will be sorted` Fr. Michael said with a nod and a wink.

Sarah and Jane could scarcely keep from crying out in rage and indignation. Housekeepers to the Parish Priests of St. Aidan`s and Davidstown, that was a fate worse than death itself, and to be separated from each other as well, was it not cruel enough that they had lost their entire family without losing each other too, and besides it wasn't just that.

Both girls had noticed over the days of the Wake that Fr. Michael had been showing them a lot of attention, and in the process of consoling them kept putting his hands on them in a way that made the girls feel uncomfortable. They couldn't say exactly what it was, but neither of them liked it, and they certainly couldn't tell anyone about it, sure who would believe two young ones like themselves prone to imagination and exaggeration, but they knew that they had no wish to put themselves in the way of further attention from him, and living under the same roof was just too awful to think about.

Sarah and Jane knew instinctively that they had to escape the fate that lay in store for them and sooner rather than later.

....

Mary McDonald`s funeral was a long and large affair, with almost everyone in the town of Enniscorthy turning out to pay their last respects. As a midwife, neighbour and friend Mary was known and liked by all, having birthed a great many of them, and besides that, there had been no chance for the town to show it's respect for Thomas McDonald, as no body had been found, so a huge crowd assembled as the long cortege made its way to St. Mary's cemetery on a bitterly cold January day in 1904 to say their goodbyes to both.

Lady Eveleen Gray had insisted on providing the finest horses in the Brownswood stables to draw the hearse. Her carriage and the carriages of many other well to do acquaintances, business associates and friends of both William and Thomas lined Main Street as the hearse moved solemnly from St. Aidan's Cathedral.

William would have been grateful to see many of Wexford's leading equestrian families represented, including the Hall Dares, the Talbot Powers, the Beattys, the Hattons, the Letts and many, many more, indeed, Elizabeth McDonald, had she been able to make it home for her mother's funeral might have been surprised to see Richard Saunders among the large attendance.

Poor little Mary and JohnJoe were oblivious to the sad proceedings but Margaret, Sarah and Jane clung to each other at the graveside wishing that their older siblings could have been there to share and divide their immense sorrow and grief. Life had changed for them forever and their terrible loss engulfed them in a dense fog allowing only ghostly glimpses behind and fearful, blurred images of the future.

As Mary McDonald's coffin was lowered into the gaping earth, her daughter Mary's voice broke the silence `I want my mammy, where is she`, she wailed.

Afterwards as people descended on the house at Court Street, where good friends and neighbours supplied what they could, pouring teas and offering cuts of freshly baked soda bread and milk scones, Mrs. McCormack was heard to remark to those in earshot: `wasn't it strange too out of all of them that the little one named for her would be the last to say words over her', and they all agreed.

Later that day the twins wrapped up little JohnJoe`s bits and pieces and handed them over to Mag and Jack McDonald who were taking him by train to his new home at Palace. JohnJoe didn't seem to mind leaving his sisters at all, he was looking forward that much to going on the train, but Margaret and the twins wept bitterly as they said goodbye not knowing if they would ever see his happy little face again.

Mai Power was having no such nonsense when the time came for herself and Mary to leave. She bundled Mary`s small belongings into her rather large bag and said: `Mary and I are leaving now and there`ll be none of that hugging or kissing or blubbering, you will see her again soon, we might just make a trip down during the summer when the weather is better`, and with that she grabbed the little girls hand and dragged her from her home and the bosom of what family she had left.

The twins would never forget the little face looking back at them and the big blue eyes pleading to be rescued from the towering woman in the long black coat and big black hat with the tight grip on her hand.

Then they were gone, down the street, the woman purposefully striding towards the Dublin train and ignoring the whimpering child running at her side, feet barely skimming the road.

Margaret`s journey would be longer and a lot less comfortable.

Her Uncle James Power had come in a pony and trap all the way from Avoca and was determined to make it back there before it got too late and began to freeze.

`It`s time for us to be off now girl`, he said to her around two o clock, `put something warm on or you`ll be frozen through and through before we reach the farm.`

Margaret wanted to run to her two sisters and cling to them pleading to be left with them, but even at ten she had sense enough to realise that that wasn't going to happen. She had no one to plead to. She had no option but to accept her fate and get on with it. Her young heart was breaking as she said goodbye to the world she knew and entered in to the unknown.

Tears streamed down her face as she looked back at the happy home that she might never see again, all her memories were there at No. 8 Court Street, Enniscorthy. As James Power`s grey mare clopped down the street she could see her mother and father standing at the front door of a summer`s evening with their arms around each other smiling as they watched her and her brothers and sisters laughing and playing in the street.

Margaret wanted to jump from the trap and run back into the arms of her family, but they were gone, they were all gone now, like dust scattered on the wind of change.

The twins couldn't even bare to watch as Margaret left, but they were proud of her going off on her own without incident, she was the brave one alright, they remembered their father often saying of her `that one has all the mettle of the McDonalds in her, you can see it in her eyes, she will let no one see her pain, she`s get on with things and suffers alone.`

`Not always a good trait to have Thomas McDonald and well you might know it `their mother Mary would reply.

`But one to be admired all the same Mary mo chroi` Thomas McDonald would retort smiling at his resilient little daughter with pride.

Margaret would need all that resilience and more in the weeks and months ahead to sustain her among a different family, in a strange household, in a different county, in a very alien world.

....

Mrs. Dempsey, who lived at No.13 Court Street wanted the twins to stay the night at her house, but they wouldn't hear of it. Then she offered to sleep at theirs. ` You couldn't think of the two of them there on their own with all the ghosts in that house tonight` she told Mrs. Quirke who lived at No.15, but Sarah and Jane were adamant that they were sleeping in their own home alone and nothing would dissuade them.

It would be their last chance to say goodbye to the home they loved as they spent the night wandering through the rooms full of the echoes of the fun and laughter of their happy childhood, caressing doors and walls and the cherished familiar items, as if in the touching, they would become imprinted on their memory and in their minds eye forever.

Under cover of darkness they left, taking the early morning train to Kingstown, where they would board the boat for England. They had the St. Anthony money with them, which should be enough to cover them until they reached Elizabeth`s house on Berkeley Square.

They had slipped a letter under Mrs. Dempsey`s front door asking her to explain to William, when he returned, that they had decided to go and live with Elizabeth and Bridget as they both wanted to finished their education and become teachers, instead of staying in Ireland and becoming housekeepers to two Parish priests.

There were many who would think them ungrateful wretches when Mrs. Dempsey made their news public, as they knew she would, but they didn't care, they would be far across the water in another land where the critical town talk would be less than a distance echo and the unsolicited attentions of a parish priest a distance memory.

Chapter 20

The ship was bigger and grander than anything the girls had ever seen or imagined, and they were nervous. Not quite sure what to do or how to go about gaining passage they dithered, watching, and observing how others were proceeding.

Unknown to Sarah and Jane they too were being observed with interest, as they gingerly approached the ticket office to purchase passage. The girls were doing their best to both act and appear older than their years, to the amusement of a well- dressed and confident looking young lady, who came up behind them just as they were being questioned on their travelling arrangements.

`Oh the girls are with me, the three of us are travelling to London together ` Margaret Cousins told the ticket officer as Sarah and Jane looked at her perplexed and startled `Yes these are my nieces, so sorry I`m late girls, we will be sharing a cabin together` she added assertively, seeing the girls obvious discomfort and confusion.

Margaret had already seen the girls counting out their money so she knew they had more than enough for their share of the cabin, and besides, if there had been a shortfall she would have been happy to cover it, there was something about these two that she was attracted to.

Sarah and Jane had no idea what to make of the self-assured young woman who had just come to their aid, as she hurried them down the gangway on to the ship, they didn't know whether to be grateful or afraid.

They certainly were not wise to the ways of the world, but they had read enough to know that there were women who trapped young girls like themselves into doing all sorts of unspeakable things on the streets of London.

Sensing their obvious unease and growing mistrust, Margaret Cousins hurriedly introduced herself. 'My name is Margaret Cousins and I am originally from Boyle in the county Roscommon but I am now living in Dublin with my husband James, who is a poet, I'm a teacher by the way, and I am heading to London for the National Conference of Women, just in case you were beginning to wonder if you were going to be abducted and sold as slaves in England ` their new friend said laughing 'and who might you two young ladies be.`

A little more relaxed, the twins related much of their story to this matter of fact stranger, who seemed to have taken them under her wing for the duration of the journey at least, and they began to feel relief and comfort to have someone in charge.

For her part, Margaret Cousins was immediately sympathetic to the plight of the McDonald sisters who seemed to have lost their entire family in one cruel swoop and she would assist them in any way she could to get them safely to the home of their sister Elizabeth in Berkeley Square.

Margaret Cousins was a young woman ahead of her time, with a passion for equality between the sexes, she liked the fact that although very young, Sarah and Jane seemed to be naturally perceptive and hadn't been prepared to allow the local parish priest to decide how they would live their lives but bravely took steps to escape and be the mistresses of their own destiny.

'How wonderfully bold and brave you two are` she said when they told her how and why they had left Enniscorthy.

'We want to be teachers like yourself`, Sarah said emphatically, 'we were getting on very well at the Convent of Mercy in Enniscorthy, before all this happened and the nuns always said we would make great teachers and that was our father`s wish for us too. There was teaching in his family, he always said, his grandfather had taught in a hedge school in Blackwater and one of his great uncles taught in a seminary in France, but he said we would be the first women in the family to teach, and he was going to be very proud of that` Sarah`s voice trailed off and tears welled up in her large violet eyes as she thought of the father she would never see again.

'He must have been a great man, your father', Margaret Cousins remarked, 'not many men think about what their daughters want to do, most, just want to marry them off as quickly as possible and certainly don't want to have to spend money on their education, any available funding usually goes to the male members of the family.'

'Well not our father.' It was Jane's turn now to stand up for the man they both loved, admired and greatly missed. 'Our father treated all of his thirteen children the same, boys or girl. We were all taught to ride and how to look after the horses, and I regularly heard my mother say that our Da got more excited on the birth of a baby girl rather than a baby boy saying: 'the man who has sons will have pride but the man who has daughters will always have love.'

'Do you know how lucky you were to have a father like that girls', and before the twins has a chance to answer, Margaret Cousins said: 'but I think you do.'

Over the course of the voyage the teacher from Roscommon was becoming more and more attached to the two girls from Wexford and felt that she was meant to be part of their destiny, and they, hers.

....

Margaret Cousins and her husband James were part of a strong, active group of educated men and women who were beginning to question all aspects of Irish Society, including women's suffrage.

The group worked closely with the British Suffrage Movement and Margaret was quite sure that some of her London friends would be happy to assist the two Enniscorthy girls in their quest for further education and training. In fact when they docked, Margaret was going to take them to meet Amelia Anderson, a formidable lady she had met on her last London trip, who was a member of the Women's Social and Political Union and ran her own school for girls in Somerset.

Margaret was convinced that Amelia would know exactly how to help Sarah and Jane McDonald fulfil their dream of becoming teachers.

When their ship pulled into the London docks the McDonald twins were completely mesmerised. Their youthful, fourteen year old eyes had never before experienced such a volume of people, such a cauldron of aromas, such a cacophony of sound, such a spectrum of life, causing them to appreciate more than ever the presence and guidance of their new and knowledgeable friend, Margaret Cousins.

Margaret was a practised visitor to London, having been there on two other occasions, and knew exactly where to go and what to do and the Enniscorthy fledglings followed on her heels like chicks after a mother hen.

As their carriage passed through the great city with its tall, elegant buildings and large statuesque monuments, the twins twisted and turned and craned trying to take it all in, the hustle and bustle, the epicentre of an Empire. They had never seen anything so grand, so busy and so exciting in all their lives and they found it hard to keep their mouths closed as they marvelled and exclaimed.

When they arrived at their destination, a large rather stately house in Bloomsbury, Margaret Cousins hurried the two girls inside and introduced them to the small gathering of women present, telling them that she had picked up two Irish strays with a history, and most definitely minds of the own. `I think these two are exactly the type of followers we`re after`, she said animatedly, `although only fourteen years old they decided to take their destiny into their own hands rather than allow the local parish priest to decide it for them.`

To the twins surprise there was a burst of applause around the room followed by whoops of "good girls" and a chorus of "well done".

The girls were quite taken aback. They couldn't comprehend what all the commotion was about. They had simply done, what they needed to do to get away. Now they listened to Margaret as she related their story to strangers even telling them about the St. Anthony money, and these women were loving every minute of it and thinking them great people altogether. `Oh my word I think you're right Margaret` a lady called Christabel laughed `these are exactly the type of girls we want, ones who aren't afraid to take bold steps to achieve their aims and take a stand against male dominated authority, regardless of the consequences.`

The twins felt like heroines and were beginning to enjoy all the admiration and attention even though they didn't quite know what they had done to deserve it.

Margaret had called her friend Amelia Anderson aside, asking her what options might be available to Sarah and Jane to further their education going forward with a view to becoming teachers.

`Well as you are aware I have my own school in Somerset for girls and would be glad to teach them there, but there would of course be the question of upkeep, do you have any money to put towards your education?` she inquired.

`We don't, but our sister Elizabeth was married to a doctor who was apparently very well off`, Sarah replied, `she may be able to help us financially`.

`You said, was married to, does that mean that she isn't married to him anymore? Could be a problem getting money for your education if there's been a divorce, unless of course, there was a pretty generous settlement`, Amelia Anderson said.

`Oh no they didn't divorce he …em…died after coming home from the Boer War ` Jane interjected `leaving her a very large house on Berkeley Square and a second house in the country outside London, could even be Somerset, we think, that's according to a letter from our other sister Bridget who is looking after Elizabeth at the moment.`

`What was this doctor's name?` Christabel inquired from the periphery of the conversation.

'It was Dr Peter Hargraves`, Sarah said. `Why?'

`Peter Hargraves!` Amelia exclaimed. `Oh I knew Peter many, many years ago and was very sorry to hear that he had died, the poor man. Yes, he has a most beautiful country home in Somerset, not at all far from my school, well isn't that the most amazing coincidence. Peter actually visited my school once, when he was spending a few days at "the cottage" as he called it.`

`Well if that`s the case`, Margaret said excitedly, `maybe the girls could stay there while attending your school Amelia.`

Before the elated Amelia could speculate, Christabel Pankhurst interjected, `Well let`s not be too hasty in our assumptions. I remember seeing something in the papers at the time of Dr Hargraves death, and things might be a little more complicated than they appear.`

This remark completely escaped the twins, but Amelia Anderson and Margaret Cousins turned inquiring glances on Christabel Pankhurst, who wasn't to be drawn any further on the matter.

....

As noone actually knew when to expect them, it was agreed that Sarah and Jane would spend the night at the house in Bloomsbury, the property of Amelia Anderson`s uncle Jerome, who was currently serving with his regiment in India.

All of the ladies present were attending the National Women`s Conference the following day, and the conversation around the dinner table that evening and afterwards in the drawingroom, revolved naturally around the rights of women.

Sarah and Jane were intrigued, fascinated and beguiled, Christabel Pankhurst was an hypnotic speaker, and they listened spellbound, as she prepared and practiced her Conference Address.

The twins had never given too much thought to the equality of the sexes living in a home where boys and girls were treated the same, but they weren't that naïve not to realise the many and varied injustices against women out there in the larger world. They had been protected from it in their home in Enniscorthy, where both their parents had exercised fairness and parity among their offspring. Sarah and Jane had always felt equal with their brothers William, Thomas Jnr, Michael and JohnJoe, but now, they were becoming incensed with all they were hearing from this amazing group of young women who were setting out to change the world in favour of the weaker sex.

At the end of the evening Sarah and Jane knew that they had to be part of this brave new world that these strong, intelligent and determined women were planning and preparing for, and the women knew that they had found two new and enthusiastic suffragettes.

Chapter 21

Elizabeth McDonald Hargraves struggled to come to terms with her husband's death and retreated further and further into her own sad, lost world, despite the very best efforts of care of her sister Bridget.

Elizabeth's tormented mind refused to allow her to move forward in any direction since Peter's passing, rather keeping her trapped, rooted rigidly in the past, over and over regurgitating the final weeks, days, hours and moments of Peter's life, constantly chastising and ceaselessly contemplating on what could have been done to prevent the wanton tragedy.

How could her handsome, kind, intelligent, steadfast man, whom she had grown to know, love and respect, be driven to such a desperate and ultimate step.

How could such a full, productive, and wonderfully caring life be reduced to such a wretched, tragic end.

Elizabeth's mind overflowed with moments, memories, regrets and terrible unanswerable questions.

If she had just left, like he wanted her too, and allowed him to be cared for by a stranger, would it have been easier for him, would it have given him a greater sense of self respect and dignity, would it have stopped him from ending it all, the way he did, leaving only devastation and a bottomless pit of sorrow in his wake?

Elizabeth would never know and tormented herself daily with harrowing self- interrogations and what ifs.

Why hadn't she been less selfish and more sensitive to his wishes?

Why had she stubbornly refused to let someone else nurse him, when she knew in her heart of hearts that he hated her witnessing the indignities that his body was forced to suffer.

Why did she continue to remain with him, when she knew he detested her seeing the bitter, tormented person he had become?

....

Peter Hargraves had been with every prominent doctor, surgeon, and consultant in England but none of them had been able to give him any real hope of recovery, and with each disappointing diagnosis he became more and more despondent, morose, and withdrawn.

Deep down he knew it was hopeless. He had treated enough young men with similar injuries in Africa to know that over 80% of them died in the first few weeks. The fact that he was still alive was testament to the excellent care he received day and night from his young, beautiful, and silently suffering wife, Elizabeth.

And he knew he couldn't continue to live like this for much longer.

It pained him to watch the life fade from those sparkling green eyes and the knowledge that it was he, who sapped that life from them, tore at him like a jagged knife, twisting and ripping through his insides and there was nothing he could do about it.

She greeted him each day with renewed enthusiasm, strength, courage and love and each day he shunned her spitefully, pushing her further and further away.

She didn't deserve to be treated like that, but he just couldn't stop himself.

He tried to reason that it was because he was preparing her for his passing, which he knew would occur sooner rather than later, but in truth, it was because he couldn't bear to look at her and feel her affection without remembering that one glorious time they had come together in total ecstasy.

Why, he wailed at the Universe, his belief in God long since dissipated, why after all the heartache he had been through, had he been granted that exquisite taste of what love and life could be, only to have it cruelly snatched from him moments later. Had he not suffered enough in the name of love. Did he not deserve love and happiness like everyone else.

He was a good man, he had lived his life well, in the service and care of others and yet the Gods had been swift and thorough in their mockery of him and his dream of love, allowing him just that one vision of paradise, before plummeting him into the dark, depths of a hell on earth.

Peter Hargraves was angry, he was more than angry, he was incensed and most, if not all, of his ire was directed at the person he loved, Elizabeth.

Every time he looked at her his mind ached for what could have been theirs. He regretted every moment that they had wasted, he lamented not having taken her in love or lust earlier in their relationship, but no, he had been too much of a gentleman for that and had lost forever all those golden opportunities on those sultry African nights, and now they would never know what magic could have manifested itself between them.

When these thoughts came to him, as they so often did in his helplessness, he wanted to lash out in anger and hurt and it was Elizabeth, who was always there to feel the bitter sting of his despair.

He hated himself, he hated the person he had become, and he hated, even more, his reactions to the person he loved most in the whole world, and still he could change nothing, each time he saw her or heard her voice or felt her presence, all the venom and bile that his weakened, crippled body and twisted mind could conjure up would rush to the surface and spew from his mouth.

And in her love and devotion she consumed it all, like the dutiful wife remaining always cheerful, kind, and caring, and he hated her for it.

Elizabeth couldn't comprehend what had happened to the wonderful man that she had known as Peter Hargraves. She was prepared to live any possible life with him but the more she tried to show her affection for him and her willingness and enthusiasm to nurse and care for him for whatever time they might have left together, the more he rejected her, scorning any love she professed to have for him, and more often than not wounding her to very her core with malicious words and actions.

But she was a McDonald, and she was stubborn and she knew his suffering and pain were intense, and the more he spurned her, the stronger her resolve became, which only further added to her husband's irritation and anger.

Peter Hargraves had been a most independent man from the moment he had been rejected at the altar, he had never appeared to need anyone after that, until almost unwittingly he had allowed Elizabeth McDonald to seep into his heart.

Now, he was determined to remove her. It was the only way he could continue to live … and die.

....

Bridget thought it despicable the way this man Peter Hargraves treated her sister. Elizabeth hardly slept or ate and was at his side all hours of the day and night and the only thanks she got from her husband were harsh, bitter, spiteful words.

Elizabeth had tried on several occasions to tell Bridget what kind of man Peter had been before the accident, but she knew that Bridget didn't believe any of it observing the bedridden monster that had become her husband.

`If only Maryanne had been here` Elizabeth thought `things could have been different.`

But Maryanne had been extremely ill, and it was taking rather longer than it should for her to recover. She wouldn't be returning to work at the Royal anytime soon, and she certainly hadn't been capable of helping Elizabeth look after her poisoned, paralysed husband.

Maryanne knew, in that part of the mind that always knows, that there was only one place she would ever heal fully: she needed to feel the soft breeze from the Blackstairs to put colour in her cheeks; she needed the rhythmic waters of the Slaney to calm her fevered mind, and she needed to be able to look to Vinegar Hill to rekindle the strength and spirit of her kind.

Maryanne had made up her mind, she was going back to Ireland and home to Enniscorthy.

....

On the night he had chosen to die Peter Hargraves did the most difficult thing he ever had to do in his life, viciously quarrel with the one person in the world he loved, because he wanted her away from him and any responsibility when the time came to put an end to the suffering for both of them.

He needed Elizabeth to hate him when she ran from his room that evening, so that she wouldn't want to return to it.

....

Elizabeth couldn't say for certain, but that day ,she thought she caught glimpses of the old affection and kindness from time to time, in the eyes of Peter Hargraves, but as soon as he noticed her observing him he would return her look with the venom and bitterness she had recently come to expect.

How odd, she thought, that this man had once been the kindest and most gentle person she had ever encountered. If she had not married him for love, she had agreed to their union because of his tender and caring nature, feeling secure that he would neither use or abuse her, and here she was now absorbing all the harshness and bile he could muster.

Towards evening she thought she heard him whisper : `Elizabeth.`

`What is it Peter, what do you need?` she asked in anticipation of some softness.

`Ask Bridget and Mrs. Patterson to come in I need to be moved`, Peter Hargraves said abruptly.

`Could I not do that for you?` Elizabeth asked hopefully.

`If I wanted you to do it, I would ask you, wouldn't I`, Peter said as harshly as he could, `and I don't want you staying in this room tonight either.`

`But Peter I stay here every night`, Elizabeth said crestfallen.

`Yes and it's high time you gave that intrusive practice up, am I to have no peace at all in my own home, not even in my own bedroom` he roared `without your constant hovering, listening, looking and attending, you make me feel like a monkey in a cage. Have you no respect for me? I asked you to leave this house but you wouldn't go. Can you now, at the very least, afford me the comfort and the privilege and the privacy of my own room.`

The look of abject hurt and sadness on Elizabeth`s face tore at Peter`s heart, with every fibre of his being he wanted to take her in his arms and wipe away all the pain, anguish and torment of the past couple of months, he wanted to kiss those soft lips and that elegant neck and stroke that magnificent auburn mane all the while whispering terms of endearment and eternal love. But to what avail, it was never going to be, the end result was always going to be the same, and it would only make it harder for both of them, he didn't want to hurt her any longer and he wanted to spare her the agony of seeing him die.

`But Peter what if you need something during the night, something administered to ease your pain`, Elizabeth implored.

`For God sake Elizabeth I'm a bloody doctor. Don't you even think I can manage that much myself, after all, you've seen me administer morphine to hundreds of soldiers in Africa.`

`I know Peter, but Dr Martin specifically said that it would be better for one of us to do that rather than leave it to yourself`, Elizabeth replied meekly.

`I know I'm a crippled, broken man and a cruel, useless husband but I have always prided myself on being a good doctor, are you determined to take that away from me now as well Elizabeth`, Peter said appealing to her sympathy.

`Oh Peter I am only trying to do what Dr Martin wanted`, Elizabeth replied.

`Well, what about what I want, do you care nothing for that`, he bellowed at her, `ours was only a marriage of convenience Elizabeth, we both know that so let's stop the pretence, there is no need for you to play the loving, dutiful wife any longer, everyone is well aware that there is no love between us it was simply an arrangement that suited us both and now it's over.`

`I know that Peter, but I thought things had changed for us just before the accident` Elizabeth stammered and before she could continue, Peter sneered.

`Oh you mean that crude, hasty fumbling in the supply tent before we left Africa, that was just a simple release of pent up animal lust and hunger, nothing more, I hope you didn't think it was anything, but if you feel that I in anyway took unfair advantage of you Elizabeth, I will be more than happy to compensate you for your services.`

Elizabeth felt that she had been kicked brutally in the stomach, breaking into uncontrollable sobs she rushed from the room.

....

The housekeeper Mrs. Patterson and Bridget McDonald were more than happy to leave Peter Hargraves to his own devices once they had changed and turned him for the night.

He was a doctor after all and was better able than either of them to administer morphine, albeit it, to himself.

They left the nightly dosage beside him on the bedside table, and happily retreated to their own rooms, both thankful not to have to sit and watch through the night.

How were they to know, that Peter Hargraves had planned for this to be the last night that he would bring pain and suffering to the household.

Chapter 22

Elizabeth McDonald promised herself that she would not under any circumstances enter her husband's room that night.

She explained, through her tears, to both Bridget and Mrs. Patterson that Dr Hargraves had explicitly requested that they both would attend to his needs that evening and that he would be left on his own for the night to administer to himself.

The required nightly dosage of morphine was to be left within his reach on the bedside table along with a bell that he would ring if he needed attention.

`Are you not going to stay with him tonight, as usual?` Mrs. Patterson inquired incredulously.

`He doesn't want me there anymore, Mrs. Patterson, his wishes are to be left alone`, Elizabeth said despondently, turning quickly for the stairs and heading for her room where she threw herself, fully clothed, on the bed and cried herself to sleep.

Bridget looked in on her later, and Mrs. Patterson took her up a tray, but when they found her sleeping, they didn't disturb her, knowing the extent of her anguish and exhaustion, they felt it was better to leave her be.

Both Bridget and Mrs. Patterson checked on Peter before retiring for the evening and he dismissed them abruptly, assuring them that he was fine and had everything he needed.

....

Elizabeth would forever wonder what woke her from her slumber that night, she just knew instinctively in the crevices of her mind that she should be with Peter.

Sitting up suddenly, she listened, but could hear nothing, except the silence of the sleeping house, then despite the promise she had made to herself earlier, she sprang off the bed and almost ran to Peter`s room.

At first Elizabeth couldn't quite make out what she was looking at in the dim light, Peter appeared to be lying calmly, sleeping, and then she spotted the syringe still sticking in his arm.

Immediately, she knew something was wrong and screaming his name ran to remove the syringe.

`You`re too late my darling`, he whispered smiling and was gone.

`Peter No! ` Elizabeth screamed, and as she pulled the syringe from his arm, she knocked a white envelop off the bedside table which slipped unnoticed between the wall and the bedhead.

When Bridget and Mrs. Patterson arrived breathless at the door, Elizabeth was standing, looking down at Peter with the syringe still in her hand.

....

Detective Inspector Christopher Hastings had known Dr Peter Hargraves before the Boer War and had difficulty equating the fine, upstanding doctor with the depressed, angry, and desperate man now being described to him by his wife, his housekeeper, and his sister in law.

As far as Christopher Hastings was concerned Peter Hargraves didn't present as a likely candidate for suicide, coupled with the fact that there was no suicide note and his wife`s fingerprints were all over the syringe, that she had been found holding, by the aforementioned sister in law and housekeeper.

Despite their unwillingness to in any way connect Elizabeth to her husband`s death, both Bridget and Mrs. Patterson were honest people and answered truthfully, albeit reluctantly, when questioned, placing Elizabeth at the scene, at the time of death, holding the potential murder weapon.

Yet, the visibly distraught Mrs. Hargraves didn't quite seem the type to commit murder and she was horrified that anyone might think she did.

According to Peter`s physician, a Dr Philip Martin, no one could have looked after him better than his wife Elizabeth. She was a trained nurse who had served in the Boer War and was no stranger to either hard work, gruesome injuries, or fatigue.

In his opinion, Philip Martin felt that Peter Hargraves had simply lost the will to live. Being a doctor himself, he would have been completely aware, that the only outcome for him was acute deterioration, resulting in a possible traumatic and prolonged death.

`He had come to hate his life`, Philip Martin told Detective Hastings, `and more than that he hated the person he had become, suicide by morphine overdose was a perfectly plausible choice for him, as a doctor he would have had his own supply of morphine and would know exactly the right dosage and would be quite capable of administering to himself.`

`But wouldn't a trained nurse be well capable of administering the required amount of morphine too?` Detective Hastings asked.

`Of course she would, Elizabeth Hargraves would have known exactly the right amount to administer, as I said she nursed in the Boer War and had lots of experience administering morphine`, Philip Martin confirmed, `but why would she do it, she seemed to love her husband and nursing him gave her life meaning and purpose?`

`But he seems to have been a difficult, bitter man in illness, I am told that he was quite cruel to her, perhaps she began to tire of nursing him and decided to speed up the final outcome a wee bit', Christopher Hastings interjected.

'Yes, but even still why risk it, Peter had left everything to her anyway, having no other relatives so it was only a matter of time before she was going to be a very wealthy lady, why would she risk all of that, and besides, I suspect that Peter Hargraves would have still had the strength to pull that syringe out of his arm before it dispersed the lethal dose if he had a mind to', Philip Martin offered.

'Any other love interest on the scene that you would have heard about?' Detective Hastings asked exploring all possibilities.

'No never heard a dickie bird about anyone else', Philip Martin replied, 'and with the amount of time she spent in that room, if there was one, he would have very quickly tired of waiting around.'

'My point exactly', Detective Christopher Hastings mused.

....

Peter had been dead for several weeks when Maryanne was well enough to call to Berkeley Square to see Elizabeth and tell her and Bridget that she was going home to Ireland.

'Are you sure it will make you happy Maryanne?' Elizabeth asked wearily. The torment and horror of the past weeks and months had taken a toll on her, and she was only a shadow of the beautiful girl she had been back in Enniscorthy only six short years before.

'I know in my heart and soul Elizabeth, that I will never get back to full strength again unless I go home, I have a peculiar notion in my head, that Enniscorthy calls to me night after night, in my dreams, and I feel that once I put my feet back on Wexford soil, some of the power and spirit of it will rise up into my body giving me renewed life and vigour, you know, like Da was always saying, that we came from the blood spilled on Vinegar Hill that flowed into the river Slaney and mixed with the very water that we drank, and the flesh and bones of our ancestors that rotted down into the soil and fed the very crops we ate, well I feel I need something like that now`, Maryanne said wistfully.

`And maybe it`s Ma and Da calling me home, or maybe it`s little Mary or Margaret or JohnJoe: I don't know what or who it is, all I know is that I hear it in my head and the only thing that would make me more content in my decision`, she continued, `would be for you Elizabeth to come home with me.`

`Well that won`t happen just now I`m afraid sister` Elizabeth said flatly.

Elizabeth had neither the will nor the energy to undertake a move at the moment and certainly had no wish to be back in Ireland where all her heartache began, she was barely able to drag herself from the bed these days and didn't know how she was ever going to continue living.

At a mere twenty-four years old all the life that once danced in her lovely green eyes had been sucked from inside her body leaving only an empty shell.

Then, without warning, two things happened that brought life rushing back into the veins and arteries of Elizabeth McDonald.

....

The day before Maryanne was due to leave for Ireland, a carriage pulled up outside the Hargraves residence on Berkeley Square and two young girls hopped out followed by a well- dressed lady in a powder blue coat and matching hat.

Bridget, who had been watching from an upstairs window ran to the staircase and taking two steps at a time arrived at the bottom just as the large knocker was dropped on the front door.

Squealing with delight, she flung the door wide and threw her arms around both twins at the same time.

Amelia Anderson, appreciating the recent bereavement in the house and the family bereavements suffered since these sisters had last met, only stayed long enough to satisfy herself that both Sarah and Jane would be in safe hands.

She had grown quite fond of the two girls from Ireland, in the short while since meeting them, and knew that with the proper training they were destined to make not only excellent teachers, but ideal suffragettes.

Quickly realising the distraught condition of Mrs. Hargraves, Amelia turned her attention to Maryanne, explaining to her that the twins had expressed a wish to continue their education. `I run a school for girls who want to do just that in Somerset`, she told Maryanne, `and I would be delighted to have Sarah and Jane enrolled there. Perhaps you could discuss it with Mrs. Hargraves at a time in the future, as her late husband Peter has a residence not too far from my school where I made his acquaintance some years ago. Perhaps the girls could stay there while taking classes.`

`That's very kind of you, Miss Anderson, to take such an interest in Sarah and Jane`, Maryanne said gratefully, `and I will certainly talk to my sister Elizabeth about it, but I am not sure of the current situation in relation to her late husband`s estate.`

`Oh yes, I quite understand` Amelia Anderson said quickly, having heard some of the story from Celine Pankhurst `the girls have my address, and I shall be in London again in two months time and could call on you all then.`

`Please feel free to call then` Maryanne replied `and thank you so much once again for all you`ve done for Sarah and Jane.`

`Not at all, I`m so glad to have met them` Amelia Anderson said honestly `they are two charming and intelligent girls and with the right instruction could go a long way, exactly the type of female the Women`s Movement needs.`

Elizabeth was glad to see her two younger sisters and happy to have them stay with her. She had been informed formally by Peter`s solicitor James Hewitt that everything had been left to her alone, apart from two small gratuities, in grateful thanks to Mrs. Patterson and Bridget for the care they had given.

`Do you understand Mrs. Hargraves`, James Hewitt went on to explain as Elizabeth sat numbly listening to him, `your husband Peter was a very wealthy man, not alone did he have the house here on the Square but also a substantial residence in Somerset, along with being a shareholder in many successful companies, the details of which I won`t trouble you with at the present time, but suffice it to say that you are now a woman of considerable substance.`

Elizabeth said nothing.

`Did you hear me Mrs. Hargraves?` James Hewitt asked a tad irritated. `Many women would be very grateful to be in your very comfortable position.`

`I did Mr. Hewitt  and I`m sure they would, but it is of little interest to me`, Elizabeth replied showing for the first time in months some of her old spirit and pride. `I never wanted anything from Peter you see, growing up in Ireland among a family of thirteen I learned from an early age to be content with very little, and I have my nursing profession which I can return to at any time, all I want is to clear my name of any wrong doing in relation to my husband`s tragic demise.`

....

Bridget was quite fed up of the heavy air of gloom that hung daily over the Hargraves residence and was determined now that she had the twins with her to do something to dispel the dreariness and bring a little bit of joy and cheer back to the house on Berkeley Square.

The very first thing she was going to do was clear out Peter`s bedroom. She discussed it with Mrs. Patterson who thought it was "high time that the stench of death was removed from what was once a beautiful room".

Elizabeth would have preferred to just close over the door, never to open it again.

Bridget and the girls got to work, pulling the curtains and opening windows that hadn't been open for quite some time, removing medicines, placing Peter's personal items in boxes and moving furniture.

Suddenly, a little lark flew through the open window and into the room.

`Get that bird out of here quickly`, Bridget gasped, `it's terrible bad luck for a bird to fly into a room and God only knows this house has had its share of bad luck lately.`

She began to whoosh and flap at the terrified little bird, who trying desperately to find a hiding place away from her whooshing, and flapping arms flew in behind the large bedhead.

`Pull that bed out from the wall`, Bridget instructed the twins, and as Sarah and Jane heaved the large bed out from the back wall the little bird flew up and out the window and a white envelope that had been trapped between the bedhead and the wall floated to the ground.

Picking it up Sarah could see that it was addressed "To my darling wife Elizabeth, the great love of my life".

Chapter 23

Elizabeth sat for a very long time holding the envelope in her hand, sometimes just staring at the words `To my darling wife Elizabeth, the great love of my life`. Other times, passing her finger over the words as if caressing and committing them to everlasting memory, before pressing them to her heart.

Mrs. Patterson, Bridget, Sarah and Jane stood silently watching her, not entirely sure if she was about to burst into tears or fall in a faint, and when she eventually brought herself to open the envelope she looked up at them with pleading eyes and they left her alone to fully absorb the last words that Peter Hargraves would ever say to his wife.

" *To my long suffering and devoted wife Elizabeth,*

Nothing I can say or do can erase the pain and torture I have inflicted on you these past few months how can you ever forgive me?

You, who have been nothing, but kindness and love did not deserve the cruel treatment that I in my anger and hurt unleashed upon you.

Our union was to be one of convenience and compatibility, but I think we both know that it was much, much more than that.

I think I loved you from the very first moment I saw you, a vision of loveliness with sparkling green eyes and wild, flaming hair dispersing kindness and gentle care to the war weary of South Africa, but my wretched fear of rejection caused me to erect barriers to protect myself from you, or what I knew, instinctively, I could feel for you.

Now I ask, protect myself from what? From love, from happiness, from life? How stupid, spineless, and wasteful I have been, living such a pretence.

All those long, lost African nights when my fear prevented me from enjoying what now could have been a lifetime of memories, the absence of which has transformed me into a callous, bitter man.

All I have are those precious moments in a hot hospital supply tent, when my whole life came together and I was totally at one with another human being, never had I experienced anything like it, Godly and savage simultaneously, exactly what I had been created for.

I have ranted and reined against Heaven and the Universe ever since, for allowing me a glimpse of Paradise before cruelly blinding me forever.

You see, I cannot be near you my Love without the memory of that one blissful physical union engulfing me in flames of desire and then rapidly in its wake the icy realisation that it will never happen again, forces all the venom, anger and hurt within me to the surface, exploding and creating a monster that I do not recognise and refuse to live with any longer.

That is not me, that is not Peter Hargraves, that is not the man I am or the man I want to be, nor the husband you deserve.

Sending you away in anger this evening is the hardest thing that I have ever had to, do knowing that I would never set eyes on your beautiful face again, but there is only one course of action open to me now, nothing can obliterate the agony I have caused you, the only thing I can do for you now my darling is to make it cease, to no longer be.

So please forgive me my Love for all the anguish and pain I imposed on you and remember me for who I was not for what I have become, and allow me the freedom to just disappear, knowing that you were the best thing that ever happened to me.

When you think of me, remember the good life I tried to lead and not this tragic end, and look for me sometimes in the night sky, or on a summer breeze or with the little birds that fly for that is where I shall be.

Yours for all eternity

Peter ".

Elizabeth sat for a very long time holding the tear stained letter.

The room darkened and the lamps were lit in the street outside, all three sisters looked in on her from time to time but she was like someone transfixed, transported to a different world, and they left her in her reverie.

....

`Well could you believe that now at all, Detective Inspector` Bridget was saying to Christopher Hastings as she showed him the letter clearing her sister Elizabeth of any hand act or part in her husband's death, `if it hadn't been for the little lark that flew through the window we might never have come across the letter and there you see it in his own handwriting *"look for me with the little birds that fly for that is where I shall be".* Isn't that remarkable altogether. Sure, it must have been himself showing us exactly where the letter was hidden` she added with all the emphasis of her Irish superstition.

Inspector Christopher Hastings did indeed think the story of the little bird a tad fanciful but there was no doubt the letter was from Peter Hargraves and no doubt that his death had been by his own hand.

`Will that be all then Inspector` Bridget inquired in her lilting voice, cocking her eye a bit playfully at him `or would you enjoy a nice cup of tea while you're here.`

Yes, Christopher Hastings had to admit, if only to himself, he was rather disappointed that this would be the end of his visits to the McDonald sisters of Berkeley Square.

196

....

A week later another little bird brought Elizabeth yet another message from beyond the grave.

The sisters were walking in the Royal Botanic Gardens at Kew, outside London, trying a day trip with Elizabeth to bring some colour back to her cheeks and some life back to her battered spirit, when a tiny robin suddenly flew out from nearby shrubbery tangling itself in the netting on Elizabeth`s hat, causing her to startle and loose her balance as she flapped her arms franticly trying to get the bird off her head and in her weakened condition fell over in a faint.

When she came round she was lying in a chair at the Tea Pavilion where she had been carried by Edward Mason, a member of the Royal Botanic Gardens Constabulary, a large, well-built man who had picked Elizabeth up as if she was no more than a child and carried her across the lawns and into the Pavilion.

`Elizabeth can you hear me `a familiar voice said, and focusing on the direction of the sound Elizabeth recognised Philip Martin, who was looking down at her anxiously.

`Doctor Martin, what happened, what are you doing here` she asked confused.

`A bird, a little robin got caught in your hat Elizabeth` Sarah began `and you stumbled and fainted` Jane continued `and wasn't it very fortunate that when that big policeman carried you in here Dr Martin who was having tea with a friend recognised you immediately.`

`Well that was very fortunate indeed and thank you very much Doctor`, Elizabeth said trying to get up but fell back down immediately into the chair as everything began to swim before her eyes.

`Elizabeth I`m not at all happy with the way you look`, Philip Martin said concerned, `I will have my carriage take you and the girls home to

Berkeley Square and I will call on you in the morning to see how you are doing.`

`But I'll be ok in a few minutes Doctor, it's nothing to worry about I'm sure`, Elizabeth began but in truth the bird had really startled her leaving her with an uneasy feeling in her stomach and a lightness in her head; she just wanted to get home to bed.

The following morning having completed his examination and questioning Dr Martin told Elizabeth Hargraves that there was a very good reason for her weakened condition and nausea, she, being an unbelievable five months with child.

With so much sadness and despair in her life with the tragic passing of both parents and her husband, Elizabeth McDonald had not even noticed or paid any attention to the changes occurring in her own body and had barely time to become accustomed to them, when four short months later, a beautiful baby boy brought life, laughter and happiness back to Berkeley Square, his besotted mother giving him the name Donald Robin Hargraves.

Donald to remind him always of his Irish blood, and Robin to remind him that the father he would never know, would always be with him.

Chapter 24

Despite the desperate pain of loss for her parents and the stark separation from her siblings, estrangement from her people and her county, Margaret was surprised by how much she liked and how quickly she became attached to the wildness of Wicklow.

Her Uncle James farm was nestled in the beautiful Vale of Avoca and although the little cottage was basic and the parcel of land small the surrounding countryside more than made up for it in lushness and abundance.

Margaret, though born and bred in the small town of Enniscorthy loved nothing better than being alone in the countryside, tramping the green fields and blue hills of Avoca with baby Sean bundled on her back.

She took to farm life with ease and vigour having always had a way with animals, regularly caring for the horses and hounds of the Brownswood Estate, now to her delight she found a fascination feeding the ducks, hens and chickens around the farm, shepherding the ewes and lambs on the adjacent slopes and even tending to the two pigs and the wild, wayward Mountain goats that her Uncle kept.

It was hard work for a child of eleven, but Margaret was strong and agile and no stranger to pulling her weight. Herself and three month old Sean took to each other immediately, she was old enough to look after him, cater to his needs and gently sooth him when soothing was needed, yet young enough to have fun with him and energy enough to be a playmate, and before long his big blue eyes followed her everywhere she went.

She found she had an aptitude for keeping house and caring for the child and took pride in having everything spick and span for her Uncle and two cousins Thomas, called Tom and Seamus, she even liked cooking for them and was well pleased with herself when they wolfed everything down in appreciation and hunger.

Her Uncle James was a progressive and kind man and not opposed to giving credit where it was due, and each week gave Margaret a few bob for herself saying `Everyone who works in this house gets paid.` The two boys were a bit on the gruff side in the beginning but it didn't take them long to soften towards her when they saw how well she looked after Sean and how much work she did around the farm greatly reducing their own daily burden.

Margaret was often lonely for those she loved and cried herself to sleep many a night thinking of times when her family of fifteen had been together at No.8 Court Street, but she was of a temperament to make the best of things, and she got on with life without complaint or sulk and that quickly endeared her to her newly acquired family.

James Power had arrived in Avoca many years before to work at the Avoca Mines. He had come to make his fortune, as it was rumoured that there was gold to be had among the Wicklow Hills.

And in truth, there was gold of a kind with the mines churning out copper, lead, sulphur and pyrites or "fools gold" as it was known, in large quantities.

And while there wasn't a fortune to be made, there was a decent living to be had by those prepared to work hard, James Power among them. Soon James had enough saved to purchase a small parcel of land along the meandering Avoca river and build a modest home for himself and his new wife Monica Casey.

Life was hard in the mines so when the chance came for James to work in the newly built munitions factory in Arklow he was happy to leave his old life behind him.

Kynochs Munitions Factory had been built at Arklow four years previously and with the outbreak of the Boer War in 1899 the demand for munitions exploded creating a corresponding demand for labour in the area.

As a hard and diligent worker James was snapped up the second, he expressed an interest.

Arthur Chamberlain, Chairman of Kynoch & Co. Lion Works of Birmingham had been a regular visitor to the Arklow area staying with the Howard Ladies of Wingfield at Shelton Abbey and enjoying their many parties, soirees and hunting expeditions with the local elite, getting to know the countryside and its prominent residents.

Ladies Alice, Joulie and Caroline Howard were all unmarried, living with their mother Lady Wicklow at Wingfield and hosting "talk of the town" tea and lawn tennis parties for the gentry of the area.

Indeed, the three ladies were the talk not just of Wicklow town but of London town as well, arriving each year for "the Season" and throwing lavish parties at their residence at Lowndes Street for their very large posse of Irish friends, the Powerscourts, Caryforts, Courtowns and Rosses, among them.

It was on such an occasion that Arthur Chamberlain first made their acquaintance and charmed by their buoyancy and exuberance promised to visit them at their home in Wicklow.

Mr. Chamberlain, ever the businessman, was enthralled with the facilities at Arklow, with pyrite, a vital component in munition manufacture, in plentiful supply from the mines at Avoca, a sandy beach to test explosives and a port at Arklow ideal for the transportation of munitions, along with a rail connection and a nearby town with a readymade labour force, the area was the perfect location for a Munitions Factory.

And perfect it was too for James Power only five miles down the road from his farm in Avoca.

Like many families in the area in 1905 the three Powers worked for Kynochs Tom Power aged thirteen and his brother Seamus aged twelve both made the five mile journey to Arklow each morning, with their father to work alongside the men, women and children of the Munitions Factory.

Margaret loved when they were gone, she would quickly tidy up after the breakfast, feed the stock then bundle little Sean in a shawl, which she tied on her back and then off to walk along the Avoca river or climb up into the surrounding hills.

Margaret loved her own company and the crisp air and exercise evoked memories of similar days with her siblings when they walked the banks of the River Slaney or climbed Vinegar Hill.

She would talk out loud sharing these treasured memories with baby Sean even though he understood not a word.

Often, she would stop to sit and stare around her when Sean fell asleep losing herself in the natural, untamed beauty of her adopted County. Sometimes she caught glimpses of deer flitting across the horizon, other times she watched as fox cubs frolicked and played in dappled sunshine, often she marvelled as birds of prey swooped and soared and trout and salmon leaped high out of the waters of the Avoca, always making sure that she returned home in time to have the baby fed and washed and a good meal ready and on the table when her Uncle and Tom and Seamus arrived home, tired and famished after a long, hard days` work.

As the days turned to weeks and months Margaret would have to say if anyone asked, which of course they never did, that she had a good life and was enjoying being part of the Power family of Avoca.

....

In 1907 when Sean was three years old Kynochs began laying people off. Since the end of the Boer War in 1902 the demand for munitions had dwindled and they simply could no longer justify the large work force.

Luckily, as skilled workers James Power and his youngest son Seamus were kept in employment, however Tom, not having the required skills was made redundant.

Tom didn't mind in the least, he had saved a nice bit of money from his work at Kynochs and now at fifteen he could do what he had always wanted to do and devote his time to the family farm, something he far preferred to working in a factory. Tom craved the outdoors and loved farming, in fact the time he spent at Kynochs had been a penance for him, but Tom wasn't the complaining type and the money had been steady and now it would afford him the opportunity to make the much needed improvements to the farm holding.

Margaret was devasted.

Her days had been her own to do with as she would not withstanding baby Sean who was happy to do whatever she did and go wherever she went. Now she would have someone else there all day watching her, and God forbid even telling her what to do.

Margaret was fond of her cousin Tom but not fond enough to have him around the farm all day, every day. She worried that her good life and happy days had come to an end and as Tom enthused full of plans and hope for the future, she determined to dislike him and everything he wanted to do.

James Power was happy for his eldest son. Tom had always missed being on the land and sometimes James wondered if some of the early animosity between himself and Margaret had been because she had the chance to be where he wanted to be.

Now it seemed the tables were turned. James had noticed that Margaret was less than happy with the prospect of having Tom, under her feet, so to speak, when she had grown used to the freedom of the farm and her own company.

James Power wasn't good with tension, it wore him down and made eating his dinner after a hard day a little less enjoyable. Little did he know that it was far preferable to what was to follow at his Avoca home.

....

Tom Power was a fine lad for fifteen, not overly tall but well built, muscular and made for work. With his wavy auburn hair and even features he was attractive if not handsome, it was his agreeable demeanour, eagerness to please and generosity of spirit that gave him an unique appeal and endeared him to people.

He was kind to animals and to the old and quite often made regular visits to elderly neighbours doing odd jobs for them, feeding their stock, and making necessary repairs to their holdings.

Try as she might Margaret found it exceedingly difficult to dislike him, despite her previous determination and his infringement on her coveted freedom she was growing accustomed to having him around the place. It was nice having someone to talk to, and little Sean simply adored his older brother and took to following him everywhere and copying his mannerisms to the amusement of Margaret as she watched them from the cottage door, Sean walking behind Tom, a tiny mirror image.

`I'm going down to the river to fish now`, Tom said one beautiful, bright Spring morning, `you can come with me if you like, you and Sean.`

`I don't really know how to fish` Margaret said uncertain yet eager.

`Sure I'll show you`, Tom said cheerily, `it's easy you'll pick it up in no time and who knows you might even catch a trout for the dinner.`

`Will I bring something to eat?` Margaret asked. `I'll have to have something for Sean anyway he's hungry all the time.`

So off they went the four of them on a warm pet day in April down to the Avoca to fish, the agile youth bounding along with the fishing rod thrown happily over his shoulder, the young girl sauntering, sometimes skipping joyfully swinging the basket of food in her right hand and the little boy and his dog running and squealing with delight ahead of them.

Tom patiently showed Margaret all he knew about fishing and being a quick learner it wasn't long until she had hooked one herself, her exuberance and excitement made him laugh as she struggled to land her catch determined not to let it get away amid her enthusiasm.

And so it was for the rest of that Spring and Summer, the boy, the girl, the child and the dog, tending to their daily chores with an energy and urgency so they could head off later with their food basket to fish and to hunt and sometimes simply just to sit and admire the wonderful Wicklow landscape.

Margaret took to hunting with the same skill and dexterity that she had to fishing and with some coaching soon became almost as good a shot as Tom. Everything killed was for the kitchen table and she developed a pride in preparing what she had shot or hooked for dinner, and basked in the praise she received from Tom, Uncle James and Seamus.

James Power was delighted each evening to have rabbit, pheasant, grouse, wood pigeon, trout or salmon on the menu, but he was even more delighted about the relationship that had blossomed between his niece and his eldest son, with Tom painstakingly showing Margaret all he knew about wildlife and farming and Margaret devouring it all with interest and relish, they were becoming quite the enterprising couple and both the farm and the little house were displaying great signs of it.

James Power often congratulated himself for choosing this particular one of his sisters` children to come live with him, it was working out well, it was working out very well indeed.

....

Margaret never thought that she would laugh and play and have fun with anyone the way she had with her siblings but herself and Tom had formed a bond very similar to what she had with her own brothers and sisters and yet it felt different. She wasn't sure how or why, she just knew it felt different and when she gave it thought it confused her, so she didn't think about it she was far too busy living and laughing and loving, yes loving, only she wouldn't know that until it was way too late to do anything about it.

....

Winter, Spring, Summer, Autumn, their days were full to the brim. Tom and Margaret were creatures of the wild, on hill, river or glen, they ran through fields, they climbed trees, they gathered mushrooms, they picked berries, they chased butterflies, they found nests, they watched otters, squirrels, badgers, hares, pine martens, bats, owls, hawks and deer with interest and intensity sometimes having to almost gag little Sean to keep him from frightening off their latest curiosity.

They were birds of a feather, childlike, loving, simple and innocent, soaring, swooping, running, and leaping with the joy of life and youth like the natural world all around them.

Their innocence preventing them from realising what was happening.

....

The early morning sun was winking through the treetops as Tom and Margaret lay sprawled, arms and legs outstretched on the grassy bank of the Avoca near the Meeting of the Waters having run all the way along the river seeking a nice spongy spot for their picnic.

`This will do nicely I think`, Tom said patting the springy grass, `now all I have to do is start the fire and gut the fish.`

`I'll just cut and butter the bread`, Margaret replied looking forward to their impending meal as she glanced around checking Sean's whereabouts.

Sean was happily throwing sticks into the river and Shep was just as happily retrieving them.

All was well with the world Margaret thought and almost had to stop from hugging herself with delight.

`What has you smiling to yourself?` Tom asked grinning, having spotted her obvious joy.

`Oh I don't know, I haven't the words to say it really`, Margaret offered, `I just feel so happy and alive all the time.`

`Well do you know Margaret I feel the same myself `, Tom said, somewhat perplexed. `Ever since I finished working in the factory and we started going places and doing things together I just feel so happy all the time. You make me happy Margaret.`

`You make me happy too Tom`, Margaret replied honestly, `you are so good to me, no-one has ever been as good to me as you have. You're always doing things for me and looking out for me and helping me with Sean and with the housework, why do you do all that for me Tom?`

`Because I want to Margaret`, Tom said his throat going dry, `it's as simple as that. I want to make you laugh and make you happy and make life lovelier for you.`

`It's not wrong Tom is it?` Margaret asked uneasy.

`How could it be wrong Margaret`, Tom said, `all we want to do is be kind to each other, how could that be wrong?'

....

Tom, just gone sixteen and Margaret at fourteen were too young, too sheltered and too innocent to realise that they had fallen in love with each other, but they had, and nothing would change that ever again.

The world with all its` rules, regulations and restrictions, sins and morals would very soon tarnish everything for the two cousins but it would never alter the love they felt for one another.

....

It was a bright, frosty morning in early January, there was snow on the hills and Sean could hardly wait for Tom and Margaret to finish their chores so that they could be off. Tom had built a toboggan for Sean who jumped up and down with excitement when he showed it to him, now he couldn't wait to be sitting in it with Tom pulling him through the snow.

`Are you nearly ready yet`, he asked both Tom and Margaret impatiently, `can we go now? Shep is getting tired waiting and so am I.`

Tom and Margaret laughed and hurried themselves because in truth they were every bit as excited and eager to begin their adventure as the child.

It was one of those splendid days when a warm winter sun casts a glistening sheen over frost, ice and snow turning the world into a wonderland of magical, mystical echoes of times long past and whispered promises of possibilities to come.

Tom and Margaret had never felt happier, it was as if the scene had been created by some Godly hand for them and them alone. Tom reached for Margaret`s hand in a friendly, almost childish way as they ran after Sean and Shep – and she liked it.

After a couple of exhaustive hours of hauling the toboggan and Sean up and down the Wicklow hills with Shep yapping alongside Sean finally got hungry and wanted something to eat, so they headed towards the Avoca where Tom would light a fire and they could have some warm bacon with bread and cheese.

While Tom went to gather twigs for the fire Margaret and Sean searched for a good position on the riverbank.
Parts of the Avoca had completely frozen over, but it didn't stop Sean from running on ahead and throwing a stick for Shep. The shrewd sheepdog had the sense not to retrieve it, but the happy, carefree child saw no danger as he raced in on the ice after it.

`Sean!`, Margaret screamed as she headed out on to the frozen waters to grab him.

Sean ran to the bank in fright, but the thin ice began to crack under the young girls` weight and suddenly she had gone under water.

Tom had heard the scream and the ice crack and came running along the bank in time to see Margaret go under, tearing off his jacket he dived into the freezing river and after several frenzied attempts he managed to get Margaret`s limp body out of the freezing river and up on to the bank.

`Margaret! Margaret!` Tom screamed, rubbing her hands, arms, legs, trying to bring life back into her lifeless form he hugged her to him and then he kissed her on the mouth. `Margaret, you can`t leave me! I couldn't go on without you. I love you, I love you, I love you`, he repeated over and over again holding her to his chest all the while rubbing her back and stroking her hair.

Sean was standing crying and shaking nearby and Shep was licking the freezing water from any part of Margaret that Tom wasn't holding or stroking, as he wailed her name to the Heavens.

When she spluttered and coughed, he kissed her again and told her that he loved her.

Margaret was weak and shaken. Tom lit a fire and tried to dry her as much as he could before setting her on the toboggan and pulling her all the way home. Sean was tired and hungry but knew better than to complain about the long trek back to the farm.

Tom put Margaret to bed when they got back to the cottage but not before holding her and telling her again and again how much he loved her and couldn't be without her.

`I love you too Tom and thank you for saving me`, Margaret managed before she drifted off.

....

Margaret was jolted from a deep sleep of exhaustion by loud voices later that night, her head was swimming, but she could hear an anger in her Uncle James voice that she had never heard before and barely recognised.

`What are you telling me Tom`, James roared. `Bad enough to come home to hear that we nearly lost Margaret to the Avoca today but now you`re saying that you and she love each other. She`s only fourteen Tom for God`s sake and she is my sister's child, she is family Tom, she is your first cousin, you can`t love her and that`s that.`

`But I do Da!` Tom cried. `I didn't realise it until I nearly lost her today. I do love her and she says she loves me. I know we`re cousins but what can we do about that.`

`I`ll tell you what we can do about it this minute`, James said angrily, `she will be leaving this house as soon as she`s able: it`s back to Enniscorthy for her I would never have taken her in if I thought something like this was going to happen.`

`But you can`t do that Da!` Tom roared. `Margaret is part of the family now - you can`t just send her back to Enniscorthy and if you do I`ll follow her there.`

`Will you now Tom`, James said, `and what will you do then I ask, she`s still only fourteen and still your first cousin, nothing is going to change that.`

`I am going to marry Margaret`, Tom said emphatically.

`Tom don't you see, you can`t`, James said a little more softly, `you have to get a special dispensation from the Pope himself to marry a first cousin, now do you think you`re going to get that to marry a fourteen year old first cousin and then there`s the question of children, you won`t be able to have any Tom, you`re too closely related, is that what you want for you and Margaret, ask yourself honestly now Tom, is it.`

Margaret held her breath waiting for Tom`s answer but it never came.

`I`m telling you Tom` James continued a little more sympathetically now he felt that his son was seeing reason `you are both young and you will both find other people to love as the time goes by and you will look back on this and say "thank God" you didn't go through with it, ye haven't have you, ye haven't done anything other than kiss.`

`No of course we haven't`, Tom said defeated. `I love her Da. I would never do anything wrong on Margaret.`

`I know you think you do now Tom and she thinks the same about you` James explained `but it`s not real Tom it`s my fault for bringing her here and allowing you both spend so much time together playing at being a family with little Sean there, it is all wrong Tom and both you and Margaret will know that as soon as you are away from each other.`

But James Power was very much mistaken, his eldest son and Margaret McDonald would love each other for the rest of their lives.

....

Margaret muffled her cries in her pillow as the harsh reality of her Uncle's words shattered the beauty of her new-found world like stone smashing glass. Her heart broke hearing the Uncle that she thought so much of demolish the utter loveliness of what she felt for Tom and what she knew he felt for her.

Uncle James had turned their gentle love into something sordid, disgusting almost unspeakable and Margaret wanted to jump from her bed and run as far away from his tarnished words as possible.

Run until she couldn't hear them anymore, but there was nowhere to get away from the reality that she and Tom were cousins in love and in the eyes of all the world immoral and wrong and yet in her heart Margaret knew that the love they had for each other was as pure and deep as the driven snow on the Wicklow hills that surrounded the sad little home that night.

What was she to do? Uncle James would send her back to Enniscorthy in the next day or two, her lovely, happy life splintered and broken forever. How would she survive without Tom, he had become father, brother and partner to her, everything he did, he did to make her happy, how could she continue without him, this was too much to bear.

Margaret wrapped herself in a blanket and ran out into the night.

Tom heard the noise, unable to sleep, he had been watching and waiting for his father and brother to slip into the deep slumber of the hard working before going to Margaret to tell her what his father had planned.

As soon as he reached her he knew she had heard everything.

`Oh Tom` she sobbed ` what are we to do, everything is destroyed.`

`Is it now Margaret` Tom said holding her in his arms `do you not love me then?` he asked.

`I do Tom, I love you`, Margaret replied honestly.

`And I love you - so what is destroyed then.`

`The lovely beauty of it Tom. Uncle James has turned it into something bad and disgusting`, Margaret sobbed.

`Margaret McDonald I know that there is nothing bad or disgusting about my feelings for you, there never has been and there never will be, I love you with all my heart and I want to be with you forever.`

`But Uncle James says its wrong and we can`t be together and the Pope wouldn't allow it and we could never have children because we are too closely related`, Margaret spluttered almost out of control.

`I don't care what my father says and I don't even care about the Pope and I don't want children I want you` Tom said holding Margaret by the shoulders and looking into her eyes `is that what you want Margaret.`

`It is but I don't want people whispering about us and making what we feel for each other ugly and shameful`, Margaret cried. `I don't want us to feel guilty for the rest of our lives.`

`Well what if we went away together somewhere no-one knew anything about us` Tom asked.

`What do you mean?` Margaret asked hopefully.

`Well if we were in England or America where no-one knew we were cousins or knew anything at all about us` Tom said.

`But Tom you don't want to leave Wicklow, you love the farm, you love what you do, you love your father and your brothers` Margaret replied quickly.

`I love you more than all that` ,Tom said simply, `my life is where you are, my future is you.`

`But what would we do, where would we go?`, the words came tumbling out of Margaret in a rush.

213

`My father wants to put you on the Wexford train as soon as you are able to travel` Tom explained. `What if you didn't go all the way to Enniscorthy but got off at the next station and got the train to Kingstown and the boat to England, could you make your way to your sisters and stay with them until I was able to come and get you?`

`I could. I have enough money saved to pay for my passage to England, thanks to Uncle James`, Margaret said, `but my sisters probably wouldn't want us to be together either`.

`They won`t know that I have come for you until we are both away on a ship to America` Tom said excited about his plan `no-one will know us there. You will need to stay with your sisters until I have it all arranged, I have a bit of money still from what I saved when I was at Kynochs, now I wish I hadn't spent so much of it on the farm, I will have to sell a few animals to have enough for our passage and to give us a bit of a start when we get to New York.`

`Oh Tom are you sure, you are so happy here among your Wicklow hills I know you never had any desire to leave them maybe you will hate me forever for being the cause of your emigration` Margaret cried.

`Hate ya, will ya whist, I will love you forever Margaret McDonald and there`s an end to it`, Tom Power said with sincerity. `Anyway, I hear the hills around Avoca are only pebbles compared to what they have in America - imagine the fun we will have in the snow there.`

Margaret allowed herself a smile of hope.

....

Two days later, Margaret stood at Arklow station with tears streaming down her face and a hysterical child clinging to her leg as she tried to board the Wexford train. She was the only mother little Sean had ever known and his distress was heart breaking both for her and Uncle James.

`I am so very sorry Margaret that it has to be this way` Uncle James began clearly very upset himself, he had grown to love Margaret, she was like the daughter he never had` but you understand don't you that I simply can`t allow a relationship between yourself and Tom it just isn't right, it`s against the law of God and man, I`m sorry` he stammered as he grabbed Sean and wrenched him away.

As Margaret stepped on to the train Tom ran to her wrapping his arms around her and whispered `Wait for word from me in London I will find you there, I promise and never forget that I love you and will love you forever.`

As the Wexford train pulled out of Arklow station Margaret watched in silent despair as once again those that she called family disappeared from her view.

If she had known how long it would be before she would see any of them again, she would most likely have thrown herself from the train.

Chapter 25

Poor little Mary McDonald was terrified of her Aunt Mai from the moment she laid eyes on her. She was everything her mother wasn't, and all Mary wanted was her mother.

Mai Power was her mother's eldest sister, but it was difficult to believe that they were from the same litter. Her mother had a softness of face and body, drills and furrows that a little person could find shelter and solace in, her Aunt Mai was all straight lines and acute angles, there was no place for a tiny, frightened seven year old to burrow into and cocoon.

Little Mary was forced to grow up quickly becoming her aunt's companion if not her confidante and friend.

But as she got older and a little less frightened of her, she began to see a lot of good in Aunt Mai and to greatly admire, if not love, her no nonsense, community conscious and civic minded relative.

You couldn't describe Aunt Mai as kind, but she was a fair and decent person and railed against injustice anywhere she encountered it, and there was plenty to encounter on the streets of Dublin in 1910.

Being a retired Matron Aunt Mai was a strict disciplinarian. Her little home on Dorset Street was run with precision and exactitude, and Mary learned from an early age what her duties were and what was expected of her.

Aunt Mai had come to Dublin to work at the Mater Hospital on Eccles Street during the cholera outbreak of 1886. Her work became her life, she never married, never having the time to devote to the onerous task of finding herself a husband, but she did strike up a lasting friendship with her landlady, a Ms. Gladys Mortimer, who rarely took in Catholic lodgers but somehow made an exception for the tall, girl from Wexford with the honest face.

When Ms. Mortimer passed to her eternal reward in 1901, Mai was more than surprised to learn that she had been bequeathed the little house on Dorset Street "in grateful appreciation for the many years of gentile and genial company, and the expert care and nurture bestowed upon me by my friend and companion Mai Power who tended to my every need most carefully and meticulously through the winter of my life".

Ms. Mortimer was the last of her line, so seemingly knew quiet well what she was doing taking in nurse Mai Power as a lodger to look after her in her old age, and apart from a sizeable donation to her Presbyterian Church, Ms. Mortimer left her home and her entire estate, including her cats, to Mai, which adding to her own savings from a rather frugal, prudent, and well spent life, transformed Mai Power into a lady of considerable consequence almost overnight.

When her youngest sister Mary McDonald died tragically Mai had decided that she would do what she could for Mary's children but by the time she reached Enniscorthy all of them had been sorted, apart from the little seven year old, called after her mother.

Not her first choice, Mai would have to admit, a little too young and too fragile, but she took Mary home with her all the same, and gradually they formed an alliance and fell into a routine, that sufficed for both of them.

Mai, to her credit, looked after the child we Mary was well fed, well clothed and well educated and stood out like a sore thumb among the poor and impoverished wretches of the Buckingham Street tenements, where she accompanied her aunt three or four times a week.

Mai Power, in grateful thanks for her own good fortune and because she was a trained and highly capable nurse, spent a lot of her time trying to alleviate the suffering of the poor of the Buckingham Street tenements, and she brought Mary with her from the beginning, as a constant reminder to the child that there were children so much worse off than she. Mai had little or no time for sympathy and refused to entertain the notion in poor little Mary that she was in any way hard done by, even if she had lost both parents and her entire family at the tender age of seven.

And in truth, what Mary witnessed in the Dublin tenements would remain with her all her years and fashion her life path and keep her forever grateful to her aunt.

Dublin was seething with disease, poverty, misery, and filth, and nowhere was it more in evidence than in the tenements.

Mary, who was a small child and underweight for her age looked extremely well nourished and cared for compared to the large eyed, pale, scrawny, ricketed children who played in the grime and squalor of the lanes and alley ways of the Buckingham Street tenements.

Tuberculosis was rampant, and Mai Power visited the sick of the tenements as often as she could, bringing as much comfort as possible to the suffering. She hadn't a great bedside manner and she certainly didn't suffer fools lightly, but she was welcomed into the homes and hovels, recognised for her expert nursing skills and her ability to get things done.

Mai Power believed strongly in the philosophy that `God helps those who help themselves` but someone had to show these poor, uneducated, tired and unhealthy people how to help themselves in the first instance, and as a former Matron this was where Mai came into her own.

The front door of the tenement building was never closed, it remained ajar all hours of the day and night, an open invitation to every undesirable, drunkard and worse, on the streets to enter and utilise the entrance hall as a squat for a few hours kip, as a lavatory and as a doss area for carnal relief.

Each morning the residents of the ground floor awoke to the most appalling, unhealthy odours of urine, excrement and vomit so Aunt Mai mobilised the entire tenement community to see to the sanitisation of the front hall as their first and most important duty of the day.

Every family in the building took it upon themselves to fetch a bucket of water from the tap in the yard to sluice down the front hall and with all hands on deck it wasn't long before they had scrubbed the disgusting horrors of the night down the street and back into the gutter from whence they came.

Aunt Mai had a great respect for these people who lived and survived and even loved and laughed in the worst urban conditions in Western Europe, living eight to sometimes sixteen people in a single room, sharing one or two beds between them, with no inside access to running water or lavatory closet, leaky roofs, sagging ceilings, broken windows, cracked walls, festering with disease, with death lurking around every corner, and yet having a clean home was so important to many of them, giving them a sense of pride and respectability even in the depths of abject poverty.

Mai came regularly armed with bars of soap, iodine and nutritious food and showed the women how to scrub the floors, wash the walls, keep themselves and their clothes clean and how to cook a nourishing meal in a fireplace.

But it was almost an impossible task for the tenement residents to pull themselves out of such poverty, the squalor was staggering, the cramped quarters unhygienic, unhealthy, rundown and depressing, and any work that the men of the households managed to get was casual and uncertain.

Mai railed against the injustice of it all and became interested in the new labour movement that had begun to take hold all over Dublin, and was soon an ardent fan and follower of the chief organiser "big Jim Larkin" and his policy "a fair days pay for a fair days work".

James Larkin was an excellent speaker and Mai hauled Mary all over Dublin to hear the big boned, large framed, broad shouldered man spread his "divine mission of discontent" with eloquence, despite his own lack of formal education.

Mary was enthralled from the very first time she heard him, with his outstretched arms and commanding voice, he was larger than life, more an out of world godlike force than a man, and she became an immediate disciple of Larkinism.

James Larkin had empathy for the poor and a hatred of injustice repeating time and again that `an injury to one is the concern of all` and that had always been Aunt Mai`s attitude, now she and Mary had a cause to rally to in the Trade Union Movement, which would surely prove beneficial to the bread winners of the tenements, the unskilled workers of Dublin.

....

The Irish Transport & General Worker's Union opened an office on Charlotte Street, Wexford at the beginning of August 1911.

As Wexford workers began to join in great numbers, local employers became nervous and adamant that no trade union members would work at their premises.

Doyles Skelskar Ironworks were the first to lockout their men on 10th August.

A little over two weeks later Pierces Foundry locked out its workforce of over four hundred men and Hearns Engineering quickly followed suite along with Thompson Engineering and Howard Rowe`s flour mill on Spawell Road.

By the third week of August, Wexford had seven hundred men out of work, impacting directly on the lives of over 3,000 townspeople.

`We need a presence in Wexford immediately` big Jim told the members at an ITGWU meeting `I am going to dispatch P.T. Daly to Wexford today, but I would like a few to accompany him, this is going to get rough before it gets better make no mistake about that.`

'What about yourself there Mai` he asked addressing Mai Power, whom he had come to know and respect `aren't you from Wexford - have you anyone down there that you could stay with while this is going on.`

'Well I`m from Enniscorthy Mr. Larkin`, Mai replied, `but I`m afraid that there are too many people depending on me on a day to day basis in Buckingham Street, for me to just up and take off like that, but young Mary here, she could go, she has family in Enniscorthy and even though she`s only fourteen she is well versed in looking after people`s needs, accompanying me as she does most days to the tenements, she can cook and clean and wash and sew and has even picked up a bit of medicinal knowledge from me along the way, I can assure you Mr. Larkin, young Mary won`t be found wanting when it comes to doing her duty and caring for others.`

Mary was startled. She wasn't used to hearing Aunt Mai speak highly of her and hadn't been back to Enniscorthy in years, but she did write regularly to her eldest brother William and sister Maryanne who were both now living in Enniscorthy. Maryanne had come home after her illness and was resident in the family home at No.8 Court Street and William was still buying and selling horses moving between Enniscorthy, Brownswood, England and Belgium.

'Well Mary` big Jim inquired `does that settle it then are you willing to go home and give whatever assistance you can to the Wexford workers and their families.`

'When you put it like that Mr. Larkin sure who could refuse` Mary said, shyly, who wouldn't have refused Jim Larkin anything, yet surprised that Mai had so willingly volunteered her, and quite excited by the prospect of being part of the Wexford lockout and seeing some of her family again.

....

There was no mistaking the tall, thin woman standing on the platform as the Dublin train pulled into Enniscorthy Station, even though she had little or no memory of her, Mary knew instinctively, it was her eldest sister Maryanne.

Maryanne had left for England when Mary was no more than a year old, but this woman bore such a resemblance to her mother that Mary would have known her anywhere.

Her dark, wavy hair was soft and luxurious, disciplined by a bright yellow ribbon but with tendrils still escaping from under her black fashionable hat, her fine featured face and creamy olive skin showing not a blemish, her velvety full lips quivering a little as her kind, soft brown eyes scanned those alighting, for the first glimpse of the little sister she had left behind so many years before.

As their eyes met the sisters ran to each other, embracing with the ease and familiarity of kin, clinging, crying, endeavouring to erase the years of separation, before recovering, and walking arm in arm along the streets of their childhood to their family home at No. 8 Court Street.

Mary and Maryanne, sisters by birth, became friends by kind. Hewn from their thoughtful, compassionate mother and tolerant, decent father they were birds of a feather, temperate and considerate with a regard and an inherent responsibility towards others, both feeling they had a duty not to be someone but to do something.

`I would join you in Wexford Mary` Maryanne said to her sister that evening eager to help in any way she could, when Mary explained that she had been sent to do whatever was needed for the locked out workers and their families `but I couldn't leave the three here on their own, dependent as they are on me for food and clean lodgings.`

Maryanne had taken in three lodgers at No. 8 Court Street to provide her with a bit of an income and to assist with the upkeep of the family home. William was away a lot and did contribute substantially when he returned but Maryanne liked her independence and particularly liked being busy.

Local women, recognising her as a good midwife, did call on her during labour and attested to the fact that she had the same birthing gift as her mother before her, but most of them had so little to live on, that Maryanne would have felt guilty accepting payment from them. She did however receive the most welcome gifts of eggs, cheese, bacon, freshly baked bread, and potatoes from time to time, and now and then there was even the odd rabbit or trout wrapped in newspaper and left on her doorstep.

Mary spent two days with her sister before taking the train to Wexford to carry out her trade union duties. The old house held many bittersweet memories for her and her first night there as she closed her eyes she imagined she could hear the voices of her mother and father and brothers and sisters floating on the air and calling to her from the walls of her long ago home.

She enjoyed meeting Maryanne's lodgers, a reporter from Dublin working for the Echo newspaper with very strong and forceful views on politics and Home Rule, Paddy Donovan, was a republican through and through and was delighted to listen to the young Mary, tell about life in the tenements and big Jim and the labour movement, though Mary was of the impression that he could tell her a lot more about it than she knew, but then she supposed that was only natural for a reporter, sure they knew everything before it happened.

Michael Furlong was from out beyond Clonroche and was working in Davis Mills and Lily O'Toole had come to Enniscorthy from Carlow to nurse at the Mental Asylum.

Maryanne kept a very neat and tidy house, and Mary could see that her sister was happy living at home in Enniscorthy, and she wondered to herself, if there might be room for her in the family home.

She was very grateful for all that her Aunt Mai had done for her and she had learned a lot in Dublin, but there was something about Enniscorthy that spoke to her heart, whispers from the ghosts of hill that floated to her across the ripples of the Slaney.

Mary had been looked after very well in the home of her Aunt, but the only place she had ever been loved was Enniscorthy, and she wanted to stay there, but how would she tell Aunt Mai without hurting her and appearing ungrateful, that was a dilemma.

....

Maryanne had made arrangements for Mary to stay with cousins of their mothers, the Nolans, on North Main Street, Wexford.

The Nolan family were sympathetic to the trade union cause, depending heavily on the foundry workers for their livelihood in the little grocery shop at No.10 North Main Street, and whilst they had to be careful not to alienate other customers, they did what they could to support the workers families and were happy to have Mary staying with them and actively assisting.

That September young Mary McDonald became a common sight on the Wexford streets carrying the much needed and very welcome food parcels to those in need.

Tensions were running high as P.T. Daly regularly addressed large gatherings of locked out workers in the Faythe area of the town, convincing them of their right to organise and combine. Violence became inevitable as employers recruited blackleg workers from Carlow and Dublin and as far afield as Scotland, Manchester, Leeds, and Birmingham, offering them wages higher than those previously paid, antagonising and infuriating the Wexford men.

Anticipating violent clashes, the RIC drafted in one hundred and fifty extra policemen from Tipperary, Waterford, Carlow, and Kilkenny to escort the blackleg workers to and from the foundries each day.

Mary generally weaved her way almost unnoticed through the crowds, stopping occasionally to hear P.T. passionately deliver the trade union message to workers to unite. She was happy, she was home, and she felt a greater sense of belonging and purpose than she had ever experienced in Dublin, even when helping her aunt in the Buckingham tenements.

These were her people, this was her place, she was of Wexford and it was of her, she became even more determined to stay.

As she turned into Bride Street, Mary McDonald froze as men and women came tumbling towards her, sending her food parcel flying into the air and almost knocking her off her feet, as they scrambled to get out of the way of a police baton charge.

One woman stopped beside her and took a stone from a bag she was carrying saying `Here, throw this at the bastards` putting the stone into Mary's hand as she withdrew another one from the bag and took aim.

About twenty baton wielding RIC Officers were coming towards them with weapons swinging in every direction, Mary watched, stone clenched in her hand, as one man received several blows to the head as he tried desperately to shield himself with his arms, taking aim Mary let fly and hit the policeman on the arm just as he was about to land another blow.

`You little bitch!` were the last words Mary heard coming from behind before she was struck in the head and tumbled to the ground.

....

Over twenty people were injured that day, some more seriously than others, Mary McDonald underwent life-saving surgery for a fractured skull, but the man she had tried to save Michael O'Leary died from his injuries five days later.

The Wexford trade union struggle continued through the winter of 1911 and into February 1912, but without Mary, who was forced to return home to Enniscorthy after her operation into the care of her sister Maryanne, a trained nurse.

Aunt Mai, who diligently cared for half the tenement population of Dublin, had little or no time to be looking after a sick niece and was happy for Mary to remain in Enniscorthy.

In February 1912 James Connolly arrived in Wexford, and within two weeks of his arrival a settlement to the Wexford lockout was achieved.

The settlement allowed for the establishment of the Irish Foundry Workers Union as an associate of the Irish Transport & General Workers Union. The foundry men, skilled and unskilled could combine and return to work.

A victory celebration was held in the Faythe on 17th February and over 5,000 people came out to cheer James Connolly and the Wexford workers, a frail Mary McDonald and her sister Maryanne among them.

Chapter 26

James Power had done everything he could to get his eldest son Tom to forget his cousin Margaret, but eighteen months later the boy, who was now almost a man, still felt exactly the same about her as the day they put her on the Wexford train bound for Enniscorthy.

James knew that she hadn't gone all the way to Enniscorthy that day, instead switching trains she headed to Kingstown and later caught the boat to England and was now living with her sisters in Berkeley Square.

How wouldn't he know, when he had foiled several of Tom`s plans to get to her, even going as far as having him arrested.

James feared that his son would never be able to forgive him, for branding him a sheep stealer, and for the indignation that he had suffered being picked up and arrested by two RIC Officers as he alighted the train at Kingstown. But accusing Tom of stealing and selling his own sheep, the ones he had bought with money saved working at Kynochs, was the only way James Power knew of preventing him from making a most grievous mistake.

James Power was both a righteous and religious man and would never be able to accept a union between his son and his sister`s child, a union that defied the law of God and nature couldn't be right and he couldn't stand by and allow it.

He had painstakingly kept his eldest son under lock and key in the hope that his love for his first cousin would somehow fade and disperse with absence, into the grey swirling mists of the Wicklow hills, but instead with every passing day Tom`s love grew stronger and more determined.

It was 1912 and Tom was approaching his eighteen birthday. Very soon James Power would have little or no say in his sons future. He had to do something and do it quickly.

A great many of the Powers had left Wexford from the 1830s onwards to fish the waters around Newfoundland or Talamh an Eisc as they knew it and some of them had settled there along with countless others from Wexford, Waterford, Carlow, Tipperary and Kilkenny.

Now a thriving Irish fishing community worked the seas and lived on the land on the Avalon Pennisula and James had cousins aplenty who would only be too delighted to welcome yet another member of kin to what was fast becoming known as the Irish Shore.

All James had to do was get the lad to them.

James had written to his cousin George Power who was unmarried and had plenty of room for another pair of hands on his boat fishing off Cape St. Mary`s. George would be happy to have Tom over and indeed would be able to come to New York to collect him when he docked.

James was surprised that he was not met with more opposition when he announced his plans to his son.

`It`s for the best Tom, you`ll see`, James said after he had told Tom what he had in store for his future, `myself and your brothers will miss you dreadfully but there are too many memories of Margaret around here. When you get away to somewhere new you`ll be able to forget all about her and begin a new life.`

`Ya think that do ya Da` Tom replied afraid to look at his father in case he would give himself away. This was exactly what he and Margaret had talked about, going somewhere new and exciting where no one knew them, where no one knew they were first cousins.

`I do son, I do, you`re a good lad and I don't want you making a terrible mistake that could ruin your life and most likely damn you for all eternity` James Power said with feeling, he loved his first born and knew him to be kind hearted and honest and wanted a good and wholesome future for him.

`Things seem good in Newfoundland and there are so many from Wexford there it will feel just like home, sure you'll hardly miss us at all. George writes that living on the Irish Shore is just like living here in Ireland, surrounded by beautiful scenery, good neighbours, friends, and kin. And besides you always did like to do a bit of fishing didn't ya`, James said smiling.

Images of showing Margaret how to fish on the banks of the Avoca flashed before Tom's eyes and he smiled too, thinking of the future that had almost miraculously materialised for them. As soon as he got to New York he would somehow dodge his cousin George and find work and lodgings in the big city before sending for Margaret to come and join him.

Tom was happier than he had been since Margaret left Avoca eighteen months before.

....

James Power travelled to Cobh with his son, it might be many years before they would see each other again, if ever, and he wanted to spend as much time as possible with him before his ship sailed.

It had been a sad house the evening before as Tom said goodbye to neighbours and friends and his two brothers Seamus and Sean.

Sean had never quite gotten over the loss of Margaret, and Tom had been a great comfort to him as the four year old cried himself to sleep many a night missing the girl who had replaced his dead mother, now he was losing his brother as well, it was heart wrenching for both of them. Tom had gotten used to sharing his bed with the pitiful little body that sometimes shook with sobs before falling asleep. He would wrap his strong arms round Sean saying over and over `Go to sleep now I'm here - but from tomorrow he wouldn't be. What would become of the poor little mite without him.'

That last night both brothers, older and younger shook with sobs before falling asleep.

With his hands on his shoulders and tears in his eyes James Power held his son`s gaze as they said their goodbyes on the Cobh quayside ` This is for the best Tom some day you will see that and maybe then you won`t hate me as much.`

`I couldn't hate you Da you`re my father I love you, I always have and I always will ` Tom said through his tears `but I love Margaret too Da and despite what you say or think I know here and now in my heart of hearts that I will love her till the day I die, it`s that simple.`

`Forgive me Tom` James Power said as his son began to embark.

`I do Da, and I hope you can find it in you some day, to forgive myself and Margaret too`.

Tom Power watched, transfixed on his father face until he could see it no longer, oblivious to all the excitement and palaver surrounding Cobh and the maiden voyage of the greatest ship ever made, the Titanic.

Chapter 27

Margaret McDonald could scarcely conceal her joy and excitement from her sisters, after almost eighteen months of torturous longing she had finally received a letter from Tom, telling her all about his plans for their future life together.

For nearly a year she had been distraught hearing no word from him but suspecting that his father was somehow intercepting their letters to each other.

The day after she arrived at Berkeley Square, she wrote to Tom sending her new address but heard nothing.

Margaret never stopped loving Tom, but everything was new and exhilarating about life in London and it was such a source of joy and happiness for her to be with her sisters again along with her new nephew, Donald, who brought pleasure and delight to all of them on a daily basis.

So the days passed not too unpleasantly for Margaret, even though there were moments in the midst of all that was new and energising, when she longed with all her young heart for the peace, beauty and wildness among the Wicklow hills and the kind and loving boy who had shared it all with her.

Her sister Elizabeth it seemed was a woman of considerable means but there was an entrenched sadness behind her eyes that Margaret suspected reached her very soul which no amount of money, status or comfort could erase. The sight of her beautiful son was the only thing that caused her face to lighten and her spirit to soar and he was never far from her view.

Elizabeth's legacy allowed her to care for and educate her sisters and that brought her tremendous gratification.

The twins, Sarah and Jane had, with Elizabeth's sanction and assistance, taken up Amelia Anderson's offer to attend her school in Somerset and after graduating would be taking up teaching positions there, residing just down the road at Honeysuckle Cottage which had belonged to the late Peter Hargraves.

Bridget, who had gone with the twins to care for them and keep house for the duration of their studies, had caught the teaching bug herself and would be completing her own teacher training as soon as the twins were qualified.

Elizabeth, often smiled, thinking to herself how amused Peter Hargraves would be to see his family's English Protestant inheritance being spent to feed, cloth and educate her Irish Catholic sisters, his ancestors must be somersaulting in their graves.

`Margaret` Elizabeth addressed her with purpose one day about ten months after she had arrived in London `have you given any thought to what you might do with yourself now that you have had the time to settle a bit.`

Margaret had told them very little about her life in Wicklow with the Powers, and certainly nothing about Tom or the love that had grown between them, that was, and would continue to be, their secret. Although, when she spoke of him a softness came into her voice describing his patience and kindness to her as he told her all he knew about farming and animals, wild and domestic and taught her to fish the Avoca river and hunt the Wicklow hills.

Sometimes she worried that her sisters couldn't help but see the love she had for him with her heart almost spilling over when she spoke of him, but if they did, they said nothing. Perhaps because it was something they simply couldn't contemplate.

She had told them that she had left Wicklow and the Powers as soon as she had enough money saved for her passage to England to be with her own family, and they seemed to accept that without question.

In fairness James Power had promised Margaret that he would say nothing to her family about her relationship with his son and she could say that she simply wanted to return to her home in Enniscorthy now that her sister Maryanne was back at No.8 Court Street.

Margaret had written to Maryanne from London explaining, that she had changed her mind, and instead of returning to Enniscorthy had decided to join the sisters in London and Elizabeth had confirmed that all was well.

`You know Elizabeth I have been giving it thought` the sixteen year old said. `I very much enjoyed looking after Sean Power when he was a small baby so maybe I should follow in Ma`s footsteps and become a midwife.`

`That's not a bad idea at all Margaret` Elizabeth said enthusiastically `and God knows it`s certainly in the family and I`ve noticed how good you are with Donald too, children are certainly your forte and I know just the person to talk to, our doctor Philip Martin has excellent connections and I`m sure will be able to get you into the Royal to do your training, shall I set the wheels in motion then.`

`Oh yes please if you would`, Margaret said appreciatively. There was no knowing when Tom would be able to come for her and it might make it a whole lot easier to get a job in New York as a trained nurse.

There was no doubt in Margaret`s mind but that Tom would come for her: she was confident that nothing but death itself would stop him from doing that.

....

Margaret was eight months into her training when Tom`s letter arrived.

Tom had found out that a friend of his from Kynochs Munition Factory was leaving to take up a position in London, and without his father`s knowledge he managed to get a letter to him asking him to post it as

233

soon as he got to England to a Ms. Margaret McDonald of Berkeley Square.

Margaret was beside herself with joy when the letter arrived and was at great pains to stop the smile that was perpetually in her eyes from spreading to her lips, lest she give the game away.

She had to be careful, now that the life that herself and Tom had talked about and dreamed of, was within their grasp, she wasn't about to destroy it:

``By the time you receive this my lovely Margaret I will be on the high seas headed to New York on the biggest ship ever made, about to lay the foundation stones for our future life together.*

I know it`s been eighteen months since we have seen each other but I am confident deep down in my heart that you still feel exactly the same way about me as I do about you.

Time and distance cannot destroy true love, rather, I believe they make it stronger.

It`s been a terrible time for me without any news of you as I am sure it has been for you without word from me, but I would ask you to please find it within your heart to forgive my father and your uncle. He is a good man and was only doing what he thought best for us.

But you and I have known from the beginning, that once we met and fell in love there was no going back. There may be millions and millions of people in the world Margaret McDonald, most of them not related to me, but you are the only one for me, now and always, death can`t even separate us I will love you throughout all eternity.

The plan is for me to meet my cousin George Power when we dock in New York and head up to Newfoundland in his boat, but New York is a large city and I`m sure when this mammoth ship docks the excitement and chaos will be something else, and it will be easy for me to get lost in the crowds and pandemonium.

Once I find a job and somewhere for us to live, I will send the passage money for you to join me.

You will come won't you, my darling, I can hardly wait to see you again, until then I will see you in my dreams dancing, laughing and skipping among the Wicklow hills.

In two days time on 11th April I will head with my father to Cobh to catch the Titanic, this ship that they are all talking about and begin the journey of the rest of our lives.

Do you know how fine you are to me Margaret McDonald.

Yours forever
Tom".

Margaret McDonald was happily walking towards the Royal Hospital when the headlines caught her eye and the newspaper boys began shouting `Hundreds drown as Titanic hits iceberg and sinks, read all about it`.

The tram driver said he did his best to avoid her, but she just kept walking towards him like someone in a trance, until it was too late.

Chapter 28

William McDonald was a Redmonite. He believed strongly in the policies and ethos of his fellow countyman John Redmond, leader of the Irish Parliamentary Party and champion of Home Rule at Westminster.

William had close dealings with the British army, through their agents, scouring and buying horses for them in both Ireland and Belgium, providing him with a job he loved and a most lucrative livelihood, which helped him maintain his family home at Court Street, Enniscorthy, the small farm his father had purchased on the Brownswood Estate, and allowed him to make regular financial contributions to the widow and family of his late friend and mentor John O`Neill.

Home Rule would give Ireland dominion status, with governance returned from Westminster to a domestic Parliament in Dublin, all achieved through constitutional methods rather than violent means.

William warmed to the concept of no violence, the country, he reasoned, had been through enough, it was time for it to emerge from the shadows of rebellion and the fetid aftertaste of famine to build an Ireland, safe and comfortable for all her citizens to reside in.

There were times though, when William's thoughts returned with emotion and pride to the day he marched as a pikeman to Vinegar Hill for the 100th anniversary of the 1798 Rebellion, and when they did, a queasiness spread across his stomach causing it to tighten and spasm with remorse and guilt.`

Was he trampling unreservedly on the graves of those who perished on the hill that day, would they understand his, and Redmond`s, new brand of nationalism, or would they think that it in some way diluted his Wexford heritage and Slaney blood.

But William wanted to live well, he had been taught to be industrious and to strive to better himself, and if Britain could be of benefit to him in this regard, then why not use it that way, he persuaded himself, and yet in the innate crevices of his mind there would always be that duplicitous niggle.

It was proving more difficult than he thought to shake off the shadow of the Hill.

William's distaste for violence as a means to an end had nothing to do with not being up for a fight, and as soon as Britain declared war on Germany in August 1914, following the invasion of Belgium, he answered John Redmond's call to Wexford men and Irish men to "don khaki and fight for little Belgium".

John Redmond was a great orator and a leader of men, and in his own dilemma, William took tremendous comfort from the fact that here was a man from Ballytrent, Kilrane, whose forebears had been hanged on Wexford Bridge in 1798 and he was now calling on his fellow brethren to assist Britain in her defence of small nations like Belgium, genuinely believing that once the war in Europe was over, it would only be a matter of time before Britain would have to grant independence to Ireland, it would be disingenuous to do anything less.

William had spent a lot of time in Belgium and had been treated well by his many friends and business acquaintances there and was willing to do his bit to alleviate their suffering and assist in their liberation.

On Sunday 27th September he attended John Redmond's recruitment rally at the Bullring in Wexford and was saddened to see the rift that had emerged between those Volunteers who wished to follow Redmond to the war in Europe, and the anti- Redmond and anti-recruitment Volunteers who would remain at home, loyal to the IRB.

`Well to be honest with you William I can see their point`, Maryanne said when William returned to Court Street later that evening to recount all. `Ireland should have first call on her sons: don't you think that we have fought enough wars for the English already without sacrificing more of our young men for them far away from home.`

`I am surprised at you Maryanne McDonald` William said quickly `and you after spending time living over there in London and receiving your training along with a livelihood there.

`I had to work very hard there William` Maryanne replied indignant `and I earned every penny I made I'll have you know, but I saw enough of war in Africa and plenty of young Irishmen wondering what the hell they were dying for over there. I don't want to see the same happen again.`

`If Irishmen are to fight and die don't you think it should be for Ireland William?`, Mary who had been listening intently asked rather timidly.

`Well you see I do think in a way that this is for Ireland Mary` William explained `if we join up and help Britain to free a small nation like Belgium from an invading army, then when the war is over, Britain would surely have to see Ireland in the same light as Belgium and grant us Home Rule.`

`But Home Rule is not independence now is it?` Mary asked.

`Well it's a step on the path to independence, isn't it`, William said, greatly surprised that his two sisters appeared to have been transformed into hard and fast republicans almost overnight and without his knowledge.

But what William didn't know, because he was at home so seldom, was that both Maryanne and Mary sat night after night listening enthralled to their lodger Paddy Donovan, a journalist with the Enniscorthy Echo and an out and out IRB man, discuss the pros and cons of Home Rule versus Republic, with their neighbour Stephen Hayes.

In fact, as their eldest brother headed for the fields of Flanders, Maryanne and Mary were heading to the Athenaeum to attend First Aid classes organised by the Enniscorthy Cuman na mBan branch in preparation for rebellion.

Michael McDonald had always harboured the spirit of adventure and yet when war was declared in August 1914 he had no great burning desire to rush out and enlist with his many teammates and friends.

Football had been good to Michael, he was a talented player who gave everything to the game, endearing him greatly to the people of West Ham and East London, many admiring his tenacity and drive, along with his talent and skill.

In everyday life Michael was a mild mannered, happy go lucky, not looking for trouble, kind of guy, but once he crossed that white line a metamorphosis occurred earning him the nickname "the Irish wolfhound".

Michael was one of the strongest and most courageous players West Ham had ever had. He played with commitment, passion and an all-consuming desire to win, so it surprised everyone, when many of his fellow footballers were joining up and heading off on the great adventure of war, that Michael McDonald wasn't among them.

In truth, the idea of being a soldier appealed greatly to Michael. He was very good at taking orders, he liked discipline, routine and training and he was also the kind of man that other men looked up to and would be happy to follow.

He watched wistfully as friends and teammates waved goodbye from platforms and docks and yet Michael just couldn't quite get his head round donning that khaki uniform, a descendant of the Redcoat that had struck terror into his Enniscorthy ancestors.

Michael had made several attempts to enlist, reassuring himself that some of his best friends, indeed almost all of his friends were Englishmen, his loyal fans in the stands and on the terraces were mostly Englishmen, and besides that, he had left Enniscorthy because of the narrow mindedness and prejudice of his own people, and yet each time he approached the Recruitment Office he would be engulfed by inexplicable emotion and the gut wrenching feeling that he was in some way turning his back on all belonging to him, and he would beat a hasty retreat.

Michael, in his rational thinking wanted to be in France and Belgium fighting Germans, he believed the English cause to be the right one, and there was a part of him that longed for the excitement, adventure and camaraderie of war, and yet each time he did an about turn and went back to playing football.

The Football Association continued to play its games throughout 1914 and 1915 and as word filtered through every day of heavy casualties and the loss of friends and teammates at the Front, Michael felt worse and worse about himself, and then to his huge relief in January 1916 Conscription was introduced.

Michael heaved a sigh of relief, the decision was no longer his, a weight was lifted from his mind, he wasn't making a conscious choice to turn his back on those who went before him, he was being forced to do a job and he would have to wear the uniform to do it, finally he could head for Flanders fields with a clear conscience.

....

His sister Margaret McDonald had no such grappling with her conscience when it came to enlisting, as soon as war was declared, she signed up for France.

No-one, but no-one, had expected Margaret McDonald to survive being run over by a tram that day, the day news came of the sinking of the Titanic, but she had, almost in spite of herself.

She could never say for certain afterwards if she had deliberately walked out under that tram or if in a state of shock, she just didn't know what she was doing or where she was and didn't see it coming.

But after three days in an unconscious state, miraculously, she came round with not a bone broken and hardly a scratch on her apart from a gash to the head which needed a couple of stitches.

As soon as she was up and about she wrote to James Power to see if there was any news of Tom, and while she waited for a reply like a great many others she scoured newspaper reports for the names of the Titanic survivors, and its dead.

She refused to believed that Tom had drowned, even though a letter eventually came from James Power who said that his cousin George had waited in New York for over a week for news of survivors and whilst he did find someone who remembered a young man answering Tom`s description on the Carpathian, Tom`s name hadn't appeared anywhere on their survivor list and George could find no trace of him.

After months of trying to find word of his son James Power, finally gave up and accepted that his first born lay in a watery grave somewhere in the North Atlantic.

Margaret went on believing that she could hear Tom`s kind, gentle voice on the wind and that somewhere he was alive and would come for her.

But she was only sixteen years old and after almost two years of hearing nothing, she had to accept that her beloved Tom was gone from this earth, if not he would surely have found a way of letting her know that he was still alive.

She had to go on living, and like her sisters before her she had the caring vocation, quickly become an excellent nurse and when war broke out it seemed the only thing to do to offer her services and skill to those who would need it most and besides she felt it was time for her to get out from under the care of her sisters, good and all as they were, and make her own way in the world.

Margaret had always had a stoic, independent streak, traits her father Thomas McDonald had recognised in her from an early age and whilst she would miss Elizabeth, Bridget and the twins, desperately,, and most particularly her nephew Donald she knew it was time for her to move on and do something with her life and she could certainly do her bit for the war effort.

The Slaney blood that flowed through Margaret's veins brought memories and stories from the Hill, but first and foremost she was a nurse and her duty was to help those in need, so history and politics didn't really cause a struggle in Margaret's mind and besides there were lots of Irish and Wexford and even Enniscorthy lads enlisting and she would be happy to look after them all.

....

Elizabeth Mc Donald had no such decision to make, her first duty as a mother was to her son Donald so she would remain to look after him and all the other London children her sisters Sarah, Jane and Bridget had given refuge to at "Honeysuckle Cottage" in Somerset.

Elizabeth knew that Peter would be delighted to see so many happy children running through his Somerset residence protected from the destruction that would possibly befall their homes in the Capital, and Elizabeth was certain that it would be good for her young son to be surrounded by so many playmates. Coming from such a large family Elizabeth often worried that Donald was missing out on so much not having siblings to interact with, well now he had more than he could count, and he was loving it.

At eleven years old Donald Robin Hargraves, was not just a fine handsome boy he was kind, loving, sensible and intelligent, he was quick to learn and made friends easily, indeed Elizabeth often looked at him and thought that she didn't deserve him, he was a wonderful mix of his father Peter and his grandfather Thomas, like his father he carried himself well, aware of both his own ability and birth right, but with the modesty and honesty of his grandfather he treated all with respect and kindness finding no-one any better or worse than himself.

Elizabeth McDonald was very proud of her boy and nothing would make her leave him.

Sarah, Jane and Bridget were in their element, "the cottage" was full to the brim with children, who had to be fed, washed, clothed and educated. It was almost like being back home in Enniscorthy again, there were so many to a room and sometimes even to a bed, but the sisters had never been happier, even if there was a war on.

Chapter 29

Kate McDonald had first met Michael Collins at King's College where they were both attending evening classes in accountancy, taxation and economics, Michael, to further his career prospects in the British Civil Service, and Kate to increase her possibilities of promotion in one of London's newest and most luxurious hotels, The Ritz.

After completing her hospitality training at the Ecole Hoteliere de Lausanne, in Switzerland, Kate returned to the Windsor Castle Hotel where she spent a further two years before applying for a coveted position at the recently opened, Ritz. Everyone in London and beyond, it seemed, wanted to work there, so Kate was more than surprised when she was offered a position. The time had come for her to move on, although leaving the Windsor had been both emotive and difficult for her with all its memories of Harry, but Kate McDonald had found herself to be both ambitious and capable and constantly in need of a challenge.

Michael Collins, beginning as a Boy Clerk with the Post Office Savings Bank, was anxious to obtain a position with the new Custom and Excise Service where the prospects were good and the pay was excellent.

Both immediately recognised ability, intellect, and kindred spirit in the other.

`So you're the Wexford girl that lives near Vinegar Hill where the 1798 Rebellion was lost`, Michael said to her when they were introduced by another Irish student at the college and cousin of Collins, Sean Hurley.

`I am`, Kate replied, `and you're from the County of Cork, from where the North Cork Militia came to help the English Redcoats beat the Wexford Rebels in that same Rebellion.`

`Well as I always say, wouldn't we be a great little country now indeed if we could all sing off the same hymn sheet at the same time` Michael Collins said with a twinkling eye.

`Well sure the man that could make that happen would be better than God himself`, Kate McDonald quipped smiling.

Kate couldn't help but like the arrogant young Irishman with the handsome face and devilish smile and Michael was attracted to the lovely, clever, confident Enniscorthy woman who wasn't afraid to speak up for herself and her kind even on enemy soil.

`Are you interested at all in the game of hurling?` Michael asked Kate.

`Well I can`t say that I`ve seen a lot of it since I came over here` Kate replied.

`Well would you like to come along and see a bit of it on Sunday then?` he inquired.

`Sure that depends` Kate said. `Who`s playing?`

`I`ll be playing` Michael answered conceitedly.

`And who do you play for?` Kate asked.

`I play for, and I am Secretary of, the Geraldine Hurling Club`, Collins said haughtily.

`And who pray tell are the Geraldines playing on Sunday then?` Kate asked, her interest very much aroused.

`The Father Murphys`, Collins said boldly.

`Well then, I guess we know who I`ll be cheering for`, Kate responded grinning, `are you still sure you want to bring me?`

And so, began a friendship that would last both their lifetimes, one an awful lot shorter than the other.

....

Kate began going to hurling matches as often as she could get time away from her very busy schedule as Head Housekeeper at the Ritz, Michael who played at midfield or in defence for the Geraldines Club was bigger than most of his opponents and tough as nails, he was an effective, if not a polished player, and very few got past him. He was a good sportsman as long as the game was being played fairly but if he got a whiff at all that foul play was the order of the day, then he would fly into a temper and all hell would break lose.

Kate loved his passion and enthusiasm for the game and being well used to the rough and tumble of four brothers, his erratic outbursts and robust temperament seemed perfectly natural to her, unlike those who criticised him profusely for his loudness and dominance of a game.

Kate loved the bones of him and began attending meetings with him at the Sinn Fein Club on Chancery Lane where they both began taking Irish Classes.

Kate knew that she was an attractive and independent woman and could have her pick from a large array of suitors, but, there had been no-one since Harry Stafford and part of her would always belong to Harry, but that part was a young, innocent girl and her first love, Kate had become a woman, confident and mature and the laughing Michael Collins had somehow burrowed his way into her heart and would hold a place there forever, spoiling her for every other man she would come across.

Michael Collins was her yardstick and very few, if any, would ever measure up.

Half of all the Irish girls in London were in love with Michael Collins, and worst of all he knew it, and Kate McDonald being from proud Wexford stock was not prepared to stand in line for any man, even one like Collins, so she kept her secret to herself and they continued to enjoy the others company at Cumann na nGael socials and dances, hurling and football matches and Sinn Fein meetings, without obligation or commitment.

In her position at the Ritz, Kate had come to know a variety of influential people and through her, Michael was drawn into a completely different social circle and got to know a great many English people in a more relaxed and friendly atmosphere than he ever had before.

He liked going places with the tall, lithe, self-assured Wexford woman who knew how to talk to people of every standing, and always had something intellectual to contribute to the conversation, indeed Michael was very proud of the fact that Kate could converse in French and German, having learned both when she studied in Switzerland. She was clever and witty, well read, and confident in her opinions, they discussed books at great length and discovered a mutual interest in the theatre, which they attended regularly together, particularly when the works of George Bernard Shaw were playing.

Kate McDonald had done much to improve herself since arriving in London and she recognised that same desire for self-improvement in Michael. She encouraged him to keep what she called a "little black book" jotting down disparate facts and figures as he chanced upon them: `You never know when the information you gather will be useful` she told him.

Little did either of them know, just how significant that information and practice would prove to be in the struggle for their country`s independence.

Michael treated most women with a certain amount of indifference, he was charming towards them and enjoyed being in their company but didn't necessarily seek them out again, but Kate McDonald was different, she was a friend who knew and understood him, he was at ease with her just as he was with his sister Hannie.

Kate for her part was never sure if she, or anyone, would ever know the real Michael Collins, but she was captivated by his magnetism and carried along by his infectious enthusiasm and wry Irish humour.

With each passing day Michael`s involvement with the Irish Republican Brotherhood became stronger and more intense, having been inducted into the organisation by his work colleague and friend Sam Maguire, the IRB very quickly became an all- consuming passion for him and when he was appointed Treasurer of the London and South England District in 1914, Kate`s administrative and organisational skills became invaluable to him.

When war broke out Collins was already drilling once a week with his IRB Company at the German gymnasium at King`s Cross, using reconditioned Martini-Henry rifles which they paid for in weekly instalments. As the threat of conscription became more and more likely Michael knew that if he stayed in London he would be drafted into the British Army which to him would be a betrayal of Ireland. His brother Pat wrote to him from Chicago urging him to emigrate to America, even sending him the fare which he returned with the message: "If there`s going to be any trouble in Ireland I intend to be in the thick of it".

He did discuss Chicago with Kate, but she knew in her heart of hearts that he was only going one place, and that was home to Ireland, and the only question was would she follow him.

`What are you going to do with yourself now Girl if I go home` he asked one day.

`What do ya mean`, Kate inquired, `sure wasn't I in England long before I knew you and doing all right for myself too I might add, do you not think I`d be able to manage without you now or what?'

`Oh I have no doubt Wexford that you`d manage quite well without any man, me included` Collins laughed `but you have to admit London will be a much duller spot without me, and besides you don't want to be missing all the fun that's about to happen at home, now do ya.`

She didn't tell him then, but she had already made an application to the Shelbourne Hotel on St. Stephen's Green for a position with them and was awaiting their reply.

She harboured no great romantic illusions for a man who had taken to calling her Wexford instead of by her name, but she knew enough to know that things were changing in Ireland and she did want to be part of whatever it was that was about to erupt and besides, he was right, if conceited, it would be like blocking out the sun's light when he left London, life would be a lot more exciting, even in his shadow.

On 14th January 1916 Michael Collins terminated his employment, packed his bags, and caught the train to Holyhead.

Kate McDonald had already beaten him to it, taking up her position as under Housekeeper at the Shelbourne Hotel, St. Stephens Green on January 1st.

Chapter 30

John Devoy and Jeremiah O`Donovan Rossa were well impressed with the young Wexford man, Thomas McDonald from Enniscorthy, when he was introduced to them by prominent Savannah businessman, John Flannery, at the gala evening hosted by William Kehoe, to celebrate the renaming of Irish Green to Emmet Park in memory of the heroic United Irishman Robert Emmet.

William Kehoe had invited the two exiled Fenians to Savannah to speak at the event, which he planned as a fundraiser for the Irish cause.

Since their exile to America in 1871, Devoy and O`Donovan Rossa had been actively fundraising for Clan na nGael and the cause of Irish freedom. Both men were part of a group known as the Cuba Five, Irish nationalist prisoners released on condition of exile, who sailed to America on a ship called Cuba.

Both men operated chiefly out of New York but were delighted to get the invitation to speak to many of the well-heeled Irish in Savannah. William Kehoe, they knew was doing much for his fellow Wexford men, bringing many of them to Savannah to work at his Iron Foundry, and John Flannery was a man of both great influence and wealth willing to do whatever he could to further the Irish cause.

Both Flannery and Kehoe were happy to be part of the Clan na nGael fundraising effort and suggested the young Thomas McDonald, as the ideal envoy to shuttle money home to Ireland on a regular basis, to be put to good use.

He was affable, confident, clever and above all trustworthy and loyal to his Wexford rebel roots. He was the perfect choice, and with both men backing him O`Donovan Rossa and Devoy were satisfied to have him in charge of the Clan na nGael operations in the Southern States of Georgia, North & South Carolina and Alabama.

Thomas McDonald was both grateful and honoured for the trust placed in him by men he revered, and happy to be given the opportunity to play his part in the struggle for Irish freedom. Settling into his new role well, he helped raise many thousands of dollars for the Irish Republican Brotherhood, and in the course of his fundraising activities came to know both James Connolly and Tom Clarke and had met with Roger Casement and Joseph Mary Plunkett on their many rallying visits to the States.

Standing on deck, scanning the horizon for his first glimpse of the Irish coast, Thomas McDonald couldn't help wondering what his mother and father would think, having sent him to Savannah in the first instance, to keep him out of trouble and away from the Fenian Charlie Kearney and republicanism, and now, here he was in 1915, in the thick of it, heading to Ireland for the funeral of his friend and mentor Jeremiah O`Donovan Rossa, with a suitcase full of money to be used to purchase a supply of arms from the German Government for another Irish Rebellion.

....

At just fourteen years old, JohnJoe McDonald was wiry but strong, agile, nimble and dexterous, the youngest of the thirteen children of Thomas and Mary McDonald, who had gone to live with his father's brother Jack McDonald and his wife Mag at the Station House at Palace, Clonroche, just outside Enniscorthy.

Young JohnJoe was the apple of the childless couples eye, and being too young to remember much about either his mother or father or his siblings, many of whom had left Enniscorthy when he was but a babe, he lived a charmed childhood on the railway. With trains continually passing his front door, every day was exciting for the young boy, there was always something happening and always things to do.

When his eldest sister Maryanne returned to Enniscorthy from London she wanted JohnJoe to move back into the family home at Court Street with her, but she very quickly found out that JohnJoe loved his life. He was a happy, active child, constantly outdoors, he loved everything to do with trains and learned very quickly about them from his Uncle Jack, who adored the boy and was only too delighted to feed his passion for them.

Maryanne couldn't in conscience take him away from Mag and Jack and the life he loved, and settled instead, for a couple of days, every so often, when the boy would come to Enniscorthy and spend time with herself and Mary and William if he happened to be home at the time.

JohnJoe was a bright young man and could have been a very good student but all he wanted to do was drive trains, until, on one of his trips to Enniscorthy, some of the lads on John Street told him that they had joined Na Fianna, an organisation set up to teach the young men of Ireland how to be ready and prepared, if and when their country would call on them.

JohnJoe McDonald joined the Enniscorthy Company under Captain John Moran, and immediately acquired the nickname "Railway Joe".

He began to spend more time with his sisters at Court Street, cycling in to Enniscorthy to drill with his Company two nights a week and on Sundays after Mass. There were about thirty boys in the Company who drilled on the Beare Meadow, opposite the Promenade. As well as drilling and military type pursuits the boys were taught first aid, signalling and map reading. Discipline was always high on the agenda as well as field trips taken to improve their knowledge of the surrounding countryside.

There was keen interest in the young McDonald boy because of his involvement with the railway, and he rapidly became a favourite with those in charge, who admired both his knowledge of trains and communications and his commitment to the Company and the cause.

Indeed JohnJoe had been weaned on the stories of Vinegar Hill and 1798, Aunt Mag being an avid republican, who's favourite phrase was `Burn everything English except its coal`, and he revelled in his membership of Na Fianna and later the Irish Volunteers who established a headquarters at the Hollow, Enniscorthy in a building that became known to all as "Antwerp".

On 23rd November 1915, Maryanne, Mary and JohnJoe McDonald attended a lecture at the Athenaeum in Enniscorthy, delivered by Sean Mac Diarmada on the anniversary of the Manchester Martyrs. JohnJoe was part of the Guard of Honour on stage with Mac Diarmada whilst Maryanne and Mary proudly sat among the large audience in their Cumann na mBan uniforms.

`Isn`t it a quare thing all the same`, Maryanne said when the three of them were together later that evening at Court Street, `here we are ready to take up arms and fight against the British for an independent Ireland, and we have one brother, maybe two, because we don't know where Michael is, and one sister fighting for the British in France and five sisters happily living in England and four of them doing their bit for the war refugees and we are all Irish and proud of it, and all from the same Enniscorthy home, how do you figure that all out I ask ya.`

`Well when you spell it all out like that Maryanne it is surely quare indeed`, JohnJoe said puzzled, `maybe some of us are more Irish than the others.`

`No that can`t be right`, Mary added, `what makes me more Irish than Elizabeth, or Sarah or Jane or Kate or Bridget or Margaret or even Agnes in Africa, or you more Irish than William or Michael or Thomas in Savannah, no JohnJoe that can`t be the answer.`

`Perhaps` Maryanne said `it`s a bit like God and religion, we all believe there`s a God, Catholics, Protestants, Presbyterians, Jews, Muslims and we all want to get to him in the end, but our different religions are the different pathways we take to get to that end, well maybe an Irish Republic is a bit like that, we all want it, but we are each favouring different ways of getting it.`

`Well I don't know if that's the case or not Maryanne` JohnJoe replied `but I do know that we are not the only house in Enniscorthy like that, a

253

great many of my fellow Volunteers have either brothers or fathers or both, fighting in Flanders, it's a bit of a conundrum all right isn't it now.`

....

Acquiring arms was a constant challenge for the Enniscorthy Volunteers who drilled with hurls, walking sticks and pikes, so a Munitions Squad was formed and a small factory set up at Pat Keegans, No. 10 Irish Street, and JohnJoe McDonald was immediately conscripted in, because his close association with the railway enabled him to give Keegan information about the arrival of consignments of powder, fuses, cartridges and other useful materials, along with alerting him to the best times to raid.

A munitions dump was hewn out of the natural rock at the back of No. 10, by the Volunteers and the young boys of Na Fianna, who spent months cutting into the stone, and JohnJoe was instructed to raid the railway huts at stations from Dublin to Rosslare for picks, shovels, axes, crowbars, anything that could be used to cut into, or break up rock. After midnight each night the women of Cumann na mBan including Maryanne and Mary would dispose of the rock, painstakingly and strenuously, piece by laborious piece.

The men and women of Enniscorthy worked continuously to stock the armoury at Irish Street, but guns were in very short supply, so in true Enniscorthy tradition three blacksmiths were commissioned, Jim Clery, Jim Keating and Davy Grace to make pikes once again in the shadow of Vinegar Hill for a people who were preparing yet again to take on the might of the British Empire.

JohnJoe McDonald was filled with a tremendous sense of pride when he was told that he was to be one of, approximately forty, Wexford Volunteers chosen to travel to Dublin to attend the funeral of the renowned Fenian, Jeremiah O`Donovan Rossa on 1st August 1915.

It was going to be a massive occasion and Maryanne and Mary had made up their minds to travel to Dublin to view it as spectators.

Marching behind the coffin all the way to Glasnevin Cemetery, for the very first time JohnJoe felt that he was really part of something big: something momentous was about to happen in Ireland that would change him and the country forever.

`Wouldn't it make the hairs on the back of your neck stand to attention` his friend Jimmy Courtney whispered to him as they marched behind the cortege, part of contingents of green-clad Volunteer companies from all over the country, pacing slowly and solemnly with rifles reversed, through the streets of Dublin, where thousands of spectators lined the route with many windows draped in black and American and Irish flags flying from buildings.

`It would surely` JohnJoe said in awe. `I've never in me life seen anything like it.`

Special trains had brought thousands of people from all parts of Ireland along with others who had travelled from parts of England and America to witness the burial of the great Fenian, who had died in New York.

It took almost four hours for the funeral procession to reach its destination where the burial prayers were recited in Irish by Fr. O`Flanagan from Sligo. Listening to Padraic Pearse give the graveside oration, JohnJoe McDonald knew, with quiet certainty, that he would never forget the spectacle or the mesmerising and inspirational words of the great orator, these would be branded on his heart and mind forever.

A volley of shots from a Volunteer firing party heralded the end of the old Fenian as the Last Post sounded and people began to disperse.

As the Enniscorthy A Company were about to take their leave, a man who had been conversing at the graveside with Thomas McDonagh and Joseph Plunkett began making his way towards them.

`So you lads are all from Enniscorthy then are ya` he said addressing them `ya wouldn't happen to know any McDonalds down there now would ya.`

`And what McDonalds would they be?` JohnJoe asked before anyone else could answer.

`Well there's a large family of them in it`, the stranger replied, `but William McDonald would be the oldest son and a little fellow called JohnJoe would be the youngest with a lot of sisters in between.`

`Well I'm JohnJoe McDonald from Court Street, Enniscorthy if that's the family you're looking for, and who exactly might you be?` JohnJoe asked tentatively.

`Well that being the case, it seems I'm your brother Thomas - over from Savannah. I don't know who I was expecting to see here today but it certainly wasn't the baby of the McDonald household: do you remember me at all?` Thomas asked.

`I'm afraid not`, JohnJoe said laughing, `I think I was barely two years old when you left. You have two sisters here today too, Maryanne and Mary, but it would be impossible to find them in this crowd.`

`I wouldn't have the time anyway` Thomas said `this was just a flying visit. I knew him you know, and I owed it to him to be here, I did a lot of fundraising with him and Devoy on the other side of the pond, and besides it gave me a chance to view the situation up close and personal and ascertain exactly what's needed. I'm heading back to New York tonight to begin another fundraising campaign to purchase a consignment of German arms but I don't have to tell you to keep that under your hat.`

Before they parted the brothers hugged each other, a little awkwardly at first, but then the years and the distance between them fell away as the blood of the McDonalds passed one to the other in a warm embrace.

`I'll be back here when the call comes` Thomas told JohnJoe who replied with pride: `And I'll be answering the same call in Enniscorthy.`

Neither brother would have to wait long for that call to come.

On 26th September JohnJoe was honoured, once again, to be chosen as part of a contingent of twenty-five Volunteers to meet Padraic Pearse at Enniscorthy Railway Station and escort him to the Barley field under Vinegar Hill to inspect and address a large gathering of Volunteers from Gorey, Enniscorthy, Wexford and New Ross.

`Oh isn't he very handsome all together Maryanne` Mary McDonald said as she stood on her tip toes to get a better view `ah you'd know he was a poet, all the same, he has that sensitive, romantic look about him and such a fine speaker too, sure wouldn't ya follow him anywhere.`

`Would ya now Mary McDonald` her older sister replied with amusement `well I've no doubt we won't have to wait too long to see just how many will follow him where he's going.`

A month later, in November, Maryanne McDonald was asked by one of the Enniscorthy leaders Seamus Doyle if she would be able to provide accommodation for a man they called John O'Reilly, who was coming down from Leitrim to take up a position at Bolger's Drapery Shop on Georges Street, Enniscorthy, and it didn't take her long to decide that there was more to Mr. O'Reilly than met the eye.

Maryanne found out a couple of weeks later that Mr. O'Reilly was in fact, Peter Paul Galligan, who had been sent to Enniscorthy by Thomas MacDonagh to take charge of advance training of the Enniscorthy Battalion, following the resignation of Company Commandant Brennan Whitmore.

`What happened between Brennan Whitmore and the Volunteers to cause him to take such drastic action as to resign?` Maryanne asked of JohnJoe, feeling that he knew a lot more than he pretended to.

`Sure didn't they fall out over something stupid altogether` JohnJoe replied. `Whitmore didn't want the lads attending dances, instead he wanted them to spend their money on the purchase of arms and equipment. Now I know, we are going to need as many guns and as much ammunition as we can lay our hands on when the Rising starts, but Whitmore should have known that most of the lads are only young fellows like myself and nothing is going to stop them having an ould knees up every now and then at a dance, and sure what harm is there in it. Some of us may well die in the fighting and never get another chance to have our arms around a girl, Whitmore should have thought of that now, shouldn't he.`

`He should have`, Maryanne agreed, `but Galligan seems like a good enough man too, how is he getting on with the lads.`

`Oh sure they`re getting on grand with him`, JohnJoe replied, `he`s a great man for the training and the field exercises, and sure he`s a fresh voice, someone they haven't heard before, and didn't they all pass with flying colours when Captain O`Connell came down from Headquarters to examine them, so the proof is in the pudding now isn't it.`

In March 1916 JohnJoe was again part of a Guard of Honour at Enniscorthy Station waiting to escort Padraic Pearse to the Athenaeum where he was due to deliver a lecture on Robert Emmet.

Maryanne and Mary who were in the Athenaeum audience swelled with pride when Pearse spoke of the Enniscorthy man, Thomas McDonald, who had been part of the Committee responsible for the renaming of Emmet Park in Savannah, Georgia in honour of the United Irish hero, and JohnJoe was surprised to hear a loud whisper in his ear shot .

`The only one of them McDonalds that was ever any good` Eddie O`Brien said audibly to Spider Dwyer `what about the brother and sister fighting for the Brits in France and the other brother making his livelihood playing football in England and all them other McDonald girls living over there, what about them now, when will they get their comeuppance.`

`But Eddie, sure, haven't you and me and half of Enniscorthy got brothers and sisters living in England and fighting in the war as well`, Spider said perplexed.

`That`s not the point Spider, Eddie snarled, `yours and mine are not doing as well as them buckoos now are they? Yours and mine are there because they have to be: them McDonalds are there because they want to be better than everyone else.`

Chapter 31

Thomas McDonald arrived back in Dublin just before the Rising, carrying with him a coded message from Clan na nGael, New York to be handed to Tom Clarke and Sean Mac Diarmaida.

After discussing the contents of the message Tom Clarke wanted Thomas to return to America before the Rising began, considering him too valuable an asset to be lost, but Thomas refused point blank, he hadn't travelled over 3,000 miles and come this close to the eve of rebellion to miss it.

No, Thomas McDonald was staying in Ireland and seeing it through now whatever the outcome would be.

Clarke relented and assigned him to the Royal College of Surgeons, in the Stephens Green area under the command of Michael Mallin and Countess Markievicz.

....

Michael Collins had introduced Kate McDonald to Countess Markievicz knowing that with her organisational skills and her position at the Shelbourne Hotel she would prove herself invaluable once the Rising began.

Kate was based at the College of Surgeons on Stephens Green from where she ferried messages back and forth to the other outposts, traveling by bicycle, initially passing herself off as a civilian just out for a cycle over the Easter holiday, but as the fighting intensified Kate was forced to weave in and out through the streets to avoid being hit by sniper fire from the roof of the Shelbourne Hotel that had been occupied by British troops.

By the third day of fighting, the College of Surgeons was under heavy attack both from machine gun and sniper fire, with bullets cracking through windows, forcing the rebels to take cover behind the thick stone walls of the building.

Kate, surprised not just herself, but those around her at how quickly she took to firing a rifle at another human being. William had taught her to shoot years before and she often went hunting with him in the fields and hills around Enniscorthy, now as she looked out across the tops of the trees and lined up British soldiers in her sights and squeezed the trigger, more than once, she saw the man she aimed at crumple to the ground.

The sniper fire coming from the roof of the Shelbourne was causing major problems for the rebels and Malin and Markievicz knew that something was going to have to be done about it.

Kate McDonald was chosen for the attack party because of her knowledge of the Shelbourne Hotel and her expertise with a rifle.

`I'd like to be part of the action if I may`, the man from America, sent over by Tom Clarke said, stepping out of the shadows.

`What's the name?` Commandant Mallin asked.

`Thomas McDonald from Enniscorthy Sir`, Thomas announced proudly.

Kate's breath caught in her throat and she was barely able to croak incredulously `Is that you Thomas!`

`It is, do you know me?` Thomas asked of the brave, attractive woman he had been admiring for the past couple of days.

`If you are Thomas McDonald from Enniscorthy who went to Savannah over fifteen years ago, then I am your sister Kate`, Kate replied shakily.

`Oh my God!` Thomas said advancing towards her . `I`ve been admiring your courage and your marksmanship since I arrived, I can`t believe that your my little sister. It seems members of the McDonald family are popping up everywhere.`

Brother and sister drew each other close in an emotive embrace, watched by teary eyed rebels most of them thinking that they might never see their own brothers and sisters again.

Michael Mallin was confident that Kate knew her way around the Shelbourne and would be the one person that could get to the roof as quickly as possible and his confidence was borne out as he watched the little unit reach the building unperturbed, in just a few minutes run.

Kate was to the fore and Mallin had to agree with her brother, she was indeed a brave and spirited woman, leading them to a small wooden door, concealed in the shrubbery and bolted from the outside which led to the basement and was just big enough from them to crawl through. Once inside Kate knew that she would be able to get them all the way to the roof undetected, giving them the element of surprise.

Just as they were making their way to the hatch the young seventeen year old, Fred Ryan who had courageously volunteered for the mission, tripped over a stone, causing his rifle to fire, alerting nearby British soldiers to their presence.

Soon the little attack party was under a hail of fire, Kate gasped as she saw Fred Ryan fall to the ground, seconds before she was shot herself.

Thomas McDonald rushed to his sister`s side, picking her up quickly and running and dodging continuous fire until he got her to the safety of the College of Surgeons.

Kate refused to be taken to hospital and insisted on being treated in the College by the doctor on duty.

Kate had been hit three times and for three days lay in a cot in the College surviving on water alone. Thomas spent as much time as he could with her.

`You're one brave woman Kate McDonald` he told her `and I am a proud man to call you sister.`

`It must have something to do with the ould Enniscorthy blood I dare say` Kate replied smiling.

`Well sure as me mother often pointed out how could we be anything other than rebels you and me, born and bred in the shadow of Vinegar Hill `Thomas said laughing `we were doomed from the very beginning.`

`Do you know what's happening around the city at all` Kate inquired anxiously.

`Mallin and Markievicz are finding it difficult to get any hard information ` Thomas answered `we seem to be fairly isolated here. But Tom Clarke did manage to get a message through for me, and he wants me to try to get out of here before it's all over and make my way back to America, he seems to think that Ireland is going to need all the friends she can muster in the aftermath of all this.`

`What are you going to do?` Kate asked.

`I don't want to leave you Kate, not like this`, Thomas said, `and I don't want to walk out on my comrades here not knowing what will happen to them.`

`Thomas McDonald`, Kate said propping herself up, with difficulty, on one elbow, `we know the Brits are bad, but they're not bad enough to shoot an already injured woman and they're hardly going to kill every one of us, have you no faith in us at all. If Tom Clarke says we're going to need friends, then we're going to need them, and you bloody well better find them for us, do ya hear me.`

`I was guessing you would say something like that` Thomas said `I will leave under cover of darkness tonight I am an American citizen that should be some help.`

`Tell me before you go Thomas`, Kate said hesitantly, `is there any word of Michael Collins and the lads in the Post Office.`

`The city centre is being bombarded day and night Kate, we`ve heard nothing but I doubt they can hold out much longer` Thomas said with sadness.

`Then go Thomas, as quick as you can and may God go with you my brother, I will always be grateful to him for giving me the chance of seeing you again` Kate said her resolve and her lip beginning to quiver.

`We will meet again sister I promise you` Thomas said as he leaned across her cot and kissed her goodbye.

Chapter 32

Activities in Enniscorthy were normal leading up to Holy Week, except for the fact that the Enniscorthy Battalion had intensified training.

It was rumoured that the Rising was to begin on Easter Sunday, but on Good Friday, Captain O`Connell arrived in town and met with Seamus Doyle, Seamus Rafter and Peter Paul Galligan telling them that he was taking no part whatsoever in the forthcoming Rising, and that it was their own responsibility what they wanted to do in Enniscorthy.

On Easter Saturday there was an air of despondency and indecision among the leaders, as well as the men, due to lack of instruction, so Peter Paul Galligan took it on himself to head for Dublin to find out exactly what the position was.

Arriving in the city on Easter Sunday morning, Galligan was told that the Rising was postponed for the present. After reading Eoin Mac Neill`s countermanding order in the Sunday Independent, Galligan headed out to Dalkey on Easter Monday, only to find out later that evening, that the Rising had indeed begun. Returning immediately to the Capital, he met with James Connolly, Padraig Pearse and Joseph Mary Plunkett at Volunteer Headquarters at the G.P.O.

Connolly told Galligan that they had enough men in Dublin and he would be better employed, returning to Wexford as quickly as possible and mobilising the Enniscorthy Battalion to take and hold the railway line, to prevent British troops coming through from Wexford, where he strongly suspected they would be landed.

Galligan was supplied with a bicycle and told to take the back roads through Wicklow to avoid being picked up.

....

Maryanne McDonald was locking the front door on Wednesday evening when she heard knocking around the back of the house at Court Street. It was her lodger Mr.O`Reilly banging on the back door.

`What are ya doing coming round to the back like that Mr. O`Reilly, sure ya frightened the heart out of me` Maryanne said, when she realised who it was.

`I can`t be seen in town yet Miss McDonald` Galligan said secretively. `I need you to bring Bob Brennan, Seamus Rafter and Seamus Doyle here to meet me, tell them I have instructions from James Connolly. Oh, and Miss McDonald, I think it`s about time you started to call me by my real name which I`m sure you know by now`.

`I won`t be long then Mr. Galligan, make yourself a cup of tea now why don't ya while you`re waiting, and by the way its Maryanne not Miss McDonald` Maryanne said grabbing her coat off the coat stand in the hall and heading out into the Enniscorthy darkness.

On receiving Connolly`s instructions from Galligan, Brennan, Doyle and Rafter decided that Enniscorthy would rise immediately and Maryanne, Mary and JohnJoe who was staying at Court Street in preparation for rebellion, were dispatched around the town tapping on doors and windows and mobilising about one hundred Volunteers through the night.

No. 10 Irish Street was the rendezvous point and scores of Enniscorthy`s young men and women leaped from their beds, quickly making their way there to be supplied with guns, ammunition, and pikes.

In the early hours of Thursday morning 27th April 1916, in uniforms, encompassing all forty shades of green, they marched four abreast through the streets of Enniscorthy to the Athenaeum at the heart of the town, taking it and declaring it as the headquarters of the Irish Republic.

Mary and Maryanne watched, hearts swelling with pride as the Tricolour was hoisted over the Athenaeum roundel by members of Cumann na mBan, Marion Stokes, Una Brennan and Eileen Hegarty, as Vice Commandant Galligan gave the order: `In the name of God, salute the flag of the Irish Republic.`

Tears trickled from the corners of Maryanne's eyes as six Volunteers let off three volleys in salutation, and she whispered to Mary: `They're the first shots fired against the old enemy in Enniscorthy since the Battle of Vinegar Hill in 1798, isn't it thrilling Mary, we are part of history.`

`We are Maryanne and isn't it great to be here among all these brave men and women`, Mary said as she looked around at the faces of freedom proudly saluting their flag.

Seamus Doyle read a proclamation, announcing the Irish Republic to the people of Enniscorthy, and calling on them to support and defend it. JohnJoe was sent to pin it to the Market House door at Market Square and Maryanne and Mary assisted members of Cumann na mBan who were busy turning the top floor of the Athenaeum into a temporary hospital.

Securing the town and all access routes was the number one priority of the new Republic. Enniscorthy railway station was of strategic importance and JohnJoe was dispatched with a unit under section commander Denis O`Brien, to take control of the station and lift the track to prevent troops coming through Enniscorthy from Wexford.

Before the track could be lifted, JohnJoe was chosen to intercept the Kynoch munitions train on its daily run between Wexford and Arklow. JohnJoe knew the driver, a Jim Doyle, from Cloughbawn and called out to him to halt.

`What's going on here at all JohnJoe`, Jim Doyle inquired when he had stopped the train.

`The Volunteers have taken Enniscorthy for the Irish Republic Mr. Doyle`, JohnJoe explained politely, `and we are taking control of the station here, stopping all trains and cutting off all communication.`

`Is that right JohnJoe`, Jim Doyle said, `sure we`ve no problem at all with that now do we lads?` he asked Paddy Murphy the train guard and Jimmy Kelly the fire stoker.

`Oh you`ll be getting no trouble from us at all JohnJoe`, Paddy Murphy confirmed, `Up the Republic`.

`But what are we going to do now` Jimmy Kelly asked a bit perplexed.

`Well we could take you prisoner and hold yez for the duration of the Rising or yez could of course head up there to Irish Street or the Athenaeum and join up with us` JohnJoe replied.

`That`s what we`ll do now for sure` Jim Doyle said as the three of them downed tools and disembarked.

`Three prisoners, is it?` Denis O`Brien called out to JohnJoe from the platform.

`Not at all Commandant O`Brien`, JohnJoe roared back, `three new recruits for the Irish Republic!`

The Volunteers dismantled the signal box at the station and Johnny Sinnott and JohnJoe were sent across the railway bridge to cut communications at the mouth of the tunnel while others were sent to cut the wires in gentlemens` houses along the railway line.

All public houses in town were locked and the keys collected, sentries were placed on outposts, and roads were blocked by trees, to the North as far as Ferns and to the South as far as Wexford, bedding, food and clothing were commandeered from all the local shops.

It was all done in a most orderly fashion with receipts given in all cases for articles commandeered.

The local RIC were put off duty and confined to their barracks, with strict orders from Rafter that they were not to be shot at, unless in defence, and no ammunition was to be squandered taking the building. `Remember`, he told the Volunteers, `it`s against the British we are, not the Irish.`

The Volunteers formed their own police force and began patrolling the town and as townspeople emerged from early Mass they could hardly believe their eyes, men from their own community, that they knew and met almost every day , of the week were now standing guard in uniform on every corner of every street armed rifles and revolvers.

All was busy at the Athenaeum with a constant stream of recruits coming from all over the county to enlist. Mary and Maryanne spent their time splitting calico, rolling bandages, decanting iodine into little bottles and making stretchers.

....

As the sun set on the first day of the Irish Republic, Enniscorthy leaders Brennan, Rafter, Galligan, De Lacy, Etchingham and Doyle were happy that the Volunteers had everything in hand, they had control of the town and the railway station, they had blocked access routes, sentries had been placed on all approach roads, all public houses were closed, they were satisfied that they could feed their troops and the civilian population, a curfew had been imposed from 6pm to 9am and there had been no looting.

All in all, a most successful takeover and without casualties.

As JohnJoe McDonald bedded down with his comrades for a few hours` sleep an aura of calm accomplishment and pride seemed to settle like a halo over the Athenaeum.

`Didn't we manage everything great today all the same lads` Tommy Foley said before they nodded off, exhausted.

`God we did for sure` Johnny Sinnott replied `and do ya know there's a great feeling of friendliness around the town for us, and so many coming in from all parts, Davidstown, Oylegate, Ferns, Monageer, Ballindaggin and Oulart to join up with us.`

`Do yez know what I'm going to tell ya ` Paddy O'Leary said proudly `isn't it a quare good feeling to be free all the same, I never knew it would feel as good as this.`

`Let's just hope it continues to feel this good is all I can say`, JohnJoe agreed.

....

Sentry duty and patrols continued throughout the town the following day, Friday 27th April, with shifts changing and Volunteers going from duty to rest, felling trees, blocking roads, and digging trenches becoming their full-time occupation.

Mary and Maryanne were on duty all hours of the day and night, and with the rest of the Cumann na mBan women they kept the Volunteers fed, tended to their laundry, and looked after the few small injuries that presented themselves.

By Friday evening many of the Volunteers were exhausted and growing uneasy as they waited for the British barrage that they knew would come.

`It's a bit like the calm before the storm` Seamus Rafter said to Bob Brennan `and it's having an unsettling effect on the lads.`

`Well I have the perfect solution` Bob Brennan said and organised a full dress parade around the town for the Volunteers not on duty, to boost morale and encourage recruitment. It was a tremendous exercise, demonstrating camaraderie and defiance and lifting the morale of participant and spectator alike.

....

At approximately 3.30pm on Saturday afternoon 29th April after five days of continuous fighting, with the G.P.O in ruins and Dublin city smouldering, realising that it was impossible for the rebels to hold off the might of the Crown Forces any longer, Padraig Pearse accompanied by Nurse Elizabeth O'Farrell, surrendered unconditionally to Brigadier General Lowe.

Enniscorthy receiving no notice of surrender continued to fortify the town in preparation for an attack.

....

`JohnJoe` Maryanne called, stopping him on the stairs of the Athenaeum on Saturday evening as he headed off to take up his sentry duty at the railway station `I heard them talking earlier JohnJoe, Rafter and Brennan, and they were talking about a surrender, have you heard anything about that.`

`I have not` JohnJoe said emphatically `and I'll tell you Maryanne none of the lads are thinking at all about surrender everyone is getting ready for a fight. What did you hear?`

`Well I'm not sure exactly` Maryanne said hesitantly `but they mentioned something about a Peace Committee from town going to meet Colonel French in Wexford to discuss terms of surrender.`

`A Peace Committee, who the bloody hell are they` JohnJoe spluttered angrily `I never heard of any Peace Committee.`
`Local businessmen and the like, and I think some members of the clergy` Maryanne replied `but I'm not sure now, so don't say anything about it to anyone in case I'm not right.`.

`I won't but you keep your ears peeled` JohnJoe instructed ` there's no stomach for surrender among the lads who'll be doing the fighting, so it galls me to think that anyone else would make that decision without even asking us.`

....

A town delegation, Fr. Fitzhenry, Pat O'Neill and Harry Buttle travelled to Wexford to ask Colonel French what the terms of surrender would be so that they could inform the Enniscorthy leaders.

Colonel French told them that the Rising in Dublin was over and that Pearse and the other leaders had surrendered. ` Dublin city is in flames the Post Office and Liberty Hall have been bombed and almost completely destroyed. I have a very large force here in Wexford, I have a big gun ready and in position on Bree Hill and if the town is not surrendered, I shall issue notice to civilians to evacuate and I shall bombard the town.`

....

`Maryanne`, JohnJoe whispered coming off duty in the early hours of Sunday morning 30th April, `have you heard anything since, there's terrible rumours around the town and among the lads, that French is ready to march on Enniscorthy with an army of two thousand men.`

`Oh JohnJoe, we haven't had a wink of sleep since I was talking to ya last` Maryanne replied `there's been ferocious comings and goings here all through the night. That Peace Committee met with Colonel French and he told them that he would bombard the town with a big gun on Bree Hill and there wouldn't be a smidgen of Enniscorthy left standing if we don't surrender.`

`Oh they will Maryanne and don't we only know it`, JohnJoe said bitterly, `they'll bomb the shit out of us if they get half a chance. Nothing ever changes in our favour here in Enniscorthy, does it Maryanne, it's still the same as it was on Vinegar Hill, a hundred years later: the Brits still have the troops and equipment to beat us and there's feck all we can do about it.`

'And that's not the worst of it, JohnJoe`, Maryanne said sadly, knowing how much it meant to her brother `the Rising is over in Dublin. The city is in ruins and the leaders have surrendered.`

....

The Enniscorthy leaders refused to believe the Peace Committee that Dublin had surrendered, and Sean Etchingham and Seamus Doyle headed to Wexford for a meeting with Colonel French.

French assured them that the surrender in Dublin was real but offered to give safe passage to them to see Pearse and take the surrender from him personally. Colonel French provided them with a military car to conduct them to Arbour Hill.

Pearse was broken hearted to have to tell Enniscorthy to surrender.

`It is hard for me to tell men of Wexford blood living in the shadow of Vinegar Hill to lay down their arms, for I know it is not in your nature to give up the fight. We fought hard here in Dublin for five days and five nights and lost some of our greatest warriors including your own brave Enniscorthy man Captain Tom Wafer. But our stand for Irish freedom has been glorious, and sufficient I feel, to gain recognition for our cause around the world.`

As Pearse was handing the written surrender to Seamus Doyle to be taken back to Enniscorthy, he leaned over out of earshot and whispered in his ear, `Tell the Enniscorthy boys to hide their arms like they hid the pikes, they`ll be needed later.`

....

When Doyle and Etchingham returned to Enniscorthy a Council of War was convened at the Athenaeum.

Seamus Doyle spelled it out to the three hundred strong Volunteers – French had two thousand troops assembled at Wexford ready to attack Enniscorthy, and he had made it quite clear that he had the artillery on standby on Bree Hill and he would shell Enniscorthy relentlessly and put the town in ruins before marching into it.

If the town surrendered at 2pm the following day, Monday 1st May, only the leaders would be arrested, that was the understanding from the Peace Committee negotiations with Colonel French.

Rafter, Doyle, Brennan, Etchingham and Richard King addressed the men telling them that they would be surrendering themselves to the British military and the rank and file Volunteers would all go free.

Fr. Pat Murphy, in tears, told them to hold on to their guns and keep their powder dry for another day.

The talk of surrender was received with mixed feeling among the Volunteers.

`I think we should take to the hills` Lar O`Toole said `we could form a flying column and be a thorn in Colonel French`s side.`

`We could`, Jack Whelan replied, `but that won`t stop French bombing the shit out of the town now will it, who`s going to thank us for that when it`s all said and done.`

`I think we should stand and fight like our people before us` Jimmy Nolan offered ` we were never gibbers here in Enniscorthy and I don't think we should start now.`

A chorus of "Hear, Hear" went up all around the hall before Seamus Doyle calmed everyone down saying: `If we surrender, the town will be spared and only the leaders will be arrested, we can use the time we have now to hide all the guns and weaponry we have acquired, and then the rest of ye can scatter, because who knows how soon the next call to arms will come. Listen and heed what Pearse himself told us: `"Hide the guns, they`ll be needed later".`

All arms were then called in and laid on the floor of the Athenaeum and the work of disposing of them continued through the night, with Fr.

Murphy raising the spirits telling the men: `We carry on in the tradition of our illustrious forefathers`, he said, `and the day will come soon again when we will shoulder these very same arms against the invader, never you fear, me boys, ya`ll get your chance yet to fight for Irish freedom.`

Mary and Maryanne watched through tears of sadness, and remorse for what might have been, as the Tricolour, that had been saluted with pride and dignity and flown gloriously defiant over the Athenaeum for the four days of the Irish Republic was taken down and given to Fr. Murphy for safe keeping.

`The dream of freedom is over for now Mary` Maryanne said despondently, as she put her arm around her sister.

`For now Maryanne` the younger girl said defiantly `only for now.`

Chapter 33

JohnJoe Mc Donald and Paddy Kehoe were on the banks of the Slaney early on Monday morning, having spent the best part of the night concealing weapons in sacks and hiding them along the riverbank.

`Well I suppose that's it then`, JohnJoe said with a sigh, `it's really all over now, the rest is only a formality.`

`What will you do` Paddy asked `will you stay around to see the leaders arrested or would that be too much to bear?`

`I hardly had time to think of it with all the running around we've done through the night`, JohnJoe replied, `my sister Maryanne wants me to get out of town altogether, she wanted me away before the Brits arrived, she doesn't trust them you know, she says she saw them in action in Africa in the Boer War and wouldn't trust them as far as she could throw them, but I'd feel kind of disloyal not to be around when they take the lads away I feel I owe them more than that, the least we can do is bear witness to their arrests.`

`Well I'm inclined to agree with your sister` Paddy Kehoe said `I think the leaders would rather see us gone and safely out of the Brits way in case they do change their mind, where would you go, some of the lads are going up Vinegar Hill.`

`Maryanne wants me to head up to a brother of my mothers in Avoca and lay low there until we know the way things are going. She has a bicycle ready for me and a change of clothes and food packed on it.`

`Hush, what's that noise` Paddy said suddenly.

`Jesus, Mary and Joseph` JohnJoe exclaimed, crossing himself as a mounted Regiment rode up along the Wexford road followed by what seemed to be an endless stream of marching soldiers.

`Your sister wouldn't have two bicycles by any chance would she` Paddy Kehoe shouted as the two Volunteers leaped from the riverbank and began to run towards Market Square.

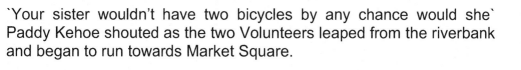

Two thousand soldiers with heavy artillery marched into Enniscorthy on the morning of Monday 1st May 1916, led by a party of the South Irish Horse Regiment just as the last load of Volunteer arms and ammunition was leaving town.

Six Enniscorthy leaders, in full uniform, Rafter, Doyle, De Lacy, Etchingham, Brennan and King surrendered the town to Colonel French at the Athenaeum, watched by a large crowd.

Colonel French accepted the surrender and handed the prisoners over immediately to the Wexford RIC, and not the military as expected.

The leaders believed their surrender and arrests to be on the condition that the rank and file Volunteers went free, but now Colonel French introduced a proviso, the Volunteers were given a choice, if all arms were handed up no one would be arrested.

All weapons were not handed up, they were already in hiding awaiting the next call to arms, so British soldiers began raiding homes and arresting Volunteers.

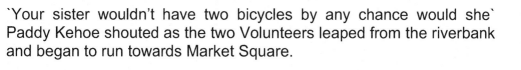

`Quick, quick JohnJoe` Maryanne said hurriedly `get out of those clothes and give them to Mary to hide, the bicycle is ready, be on your way now as speedily as you can.`

`But what about you and Mary` the young man asked uncertain. `What about us`, Maryanne replied, `they're hardly going to start arresting women now are they.`

`They might Maryanne` JohnJoe answered `there's no telling what they might do, sure haven't they gone back on their word already arresting the Volunteers.`

`Well that was hardly a surprise now was it` Mary said coming from the kitchen with more food for JohnJoe's already bulging parcel `when was their word ever worth anything here in Enniscorthy`.

`Don't worry about us JohnJoe, we'll be alright`, Maryanne said comfortingly to her baby brother.

`On yer bike now and out of here before they come banging on the door. When you get to Uncle James tell him to let us know some way or other that you are safe, but no letters now mind, they'll surely have control of the Post Office here in town for the foreseeable future.`

`Jesus protect us`, Mary spluttered as one of the back windows was tapped, `it can hardly be them already`.

`Its only me JohnJoe`, Paddy Kehoe said anxiously ,` let me in quick, the bastards are all over the bloody town.`

`What is it Paddy?`, JohnJoe asked as Paddy slipped quickly through the back door.

`I'm coming with ya JohnJoe`, Paddy said agitated `that is, if you have another bike Maryanne I'd be more than grateful for it and you'll be in my prayers til the day I die, which won't be too far away I'm afraid if we don't get out of Enniscorthy soon. There's a bit of a commotion going on up on the Hill which might keep them occupied for a little while giving us a chance to get away.`

Maryanne ran into the back yard and came back with another bicycle.

`It belongs to Peter Paul Galligan` she said, `but sure God only knows where he is now, we might never see him again, so take it Paddy and

278

may God and his Blessed Mother go with the two of you to guide and protect you.`

`Have either of you got a gun?` Mary asked. `Ye can hardly head off unarmed.`

`Sure aren't we only after spending the entire night hiding them` Paddy replied exasperated. `What are we going to do now`.

`Is there anything here in the house Maryanne?`, JohnJoe asked looking to his older sister.

`No I brought anything we had here to Antwerp last night` Maryanne said `they were hiding guns and ammunition in a cavity in the wall, to be boarded up and papered over I think. What will yez do now Mary is right it would be foolish to leave without any protection.`

`Sure the only thing we can do is head down to the riverbank and retrieve them` JohnJoe said matter of factly.

`But sure ye can`t be seen around Enniscorthy` Mary insisted `there`s that many informers in this town you`d be shopped immediately, and ye surely can`t bring the bikes with ya, that`d be a dead giveaway.`

`Oh a dead giveaway Mary` JohnJoe smiled amid his anxiety `look we can`t stay here either sure the Brits are going door to door as we speak. Paddy and myself will head out the back and down to the river and make our way along the bank up towards the bridge where we hid the guns, I hate to ask you girls but would ye take the bicycles down to the bridge and meet us there. That`s our best chance, ye might get away with walking through town with the bikes and when we`re armed we will head up the river until we`re out of town.`

`It`s the only chance we have now so there`s no choice` Maryanne whispered as though the walls had ears.

Chapter 34

Shortly after Conscription was introduced in January 1916 Michael McDonald received his call up.

By that time he had just about resigned himself to the fact that he was going to be a soldier in the British army, justifying it to his Wexford conscience by acknowledging the debt he owed to the country that had provided him with a good living for the best part of his adult life, and appreciating that, at least this time, the Brits were on the side of right, defending the freedom of small nations and besides which, he had no choice, he hadn't volunteered he had been conscripted, and yet in the dark folds of his Enniscorthy soul something stirred, an uneasy queasiness of disloyalty to his Slaney heritage.

At his assessment it had been discovered that he had several years of experience with horses and to his delight he was dispatched to a mounted regiment, the South Irish Horse.

Happy to be part of a mainly Irish contingent, Michael settled into his new life well, revelling in the training, and quickly proving himself to be an agile and adept horseman with strength and daring, an excellent combination. He had a way with horses and like all the McDonalds was meticulous in the care of them. He was well liked and admired by both men and officers, and it could be said that Michael McDonald was almost looking forward to getting to France to fight Germans.

So, it came as a terrible shock to him when his regiment received orders that they were being dispatched, not to fight Germans on French soil or in Flanders fields but to quench the Rebellion in Ireland.

Michael along with many of his comrades in the South Irish Horse were unhappy with the order to say the very least. They had joined up for a variety of reasons, some because they believed in the war, some because they believed their participation would force England to grant Home Rule for Ireland, some to simply feed their families, some of the younger ones for adventure, some like Michael were conscripted, but none had joined up to turn on their own and it wasn't sitting well with any of them.

No, the South Irish Horse were not relishing the thought of supressing the Irish rebels, least of all Michael when they found out that their destination was to be Wexford.

As they rode along the Wexford road towards his hometown of Enniscorthy Michael's heart palpitated, and his stomach churned, when they came in sight of Vinegar Hill.

What was he to do? The little voices in his head seemed to come from the long dead corpses of the Hill, his ancestors chastising him for being on the wrong side. What could he do he wondered. Could he desert and go on the run. Who would hide him. He hadn't been in touch with home almost since he left it. Who would know him here in Enniscorthy now, as anything other than the enemy. Were the McDonalds still living at Court Street, could he go there seeking shelter and help. Would they even know him, would they want to know him, would they help him, were some of them involved in the Rising.

At that moment in time, ridding towards Enniscorthy with the South Irish Horse, the one thing, Michael McDonald knew for certain, was that there was no way he was going to be able to raise a hand against his own people.

`You're from here Mick aren't you`, the rider to his left, Tim Corrigan said, just as they came to the outskirts of the town.

`I am`, Michael said glumly. `I was born here in Enniscorthy in the shadow of Vinegar Hill and I have to tell ya every step we come closer to the town the more the knot in my stomach tightens`.

`Jaysus, I'm not surprised` Corrigan went on `will they know you here in town? Do you still have family here?`

`Yes, as far as I know, but God forgive me, I haven't been in touch with them for a long time. I never imagined coming back home like this`

Michael said looking down in dismay at his British uniform. `I thought I'd be fighting Germans in Belgium and France not riding into Enniscorthy to overthrow my own people.`

`I can only imagine how you feel Mick` the rider on his right Billy Reid offered. `I'm from Dublin and I have two younger brothers out with the rebels, and saving your own dilemma, but I'm damn glad I am, that we're riding into Enniscorthy and not down Sackville Street I can tell ya.`

`I'm from Galway lads` a voice said coming from behind `and the rebels are out there too, and I don't feel good about this at all, so I don't.`

`I grew up hearing about Vinegar Hill and 1798 and all my forefathers who were pikemen` Michael went on sadly ` and here I am about to be part of the first battle in my town since then and I'm wearing the wrong bloody uniform.`

His comrades in the South Irish Horse could find no words to console him, or each other.

To Michael's eternal relief and that of his comrades the Enniscorthy leaders surrendered the town to Colonel French and were promptly handed over to the Wexford RIC.

There would be no blood shed in Enniscorthy.

There was a collective release of tension and apprehension among the South Irish Horse until they were given orders to round up the rebels, arrest them and confiscate their arms.

`Jesus Christ`, Michael thought his heart starting to pound again in his chest, `I'm surely going to know some of them if we are to knock on every door and search every house in town.`

So he volunteered for the reconnaissance party to scout the riverbank for rebels trying to escape or conceal their weapons, at least he felt that would be a little less up close and personal, and maybe he would even get away with turning a blind eye.

Near the bridge he noticed two girls standing with bicycles, they were trying to give the appearance of having a casual chat but all the while their eyes were watching him and scanning the riverbank.

As they began walking down along the river one of the women started to look very familiar to Michael, watching her intently as he began following them, the dark hair, the slim figure, the sprightly gait. `It couldn't be, could it?` he thought to himself. `Could that possibly be Maryanne?`

....

Mary and Maryanne watched with trepidation as the young soldier followed behind getting closer and closer.

`What are we going to do Maryanne` Mary asked, glancing over her shoulder.

`Just keep calm Mary and let me do the talking` Maryanne said with more confidence than she felt.

`Can we help you at all` Maryanne turned and called when Michael was close enough to them to hear.

Her voice was all the confirmation Michael needed.

....

`Do it now JohnJoe`, Paddy Kehoe said as the young soldier approached the two girls. `If you don't do it now, he'll have them arrested or worse.`

'Shoot the British bastard before he arrests your sisters`, Eddie O`Brien goaded, `ya have a gun, just do it, you`re not afraid are ya.`

JohnJoe and Paddy Kehoe had been lying in wait along the riverbank near the bridge for the two girls to arrive with the bicycles when they happened on Eddie O`Brien who had been trying to make his way across the river to Vinegar Hill.

The three had seen the girls arriving and were about to make their move when they spotted the British soldier following them with intent.

....

JohnJoe, Paddy and Eddie O`Brien leaped from the riverbank where they had been concealed when they saw the soldier questioning Mary and Maryanne.

`Leave them alone or I`ll blow yer fucking brains out`, JohnJoe said coming up behind the soldier and pointing the revolver at his head.

`Shoot the bastard JohnJoe`, Eddie O`Brien roared, `they wouldn't think twice about shooting you if the boot was on the other foot.`

`For the love of God don't shoot him JohnJoe` Maryanne screamed. `He`s your brother.`

JohnJoe`s hand dropped, as he stood staring at the young man in the British uniform who was staring back at him.

`It`s Michael, JohnJoe`, Maryanne said softly, seeing the abject look of shock tinged with horror on JohnJoe`s face `you don't remember him - you were only a little fellow when he left for England.`

`But what`s he doing in that bloody uniform` JohnJoe spluttered when he finally found his voice somewhere between the terror of having almost shot his own brother and the terrible realisation that they were on opposing sides.

`I`ve been asking myself the very same question ever since I set foot back on Irish soil` Michael said sadly.

`You were never any fucking good!` Eddie O`Brien spat at him. `You wouldn't play football for the Vinegar Hill `98`s or for your own county, instead off you went to play soccer in England, thought yerself bigger and better than anyone else, ye did, just like yer old fellow before ya, well he got what was coming to him down here by the river and by Jesus you`re going to get the same now.`

Eddie O`Brien drew a knife from his boot and before anyone knew what was happening lunged it at Michael, who saw it coming just in the nick of time, side stepping the thrust and knocking Eddie into the rapid moving waters of the Slaney.

`Jesus Christ!` Paddy Kehoe gasped as Eddie was swept down river disappearing out of sight.

Michael was the first to react and removing his boots and jacket dived into the river. JohnJoe was about to follow suite when Maryanne grabbed him by the arm. `Don't be stupid now JohnJoe` she said in earnest `if anyone will get him, Michael will. He was always a strong swimmer: you and Paddy need to hop on those bikes and get out of town quickly before half the British army are breathing down our necks.`

`But Maryanne` JohnJoe said agitated `we can`t just leave now, what about Michael and Eddie, I have to know what happens to them and what did Eddie mean about Da getting what was coming to him here at the river, what is that all about.`

`Jesus, JohnJoe`, Maryanne said sharply, `how do I know.`

`Well I want to know before I leave` JohnJoe replied `I can`t just walk away.`

'Well ye won`t be walking anywhere if ye don't go soon`, Maryanne said grabbing him again and steering him towards the bicycle, `the two of ye will be rotting in an English prison, you held a gun to a British soldiers head JohnJoe, do you not realise that.`
'She`s right JohnJoe` Paddy Kehoe said shaking `if we don't get out of here now, we`ve lost our chance, come on, I`m going anyway whether you`re coming with me or not.`

Paddy grabbed the bike from Mary and looking around to see if the coast was clear began walking down the riverbank towards the edge of town.

`Go JohnJoe, for Gods sake go, will ya` Maryanne said exacerbated. There was no sign of Michael and she was beginning to get concerned, but she needed to get her younger brother out of town and away, before she could begin to think about anything else.

....

Michael was a strong and capable swimmer but he could see nothing of Eddie O`Brien as he scanned the river ahead of him.

He wasn't sure how far upriver he should swim, Eddie O`Brien couldn't be too far in front of him, sure he had jumped in almost immediately after him and yet there was no sign.

Perhaps he should swim in closer to the riverbank maybe Eddie got tangled up trying to get out, but as each moment passed with no sighting, Michael became more and more concerned for the wellbeing of the rebel.

Michael had never liked the man, the little he knew of him when he lived here in Enniscorthy was enough to know that he was a troublemaker and one to avoid.

There was a maliciousness of nature in Eddie O`Brien causing him to revel in the misfortune and tribulations of others, a man who, for

286

whatever reason, could get little or no pleasure in his own life and begrudged others any pleasure in theirs. A waste of the gift of life but worse, much worse than that a danger to the happiness of those around him as his wife and family could well attest to.

And yet Michael continued searching driven by responsibility and struggling with the belief that all life is precious.

Diving under the water he thought he saw something close to the bank and began swimming towards it. It appeared for all the world like a hole in the riverbed and there was definitely something or someone in it.

Michael swam in as far as he could and grabbed hold of the lifeless Eddie and began to pull him upward, but he appeared to be held back by something.

Michael swam round him and underneath him trying to find what the problem was before coming up for air. On his third attempt he found it, Eddie`s belt seemed to be caught on some kind of a metal hook sticking out of the mud on one side of the hole, Michael tried frantically to release the belt without success so in a last desperate effort he yanked once more and brought Eddie, belt and hook to the surface.

By the time he hauled him out on to the bank Mary and Maryanne had reached them.

Her nursing vocation kicked into action, Maryanne dropped to her knees and began working on Eddie but it was apparent to the three of them that it was futile.

Eddie O`Brien was long gone to meet his Maker.

`There`s a pretty deep hole down there` Michael told them when he regained his breath `the current must have carried him into it and then it seems he couldn't get out because his belt got caught in that hook that was jutting out from the side of the hole.`

`Jesus, Mary and Joseph take him to God the Most High` Maryanne said before she whispered an Act of Contrition into his ear.

When she looked up Michael's face was ashen, as he stared at the metal hook that he had just released from Eddie's belt.

`What is it Michael?` Maryanne asked in trepidation.

`Do you recognise it Maryanne?` he asked, his voice quivering as he held out his hand for her to see the hook clearly.

`Oh Sweet Jesus!` Maryanne exclaimed turning it over and reading the inscription.

`What is it?` Mary asked, looking from brother to sister.

`It's a hoof pick for horses Mary` Michael told her gently `an essential piece of equipment for a horse dealer but this one is particularly special because it was presented to our father, by Lady Gray, when he became Manager of the Brownswood Stables. She had it inscribed in Dublin: "Thomas McDonald, Stable Manager, Brownswood Estate".`

Maryanne had her hand over her mouth and tears were streaming from her eyes, looking at Michael she said `He was so proud of that hook it was a treasured possession, he never went anywhere without it from the day she gave it to him. Was there anything else down there in that hole Michael?`

`I saw bones Maryanne from what could be a skeleton` Michael said almost choking in disbelief.

`No wonder his poor body was never found`, Maryanne cried, `down in that great hole all these years. Ma never believed that story from Eddie O'Brien and his cronies: she always knew that they had something to do with Da's disappearance, and now it seems she was right`.

`I know it's frowned upon to speak ill of the dead Maryanne`, Michael said, `but there's nothing good that I would have to say about that man lying there in front of you. I can`t even say that I`m sorry he`s dead, in fact - there`s a tremendous sense of rectitude and righteousness in his end.`

`I know Michael`, Maryanne almost whispered, `it`s uncanny - like Da sought and executed justice from beyond the grave.`
As sisters and brother stood on the banks of the Slaney in the shadow of Vinegar Hill with the town once again flayed in the aftermath of rebellion, Michael looked around him and replied `Yes it's fitting. Da was a great man for justice alright and he`s finally got his after all these years - but will we ever see it here in Enniscorthy.`

The End

Printed in Great Britain
by Amazon